THE OFFERING

ISBN: 978-0-9883316-0-0

The
Offering

MARK BRADLEY

POIGNARD PRESS

A NOTE TO THE READER

Because the adjectives *Maya* and *Mayan* appear often in this novel and their correct usage is a frequent source of confusion, a word of explanation is in order. Mayanists—that is, scholars who specialize in the study of the ancient Maya people and their culture—use *Mayan* when referring to the spoken languages, and *Maya* when referring to everything else, including the written word. I have some of my characters use *Maya* and *Mayan* interchangeably because that is what non-specialists—most of whom are blissfully unaware of this crucial distinction—tend to do.

Then they put them into the House of Bats. There was nothing but bats inside this house, the house of Camazotz . . . and instantly those who came into their presence perished.

From *Popol Vuh: The Sacred Book of the Ancient Maya*

Chapter One

DISCOVERY

A ndy Brower pulls up to the gated entrance in his mud-caked Land Rover and catches his first glimpse of the main temple-pyramid through the trees. The sign above the entrance reads: "*Bienvenido a Ciudad Antigua.*" He smiles. *Ancient City. Was that really the best you could do, Hector?* Andy is addressing Hector Nuñez, the long-dead archaeologist who gave the site its generic-sounding name. He drives for half a mile over a bumpy dirt road and pulls into the parking area, where he gets a closer view of the grass-covered pyramid. Behind it the Santa Ana volcano looms on the horizon, shimmering in the late-afternoon heat. Andy gets out of the Land Rover and walks up to the ticket window. The young man sitting behind the counter is sound asleep. The brim of a New York Yankees ball cap is pulled down over his eyes. Clearing his throat, Andy says in a loud voice:

"*Perdóname. ¿Dónde está Susan Stanley?*"

Although his chair back is propped against the wall at a perilous angle, the young man somehow manages to awaken without falling on his ass. "Professor Brower!" he says, jumping to his feet. "Hi. I'm Chad Wilkinson."

"Pleased to meet you, Chad," Andy says as they shake hands.

"I've been looking forward to this ever since Susan told us you were coming here. Your book on cracking the Maya code is like my Bible. I take it everywhere." Chad produces a dog-eared copy and places it on the counter. "Would you do me the honor of signing it?"

"Gladly." Andy fishes through his pockets for a pen but comes up with only a small flashlight.

"That's okay. I've got one right here." Chad puts the pen down next to the book. As Andy writes, Chad continues, "Susan says you taught her more about epigraphy"—in this case, the study of ancient Maya hieroglyphs—"than she could ever teach you."

Andy hands the book back. "She's just being modest. Now where do you think I might find her?"

"I'll take you to her in just a second." Chad places a sign on the counter that reads "Back in a few minutes." "I'm the only one minding the store today," he explains.

Andy follows Chad to the turnstile. A uniformed security guard armed with a short-barreled, pump-action shotgun stands near the entrance. Andy gives him a nod. Then he takes a brochure out of a small wooden bin and starts to read:

In what is now western El Salvador, a huge trading center sprang up in the shadow of the Santa Ana volcano and flourished for two centuries before it was destroyed by fire a thousand years ago. The first archaeologist to study the ruins of the ancient city named the site Ciudad Antigua. Ever since, Mesoamerican scholars have puzzled over its mysterious downfall. Like the great city of Chichen Itza to the north, Ciudad Antigua was a latecomer to the ancient Maya world. It was established sometime in the ninth century, during the Late Classic period. While many classic Maya cities were abandoned and reclaimed by the jungle, Ciudad Antigua grew and prospered into the early Postclassic period before disaster struck around the turn of the eleventh century.

"There she is," Chad says, pointing in Susan's direction.

Andy walks over to the dig site and surveys the area that Susan's team is excavating. It is laid out in a large grid composed of thick string held in place by wooden stakes driven in at regular intervals. The grid enables Susan and the other team members to record the precise location of the artifacts they uncover using the grid coordinates assigned to each square.

The workers are all busy with their tasks. Susan is on her hands and knees chipping away at the ground with a trowel. Nearby, a young woman in cutoffs and a tank top uses a toothbrush to clean off an oblong brooch, while a young man in cargo shorts and a Radiohead T-shirt jiggles dirt through a shaker-sifter, only to come up empty-handed. Andy assumes that the latter two are

3

student-volunteers from the States. Just outside the grid, a Salvadoran laborer armed with a pick hacks fresh gashes into the grassy earth while another worker shovels piles of rich brown soil into a wheelbarrow.

Susan is so intent on her work that she fails to notice Andy until Chad says at last, "Hey, Susan. Look who's here."

She rises to her feet and turns around. "Why, Andy! How in the hell are you?" She drops her trowel and gives him a hug. As Andy bends over to hug Susan, her flowered sunhat falls to the ground.

"Gather 'round, everyone," Susan shouts to all and sundry. "We have a very special visitor." In less than a minute, fifteen sweaty, grimy-looking people are standing in a semi-circle before Susan and Andy. "Everybody, this is Professor Andrew J. Brower of the University of Maryland. Andy, this is everybody."

"Welcome to Ciudad Antigua, Professor Brower," says the young woman in cutoffs and tank top. Everyone else chimes in with a *Hello* or a *Buenos*, which is Salvadoran shorthand for *Hi*.

"I'm now going to embarrass Andy by telling you all a story about our first meeting," Susan announces. "I had just started working with Andy's father on a dig at Dos Montañas in Guatemala. When I arrived there, the first thing I noticed was this twelve-year-old kid with colored pencils and a sketch pad scribbling away from dawn to dusk. Only he wasn't scribbling. This boy was doing these amazingly detailed drawings of the stelae"—or slab-like stone monuments—"that stand in front of the main pyramid. At the time we couldn't decipher most of the glyphs"—or hieroglyphs—"on the stelae. So I told Andy's dad, 'Look Tom, why don't you put the kid to work on the stelae and see what he can do.' 'Well, I suppose it couldn't hurt,' he said. Anyway, the rest is history. Andy kept at it day-after-day, and damned if he didn't decipher them all! I'll never forget when he showed me his work. He'd identified an entire royal dynasty that lasted four centuries. All I could say was, 'Congratulations, kid. I think you nailed it.'"

The group breaks out in a mixture of laughter and applause.

"Aw shucks, it was nothing," Andy says, playing along.

"All right, everyone. Back to work. Andy's had enough adulation for one day."

While everyone else goes back to work, Susan and Andy continue talking.

"So this must be the palace complex you were telling me about," Andy says.

"Yep," Susan nods. "These people were probably royalty. Only the fanciest dishes for them. Just look at these polychrome sherds." She holds up two colorful pottery fragments. One piece depicts the front half of a black shark swimming in a brilliant Maya blue sea. The other reveals a pair of dancing legs clad in jaguar-skin leggings with brown and red spots. "This structure is like most of the others here," Susan continues. "It burned to the ground. There are signs that the occupants left in a hurry. We found a jug that was smashed to pieces, as though it were dropped." Shielding her eyes, she says, "Well, I'd better get back to my crockery while there's still some light. If you can entertain yourself for another hour, we'll be heading into town for dinner. How does that sound?"

"Sounds great. Mind if I take a look around in the meantime? I'd like to see the view from up there." He gestures toward the pyramid.

"Be my guest. But watch out. One of the workers ran into a huge wasps' nest while trimming it the other day."

Andy walks over to the sixty-foot-tall temple-pyramid, which dominates the landscape. Though modest by Maya standards, he finds it impressive just the same. Earth and grass cover much of the structure, with a section of the steep stone stairs revealed along the base, thanks to a recent excavation. Closing his eyes, he tries to visualize how it might have looked a thousand years earlier, before the fire: the exterior painted in soft rose and turquoise pastels, massive incense burners perfuming the air with the citrusy scent of copal, and a shaman inside the thatched shrine on the pinnacle, chanting a summons to assemble for a human sacrifice. Andy clambers to the top and spies the Santa Ana volcano in the distance. As he scans the horizon, something close at hand arrests his attention. He notices a large mound covered by trees and brush next to the North Ball Court a few hundred yards off. He recalls Susan telling him that the area once contained a cluster of sacred buildings and a sacrificial platform. He scrambles down the pyramid's steep slope and dashes over to the mound.

As Andy examines the mound's surface, he notices a small, bare depression where erosion appears to have uncovered an artifact. To his amazement, he finds himself face-to-face with Camazotz the bat god, bringer of death and destruction. Perhaps, he thinks, the mound once held a shrine to the fearsome deity. As he kneels to study the fanged effigy more closely, the ground gives way under his feet. The next instant, he's tumbling into a dark void. He lands with a sickening thud that knocks the wind out of him. For a minute or so, Andy gasps for air. Catching his breath at last, he rises unsteadily to his feet. In the shaft of light from above, he inspects his body for injuries. Aside from a headache and some sore ribs, he appears to be okay. But he notices that the fall has shattered his watch crystal. As his eyes adjust to the darkness, they begin to trace the jagged outlines of a cave. He assumes that it was no accident that the ancient Antiguanos built their Camazotz shrine above this spot, for the god was closely associated with caves. Andy also realizes that he must have blundered onto the remnant of a manmade air shaft that once fed into the cave. The Maya regarded caves as portals to the Underworld, which they called Xibalba—the "Place of Fear."

"Help!" he cries. "Help!" He calls out several more times, but no one seems to hear him.

With the aid of his pocket flashlight, Andy begins to scan the cave walls but finds nothing remarkable. Training the light on the ground at his feet, he sees the Camazotz effigy and, beside it, a human skull staring up into eternity, its jaws frozen in a silent scream. He notes the classic Maya facial features: a sloping, flat forehead and teeth filed into various shapes. The Mayas' efforts to improve on nature began at infancy, when two boards were tied to a baby's malleable head, one in front and one in back. Within a few days, the forehead attained a beautiful flatness that would last a lifetime. Similarly, they altered the nose by means of an adjustable wooden bridge and developed crossed eyes by attaching tiny balls to strands of the child's hair and then hanging them between his or her eyes. Men and women alike tattooed and painted their bodies and pierced their ears. In addition to filing their teeth, wealthy Maya adorned them with jade inlays, a practice that had all but vanished by the Postclassic period, thanks to a dearth of the precious stone.

With his flashlight, Andy studies the skeleton at his feet. Eyeing the small skull, slender frame, and wide, bowl-shaped hips, he judges the skeleton to be that of a young adult female. As he scans the cave floor, other female skeletons come into view, along with a host of scattered artifacts. Sifting through the debris, he uncovers turquoise and shell fragments, probably the remnants of bracelets, earrings, and necklaces. Based on the jewelry, he guesses that at least some of the women belonged to the elite class. He finds several small skeletons, probably those of young children, scattered among the women. A cluster of tiny bones indicates an infant. Because the children have not reached sexual maturity, Andy knows that determining their sex using only skeletal remains will be difficult, if not impossible. Lying beside one child is a toy dog on four wheels.

One dark corner of the cave resembles a slaughter-house. He finds several contorted skeletons that bear evidence of severe trauma: fractured skulls, cracked or perforated ribcages, shattered limbs. The ground around them is littered with obsidian blades and projectile points. One skull differs from the others, for it lacks the usual flat, sloping forehead. Andy counts eighteen skeletons in all—twelve adults and six children.

He begins formulating a hypothesis to explain the carnage on the cave floor. The scene probably dates from the fall of the city. The evidence suggests that the women and children were brought here against their will. Perhaps the conquerors of Ciudad Antigua decided to offer some of their captives to Camazotz. He guesses that the victors chose several members of the royal family and their retinue. A shaman may have torn out the beating hearts of the first victims, or perhaps some soldiers simply cut their throats or eviscerated them. In any event, the battered skeletons indicate that a few of the women went down fighting. Perhaps one of the skeletons belonged to the queen herself.

His flashlight shines on a smooth section of the cave wall that appears to be smudged. Upon closer inspection, the smudges prove to be paint. Andy brushes away a layer of dirt from the wall and finds himself staring at the faded image of a woman dancing. The face staring back at him is familiar—*it's Luisa Santiago.* He would recognize those eyes anywhere.

Andy leaves the image partially uncovered rather than risk damaging the remainder. Besides, the cave is growing dark, and he's feeling a bit light-headed. He assumes that it's just fatigue—the result of a long day compounded by too little sleep the night before and nothing to eat since breakfast. And his ribs are really aching. Confident that Susan will find him soon, he decides to rest in the meantime. He sits against a cool, soft curve in the cave wall and drifts off to sleep with the disquieting thought that his own remains might be discovered down here some day.

He dreams of hearing strange noises—high-pitched chattering interspersed with faint rustling sounds. He blinks and rubs his eyes but can see nothing in the inky blackness. Turning on his flashlight, he spies a dark cloud approaching from the depths of the cave. The cloud is alive with hundreds of flapping wings, and it is coming straight for him.

"*What the—*" As he ducks, a vampire bat with shining red eyes swoops down to within a few inches of his face, baring a pair of razor-sharp fangs. *Jesus Christ!* He covers his head with one hand and swats at the bat with the other. Hearing a familiar voice from somewhere outside the cave, he tries to answer but can't speak. Then he awakens with a start.

"Hey, Andy! Are you down there?" It's Susan.

"Yeah!" he shouts back.

"You okay?"

"I'm a little banged up, but I think I'll live."

"All right, hon. Just hold on. We'll get you out of there in a jiffy."

Andy laughs despite the pain in his ribs. "Wait a minute. Why don't *you* come down *here*? You'll never believe what I've found."

Chapter Two

BECOMING FAMOUS

Just before airtime, Luisa Santiago asks herself why she agreed to do a national television interview on this morning of all mornings. A few more hours of sleep would have been far more beneficial than five minutes under the hot lights of a TV studio. But Luisa tells herself that it's too late to back out now, so she'd better make the most of this opportunity.

As the producer counts down the seconds, Luisa chants a mantra to herself that she uses to overcome pre-performance jitters: *Everyone's watching, Luisa. For God's sake, don't fuck up.* The pop-jazzy *Top o' the Mornin'* theme music plays in the background. From New York, the host wishes everyone a cheery "top of the morning" and then announces that the show is switching to its Washington, DC, affiliate. Luisa stipulated that the interview take place in her hometown.

"Good morning, everyone. This is Amanda Donovan. I'm chatting with Luisa Santiago, a young dancer-choreographer with the Capital Ballet. This is a big day for you, isn't it, Luisa?"

The high-definition camera closes in on Luisa's soft, round face. "Yes, it is, Amanda. The world premiere of my first ballet is tonight."

"Congratulations! You must be very proud and excited. What is the name of your ballet?"

"It's called *The Offering*. It comes from the Maya word for 'dance,' which also means 'offering' or 'sacrifice.' I got the idea for my ballet from a Maya sculpture I saw at the National Gallery of Art." An image of the limestone relief appears onscreen. "The kneeling figure on the right is the wife of a Maya ruler. She is performing a sacred blood rite. Using a stingray spine, she has perforated her tongue. The sculpture shows her drawing a thorny rope through the perforation."

"Ouch!" Amanda grimaces. "I don't think we need to warn our viewers not to try *that* at home."

Luisa smiles. "Yes, blood rites must have been very painful, but that was how Maya rulers communed with the gods and their ancestors. My ballet is an imaginary recreation of a two-part Maya religious ceremony. The first part depicts a blood ritual, and the second part a human sacrifice."

"Sort of a Mayan *Rite of Spring*?"

Although Luisa dislikes the analogy, she goes along with it anyway. "Yes, but without the opening-night riot, I hope."

"You've done an amazing amount of historical research for your ballet."

"Well, I wanted it to be as accurate as possible. I have Professor Andrew Brower to thank for steering me to the best sources. Even though dance was a crucial part of Maya rituals, we can only speculate as to the form the dances took. Chances are, the ancient Maya would find my choreography very strange."

"Has it been difficult being the choreographer *and* dancing the female lead in your ballet?"

"I'd have to say yes and no to that one, Amanda. It does make me wish sometimes that I could be two people, but as the choreographer, I don't have to worry about the prima ballerina ignoring my directions."

"Luisa, you're a native of El Salvador. How old were you when you came to America, and why did you move here?"

"My parents sent me here to live with my aunt when I was two. It was during the Salvadoran Civil War; they feared for my safety. I never saw them again. Their village was wiped out by a government death squad just after I left." Luisa braces herself for the inevitable follow-up.

"I also want to offer my condolences for the tragic death of your aunt."

"Thank you, Amanda." Luisa pauses for a moment to collect her thoughts. The high-def camera slowly closes in to reveal any tears, but she remains dry-eyed. It has been six months since her Aunt Rosa was gunned down in a turf battle between two rival gangs. Luisa no longer cries at the mention of her aunt, but a burning desire to avenge her murder has taken hold and won't let go. "I'd rather not discuss it. It's still a difficult subject for me."

Taking the hint, Amanda adroitly shifts gears. "You began your ballet studies at the age of seven. You were nicknamed 'La Mariposa,' or 'the Butterfly,' by your first ballet teacher. Why was that?"

Luisa laughs. "I was the smallest girl in my class. My teacher said I looked so fragile that I reminded her of a butterfly. The nickname caught on and has stayed with me ever since."

"You went on to study ballet and modern dance at the Duke Ellington School of the Arts right here in Washington, and then you studied dance at George Mason University before joining the Capital Ballet. And now you're premiering your first ballet at the Kennedy Center. So what's next?'"

Luisa smiles. "I have no idea. I'm just focused on tonight."

"Thanks so much for coming to visit, Luisa. Break a leg!"

"Actually, Amanda, dancers consider it bad luck to say that. They say *merde* instead."

"Oops! *Merde* it is."

"Thank you."

They shake hands. End of interview.

After Amanda and the producer congratulate her on a job well done, Luisa takes a deep breath and exhales.

Thank God that's over. She feels as if she's just emerged from a strange dream.

Like the young Lord Byron, Luisa awakens to discover that she is famous. People recognize her in the elevator and on the street. During the cab ride to the Kennedy Center, she receives dozens of voicemail and text messages on her cell phone and later finds even more messages on her office phone—her office at the Center being little more than a broom closet with two chairs and a desk. Many calls are from strangers and a few from people whom she hasn't seen in years. Some callers wish her luck, while others make business or more personal propositions. A few even take her to task for saying *merde* on a family program. One phone call is from Rob, her ex-boyfriend, who says that he just wanted to tell her how great she looked on TV, and that he hopes that they can get together for dinner. Another call is from Andy Brower. He's babbling on about a mural he just found in a cave somewhere in El Salvador. "It looks just like you!" he yells. The rest of the morning is spent attending to a host of last-minute details with the artistic director, the costume and set designers, the technicians, the conductor, and the composer of the ballet score, Jorge Morales. Luisa has known Jorge since their student days at the Ellington School and considers him a genius. She once had a schoolgirl crush on him, until he confided to her that he is gay.

Luisa returns to her Dupont Circle apartment around noon. Her home answering machine is jammed with messages. She ignores them, eats a salad, feeds her Siamese cat, Mauricio, and then tries to rest, but the phone keeps ringing. She finally unplugs it and manages to get some shuteye before it's time to go.

Several hours later, it seems to Luisa that all of DC has turned out to applaud her ballet. The premiere is sold out, and the audience, bowled over by the sixty-minute tour de force, responds with a long standing ovation as admirers toss bouquet after bouquet onto the stage. After the final curtain call, Luisa gathers up her bouquets and heads back to her dressing room. Overall, she's pleased with the performance but thinks that the finale needs work. In the closing *pas de deux*, Roger almost dropped her, and the sacrifice scene briefly lapsed into confusion. (One unsuspecting critic later praises it as the most inspired moment of the ballet.) But Luisa's concerns can wait until tomorrow. For the moment, she wants to savor her opening-night triumph.

Chapter Three

MIGUEL

The premiere party is an invitation-only affair at the L2 Lounge in Georgetown, where young women in short, strapless dresses hold court and mojitos are the social lubricant of choice. The place is pulsing with bass-heavy rock music, punctuated by the buzz of animated conversation. For an hour or so, Luisa mingles with members of the Repertory, young and upwardly mobile supporters of the Capital Ballet. She talks briefly with Jorge Morales about his idea for a ballet based on the life of Lola Montez, the nineteenth-century Irish dancer who gained notoriety as the mistress of Franz Liszt and King Ludwig I of Bavaria. Luisa tells him that she'll think about it.

As she heads for the door, John Mitchell, the executive director of the Ballet, comes over. "Luisa," he says, "I know it's late, but could you stay long enough to meet our newest patron? His name is Miguel Maldonado. He's from El Salvador like you."

She's heard the name before but can't recall where or when. A lean fellow with a ramrod-straight posture, Miguel wears his lank, jet black hair in a ponytail and stands six inches taller than Luisa, who's about five-four. He's also strikingly pale.

"My full name is Miguel José Napoleon Maldonado y Vargas," he says. "But you can call me Miguel." When Luisa offers her hand, Miguel kisses it the old-fashioned way. His profile reminds her of Pakal the Great, the ancient Maya ruler whose portrait bust she recently saw at the National Gallery of Art. *Now I know what a Maya king would have looked like in an Armani suit.*

"Luisa," John Mitchell says, "your ballet so impressed Señor Maldonado that he has offered to underwrite our expenses for the rest of the season."

She, in turn, is impressed by his generosity. "*Estoy halagado. Muchas gracias.*"

"*Mucho gusto,*" Miguel says. Much to her surprise, he resumes speaking in English. "For one so young, you have a strong affinity for the old ways. But you still have much to learn about ancient Maya dance."

"So what makes you such an expert?" Luisa fires back. John gives her an admonishing shake of the head, which she ignores. "You don't appear to be much older than I am."

"Believe me. I'm older than I look."

"Okay, but that doesn't mean you know what you're talking about."

He hands her his business card:

MALDONADO Y COMPAÑÍA, LIMITADA
Antiquities Dealer
Specializing in Rare Pre-Columbian Artifacts

"So now I'm supposed to be impressed?"

"Why don't we just agree to disagree?" John Mitchell says. "After all, this isn't an argument that can be settled by Wikipedia."

"He's right," Miguel says, placing his hand on Luisa's arm. She notices that his gold ring bears the likeness of a fanged monster. "Allow me to buy you a mojito."

"Thank you, but I was just leaving. It's been a long day. I'm exhausted."

"Please stay." Miguel grips her arm gently but firmly. "I'll drive you home. Besides, we have so much to talk about."

Finding it useless to protest, Luisa relents. She also has to admit that Miguel intrigues her.

Mojitos in hand, Luisa and Miguel enter a long room with high brick walls and lime green sofas arrayed in a semi-circle. They're alone. Miguel touches her hair, which is pulled back in a thick braid that reaches down past her shoulders. "Your hair appeared dark in the other room," he says, "but in here, the red strands shine so beautifully." His intense stare makes her self-conscious. "You look familiar," he says. "Your eyes remind me of someone I knew long ago. I had the same sense of déjà vu when I saw you on TV this morning."

For what seems the first time in years, Luisa blushes. "There must be many women in El Salvador who look like me."

"Maybe," he says, too readily for her liking. "There was a time when your face would not have been considered beautiful."

"Thank you for bringing that to my attention."

"But I happen to find you irresistible." Miguel leans forward to kiss her, but she pulls away. He continues talking as if nothing happened. "It's just that the ancient Maya preferred elongated features, angularity. They wanted to resemble ears of maize. Corn was the stuff of life."

"And what about blood?"

"To the ancient Maya, human blood was the ultimate elixir. It enabled them to commune with the gods, to be like the gods."

"Or so they believed." Luisa notices that Miguel hasn't touched his glass, while hers is nearly empty.

"No, no," he says with emphasis. "You don't understand. The ancient Maya discovered that under certain conditions, human blood endowed them with tremendous power. It could even make them immortal."

"You're joking, right?"

Miguel says nothing but looks deadly serious.

Luisa drains her glass. "I'll need a lot more of these to buy what you're selling. Anyway, I think it's time to go."

Miguel is staring at her and speaking in a strange tongue—only his lips aren't moving.

"Did you say something?" she asks.

"No. Why?"

"I guess that mojito went straight to my head."

On their way out, Luisa runs into Karen Silber, her best friend and roommate. A former dancer with the Capital Ballet, Karen has just opened her own studio and is struggling to make ends meet.

"Sorry I'm late," Karen says, giving Luisa a hug. "Congratulations! You were wonderful. I'm so proud of you." Then, eyeing Miguel, she whispers, "Are you sure you know what you're doing?"

"Don't worry," Luisa whispers back. "I'll be fine."

As they head into the night, Miguel turns to Luisa and says, "I get the feeling she doesn't like me."

"Who?"

"Your friend."

Luisa laughs. "Oh, that's just Karen. She likes playing the big sister."

Luisa is not surprised by the fact that Miguel drives a sleek black Mercedes or that he drives it fast. But she is floored by the discovery that they share a passion for Puccini.

"*Tosca* is my favorite opera," he announces above the *Te Deum* scene at the end of Act I.

"And *'Vissi d'arte'* is my favorite aria," Luisa says.

As Miguel pulls up to Luisa's apartment building, she's saying goodnight and thanking him for the ride. "Not so fast," he says, turning off the ignition. "I have some unfinished business with you." He leans forward and kisses her on the mouth. This time, she doesn't resist. He moves lower, nibbling her neck and throat. Tosca's final words to Scarpia—*"Muori, dannato! Muori, muori!"*—resound in her ears. *Die, damn you, die!* As Miguel nibbles at Luisa's neck, her head begins to swim, and she feels as if she's floating away. All of a sudden, she's climbing rapidly and looking down on the city from a great height . . .

"Miguel!" For the second time that day, Luisa feels as if she has emerged from a strange dream. "It's late. I have to go." As he nibbles at her throat, she struggles to break free of his iron grip. "You're hurting me!" When that fails to get his attention, she orders him to stop—only the sounds that she makes are utterly foreign to her.

Miguel appears to snap out of a trance and become himself again. "Please forgive me." He gets out of the car, hurries over to the passenger side, and opens the door for her. "Allow me to walk you up to your apartment."

"That won't be necessary."

"Don't be angry with me."

"I'm more scared than angry."

"I'm so sorry, Luisa. It won't happen again, I swear."

He tries to kiss her, but she pushes him away. "Good night, Miguel."

"May I call you tomorrow—I mean, later today?"

"Okay." Luisa hands him her business card. "Now good night."

She turns and heads up to her apartment, feeling light-headed with fatigue—or so she thinks. She drops her duffel bag by the door and heads for the bedroom. She undresses, slips into bed, and immediately falls asleep.

Later that morning, she awakens with a throbbing head and a queasy stomach. Putting on her robe, she pads into the bathroom and takes two Advil, followed by a couple of Pepto-Bismol tablets.

As Luisa gazes into the mirror, something on her neck startles her—two dime-sized spots of dried blood about an inch apart. She wets some tissues and wipes off the blood, only to find a pair of angry welts underneath. *So this is why Miguel was so apologetic. The horny bastard drew blood!* At first she thinks that they're two of the weirdest-looking hickeys she's ever seen, but closer inspection reveals a small puncture wound within each swelling. *If I didn't know better, I'd say it looks like a . . .* Tossing the blood-stained tissues into the sink, she snarls, "*¡Hijo de puta!*" She can't wait to give him a piece of her mind. She sticks a Band-Aid over the wound and then adjusts her braid to conceal the Band-Aid.

In the kitchen, Luisa empties a can of cat food into Mauricio's bowl while the yowling Siamese paces back and forth and rubs against her legs. Then she pours a glass of orange juice and drops a bagel into the toaster. She's surprised to see Karen emerge from her bedroom. "I thought you were spending the night at Roger's." He dances the role of the King in Luisa's ballet.

"We're on the skids again," Karen sighs. "Apparently, he's chasing a new piece of tail this week." She pours some water into the coffeemaker. "So how'd it go with the drug lord?"

"You mean Miguel?" Luisa sips her juice. "He's a strange guy—old-school polite but very aggressive."

"I think he's creepy."

"Why do you say that? You haven't even met him."

"I have eyes, don't I? He looks like trouble with a capital T." Karen gives Luisa a concerned look. "You're looking a little pale this morning. Are you all right?"

Luisa studies her image in the hall mirror and realizes that Karen is right. "I'm feeling drained. It's probably just a post-premiere hangover. At least I have an excuse to skip my workout today." She sits down opposite Karen at the kitchen table.

"Where's the newspaper?" Karen asks. "Have you read the review yet?"

"No, I totally forgot." Luisa goes to the door and retrieves the morning paper. She opens it to the Arts & Leisure section and finds the review. The headline reads: "*Rite of Spring* Revisited." Luisa can't bear to read further: *Oh no, not another comparison to* The Rite. . . . "Here, you read it." She slides the paper across the table. Karen picks it up and starts reading.

"The title sucks, but the review's pretty good."

"Then read it to me, for God's sake!"

"Okay, okay." Karen clears her throat and begins, "'Any choreographer working today must be very brave or very foolish to remake *The Rite of Spring*. The wild beauty of Stravinsky's incomparable score, the legend of Nijinsky's original ballet, the countless reinterpretations—what is left to add or improve upon? Perhaps only a pair of ambitious, twenty-something neophytes such as composer Jorge Morales and choreographer Luisa Santiago would attempt to surpass the unsurpassable. Their audacious new ballet is called *The Offering*, and it premiered at the Kennedy Center last night.'"

"Enough!" Luisa says, raising her hand. "I get the message. The critic thinks my ballet's derivative."

"Just be patient," Karen says. "It gets better." She returns to the review. "'In the hands of less skilled creators, *The Offering* might have been nothing more than a grotesque parody of *The Rite*. Fortunately for last night's sold-out house, such was not the case. Morales and Santiago reinvented the Stravinsky-Nijinsky ballet by utilizing ancient Maya themes, lending their own ballet a distinctly New World flavor. The stark contrasts in Santiago's imaginative choreography complemented the abrupt mood shifts in Morales's Revueltas-inspired score, ranging from barbaric savagery to heartbreaking lyricism. The costumes, magnificent recreations of Maya ceremonial garb, made the dancers appear as if they had leapt directly from an ancient mural onto the Kennedy Center stage. The sets were monumental recreations of a Maya acropolis, complete with a massive temple-pyramid that served as the backdrop for the final human sacrifice.'" Karen looks up from the paper and says, "Not bad, huh?"

"Yeah, but what about my dancing?"

"I'm getting to that. Let's see, where was I? 'As the King, Roger Cavanaugh displayed his usual sturdy athleticism, though he appeared a bit shaky in the final *pas de deux*.'"

Karen cannot resist commenting, "That's the price he paid for staying up night before last, and I do mean *up*." She turns the page and says, "Now, here's the payoff: 'Luisa Santiago's sublime performance as Lady Xok revealed that she has blossomed into a world-class ballerina. In addition to her flawless technique, she brings irresistible joy and exuberance to her dancing. This has earned her a large and loyal following, as last night's thunderous standing ovation attested. One can only hope that she will not abandon her true calling in a misguided attempt to win fame as a choreographer.'"

"¡Coño!" Luisa snaps, infuriated at the reviewer's final comment. "Why did he have to spoil it?"

"Because *she's* a critic." Karen suddenly looks concerned again. "What's that on your neck?"

"It's just a Band-Aid." Luisa shrugs. "Miguel got a little carried away last night."

"Don't say I didn't warn you," Karen says. "You're not planning to see him again, are you?"

"I don't know . . ."

"Jesus, Lu. Promise me you won't see him again."

"Okay. I promise," she says with no intention of keeping her word.

Miguel calls around 11 a.m. Before she can launch into a carefully rehearsed tirade, he apologizes yet again for his misbehavior and asks if they can get together for dinner. "We have to talk," he says.

"That's the understatement of the year," she replies. "As Ricky Ricardo would say, you got some 'splainin' to do."

Luisa tells him she has a performance that evening but can meet him for supper afterward.

"Excellent! All will be revealed tonight," he promises.

Chapter Four

Q&A

It is midnight when Luisa and Miguel enter The Diner, an all-night eatery in the Adams Morgan section of DC. They occupy a booth near the back. The place is noisy and crowded as usual, with light jazz playing on the sound system. Ravenous after a performance on too little sleep, Luisa orders a steak and two eggs. Miguel tells her that he's already eaten and then orders a Bloody Mary, which he doesn't touch. As Luisa wolfs down her supper, Miguel tells her to eat slowly and savor her food. She ignores his advice.

"*Diga me*," she says at last. "*¿Por qué no quieres hablar conmigo en Español?*"

"It's simple," he answers. "Spanish is neither my first language nor my favorite."

"So what *is* your first language?"

"Nawat."

"I thought it was dead."

"It almost was, but it's making a comeback. When did you learn it?"

Luisa laughs. "What are you talking about?"

"You spoke it last night. Don't you remember?"

She thinks for a moment. "I remember saying something that sounded like total garbage."

"Well, you were speaking Nawat." Miguel asks the waitress for the check. "Come on. Let's find a quiet place to talk."

"Where can we go at this hour?"

He smiles vaguely. "I know just the place."

"I'll bet you do."

Miguel guides the black Mercedes through the streets of downtown Washington.

"Where are you taking me?" Luisa asks.

"I thought we might drive for a while," he replies, "if you don't mind."

"Okay."

Within a few minutes, the Mercedes is streaking along I-95 North at 120 miles per hour. The stormy opening chords of Brahms's D minor Piano Concerto are playing on the sound system.

Luisa casts a nervous glance at the speedometer. "You're going way too fast."

"The car is built for comfort *and* speed," he says. "Just like the driver."

"Slow down, dammit!"

Much to her relief, Luisa watches the speedometer drop to seventy-five. No sooner does Miguel slow down than the Mercedes runs into a cloudburst, which provides a fitting backdrop to the Brahmsian *Sturm und Drang*.

"All right," Miguel says at last. "It's time for Q&A."

"So what's the deal with biting my neck?" She points to the Band-Aid.

"What do you mean?" He draws Luisa's hair away from her throat and peels off the Band-Aid with one hand while steering with the other. "I see no bite marks."

"Pay attention!"

He begins to caress her neck. "All I see is some very lovely skin."

"Miguel!"

"Don't worry." He turns to face the road. "I have excellent peripheral vision."

"Look, I'm not making this shit up. The bite marks were there."

"Yet by some miracle, they vanished, is that what you're thinking? Only it wasn't a miracle. All it took was a few drops of my saliva." His eyes turn red as he flashes his fangs. "You see, that which kills can also cure."

"Just take me home," she pleads. "I swear to God I'll never tell anyone."

"Relax," he says in a calm voice. "I'm not going to hurt you. Look—both my hands are on the wheel and my eyes are on the road."

Luisa somehow manages to settle down, only to notice that the speedometer is back up to 120 MPH, even though the downpour is so heavy that she can barely see beyond the hood of the car.

"Slow down, you bastard!" She tries to stomp on the brake with her left foot, but he shoves her back against the passenger seat with his right hand, which she bites hard enough to draw blood.

"Don't do that again," he warns, his red eyes indicating that he means business.

"I just want to go home."

"Not yet. I'd like you to meet a friend of mine." He exits the Interstate and turns onto a two-lane country road choked with fog.

"Where are you taking me?"

"You'll find out soon enough."

"You're going to kill me, aren't you?"

He smiles. "I would've killed you last night had I wanted to. But I brought you here for a different purpose. I want you to be my companion."

She glares at him. "You must be out of your fucking mind!"

Miguel ignores the rejoinder. "If you accept my proposal, I will help you bring your aunt's killers to justice."

"The police are already searching for them."

"The police won't find them. I will."

"Prove it."

"All right, I'll bring you the head of Rafa Herrera."

"Are you serious?"

"Of course I'm serious."

"What about my dancing?"

"I think you already know the answer to that."

Luisa folds her arms across her chest and sets her jaw. "Then there's nothing more to discuss."

The ensuing lull in the conversation lasts until the first faint rays of sunlight appear on the horizon. "Hey," Luisa says, "shouldn't you be looking for a coffin about now?"

Miguel laughs. "My dear, I wouldn't be caught dead in a wooden box."

The sun burns off the morning fog but not Miguel. They are driving through a quaint little town filled with stately old houses.

"Where are we?" Luisa asks.

"Concord, Massachusetts. My friend lives here."

"Don't you think it's a little early to be making social calls?"

"She's expecting us."

They pull into the driveway of a gray, two-story wood-frame house with a mansard roof. Miguel says that the house is about 150 years old. They are met at the door by an elegant, dark-haired woman in a little black dress and high heels. She introduces herself as Constance Bennett. Though she could pass for thirty-five, Luisa assumes that she is much older.

Constance gives Luisa a tour of the house. The interior is bright, open, and cheerful—not at all what Luisa expected. She immediately falls in love with the high ceilings, oversize windows, ornate crown molding, and marble fireplaces. When they return to the first floor, Luisa realizes that Miguel has vanished. Standing alone in the living room with Constance, she feels a sudden urge to bolt for the front door. As though sensing Luisa's distress, Constance offers to fix her some breakfast.

"To tell you the truth, I'm starving!" Luisa replies.

They walk into the kitchen. As Constance removes a carton of eggs and a package of bacon from the refrigerator, Luisa asks if she had to make a special trip to the supermarket.

"I have people over all the time," she says, cracking an egg on the skillet. "So I'm used to feeding them as opposed to feeding on them, although I must admit that I've been known to combine the two."

"Am I on the menu?"

"Not to worry." Constance places some bacon strips in a pan. "I fed last night, so I'm good for at least a day or two. The older I get, the less I seem to need." Constance pours some coffee into an exquisite Wedgwood china cup and hands it to Luisa. "But from time to time, I still feel the old craving. Has Miguel been filling you in on the gory details?"

Luisa sighs. "Actually, he's been less than forthcoming."

"Miguel's not much of a talker. I guess that's why he asked me to step in." Constance serves the bacon and eggs on a matching Wedgwood china plate. "Why on earth do you want to become a vampire?"

"I never said that I did," Luisa says between bites.

Constance arches her eyebrows. "He's pressuring you, isn't he? But I suppose that's better than waking up and finding yourself changed."

"Did *you* have a choice?" Luisa asks.

"No, but I suspect few of us do."

"How did you become a vampire?"

"It's a long story. Ever hear of the Salem Witch Trials?"

"Sure. I had to read *The Crucible* in high school."

"Well, then you have some idea of what a nightmare it was for the accused."

"How old are you, if you don't mind my asking?"

"I was born in Ipswich, Massachusetts, around 1675."

"Wow!" Luisa laughs in spite of herself. "You don't look a day over two hundred."

"Thank you." Constance picks up Luisa's cup, plate, and silverware. "My looks nearly got me killed more than once. The first time, I was a servant for a parson and his family. The good parson liked to preach hellfire and damnation on Sunday and chase after me the rest of the week. One night, he became a little too frisky. He entered my cell and threw himself at me. I was terrified. Without thinking, I hit him over the head with my chamber pot and hid out in the woods. I later learned that he accused me of witchcraft. Had I returned, he would have had me arrested. Of that I am certain."

"Where did you go?"

"To avoid being seen, I slept in the woods by day and traveled by night. In those days, teenage girls did not wander about unescorted. As soon as I thought I had put enough distance between the parson and me, I hired myself out to a farmer with two small children. My new employer was a widower whose wife had died in child-birth. He treated me so kindly that when he proposed,

I gladly accepted. A few years later, we moved west. We lived on a large farm and were as happy as any family had a right to be. But then disaster struck."

"What happened?"

"The Deerfield Massacre. The year was 1704. England was at war with France, and Massachusetts was an English colony within striking distance of New France, as Canada was called back then. An Indian raiding party led by some French officers swept down from the north and attacked us before dawn on Leap Year Day. We were staying in Deerfield at the time because it was protected by a stockade and a small garrison. But the snow was so high that the raiders easily climbed over the fence and were in the village before the night watchman could raise a cry. But I think he just got drunk and fell asleep. An Indian tomahawked my husband as he was loading his flintlock. The savages murdered our two boys before my very eyes. Fearing that I would be raped, I begged the Indians to kill me, but they kept me alive for ransom. The journey to Canada was in the dead of winter, and it nearly finished me." She pauses to collect her thoughts.

"I remained in Canada for several years," Constance says. "I can't recall exactly how long. I do know that I went native and refused to go back to Massachusetts when I had the chance. I became the wife of an Abenaki warrior instead and bore him a son. Call it Stockholm syndrome, but I stayed of my own free will. It was during my time in Canada that I became a vampire."

"What was it like?" Luisa asks.

"Living among the Indians?"

"No, the transformation."

"Oh, that." Constance wrinkles her forehead. "It was like a dream—an erotic dream. On the night it happened, my Abenaki husband and our young son were away on a hunting trip. I wasn't feeling well and went to sleep early. I dreamt that a handsome stranger entered our wigwam and began to make love to me. With each thrust, I could feel my life ebbing away. But," she says with a wicked smile, "I found the experience positively exhilarating."

"You did?"

"Just think—climaxing on the very brink of death." Constance's eyes flash a brilliant red. "Even after three hundred years, I get chills just thinking about it."

Luisa grimaces. "So what happened next?"

"When I awoke, I was drinking from an incision in my maker's forearm. After draining the life from my body, he was reviving me. As his blood began to flow through my veins, I became conscious of a heightened awareness and power I had never known before. I was a vampire."

Luisa gives a disappointed groan. "That was it?"

"What did you expect?"

"I don't know—something magical."

"Believe me, there's plenty of magic. *Wild* magic."

"Such as?"

"Well, your body undergoes some wondrous changes. Your special powers seem truly amazing at first."

"What kind of powers?"

"You'll be the fastest, strongest, and stealthiest predator on the block—unless, of course, you happen to run into another vampire."

"Are vampires immortal?"

Constance smiles. "Not exactly immortal—let's just say damned difficult to kill. At the age of a hundred, I watched the Minutemen chase the Redcoats out of Concord. I was well into my second century when I read Shakespeare with the Alcotts and the Emersons and went skinny-dipping with Thoreau in Walden Pond. I've seen the Boston Red Sox win the World Series with Babe Ruth *and* with Manny Ramirez. And I'm still pretty young as vampires go."

"What happened to your family?"

"I never saw them again." Constance stares out the back window into the Japanese garden. "For all they knew, I was dead and gone. They, in turn, were dead to me." Turning around, Constance seizes both of Luisa's hands and draws her close. "If you decide to go through with this," she says, baring her fangs, "you'd better turn your heart into granite, or you'll regret your decision for the rest of your days." Constance gazes at Luisa with imploring eyes, her fingers entwined as firmly as steel cords around Luisa's. "I would not hesitate to trade places with you if I could." Unable to break free of Constance's grip, Luisa begins to panic. Just then, Miguel appears beside her.

"Constance," Miguel says. "We've enjoyed our visit, but I'm afraid it's time to go."

Constance relaxes her grip, and as soon as her aching hands are free, Luisa slips behind Miguel. "Come, Luisa," he says. "You must be exhausted."

As they leave the kitchen, Constance flashes past to wait for them at the front door. "It was a pleasure meeting you," she tells Luisa. "Please feel free to drop in anytime." Turning to Miguel, she says, "You'll take good care of her, won't you?"

Once they're on the road, Miguel says, "Had I not appeared when I did, I believe Constance would have killed you."

Luisa stares openmouthed at Miguel. "What makes you say that?"

"She envies your youth, your beauty, and above all, your vitality. Without knowing it, you sparked a fire that nearly engulfed us all. Had I waited another minute or two, she would have drained you, and then I would have had to kill her."

"Gee, thanks. I so needed to hear that," Luisa says with a scowl. "I'll definitely sleep better now."

Her sarcastic comment is a self-fulfilling prophecy. As the Mercedes speeds through another rainstorm, Luisa becomes drowsy and dozes off. She awakens once during the drive home, just long enough to become aware that her head is resting on Miguel's shoulder. The second time she awakens, Miguel is carrying her up to her apartment. He manages to open the door and then gently lowers her onto the bed. She slithers out of her clothes, too sleep-drunk to care if he is watching. Then she pulls on an oversized

T-shirt with a Maya pyramid on the front and "CIUDAD ANTIGUA" emblazoned in a semicircle above it. The T-shirt was a gift from Andy Brower. When she wakes up, her bedroom is dark. As she fumbles for the alarm clock on the nightstand, she finds a sheet of paper. Switching on a lamp, she sees that it's a note from Miguel. *Be sure to watch the 11 o'clock news*, the message instructs. *See you at midnight.*

Chapter Five

CRIME AND PUNISHMENT

As Detective Sergeant Bill Cochrane pushes through the crowd, a TV reporter—no doubt eager to break the story on the 11 o'clock news—asks him a question. "No comment," is his terse reply. He ducks under the yellow crime scene tape. The first thing that catches his eye is a severed hand on the sidewalk—the lifeless fingers wrapped around a 9-mm. Beretta. A few feet from the hand, a headless corpse lies in a pool of thick, dark blood. A crime scene technician named Phil Lewis is preparing to take some photos. He places numbered yellow plastic cones beside the hand and the body.

"What have we got here, Phil?" Cochrane asks.

"Somebody went totally medieval on this dude," Lewis replies. "Looks like the assailant severed the victim's right hand before he could squeeze off a shot. Then he cut off the head. He apparently took it as a trophy." Lewis shakes his own head and mutters, "Just when you think you've seen it all."

Cochrane joins Detective Jack Reynolds, who is standing over a second corpse while a forensic scientist named Linda Battista uses tweezers to recover hair, fabric, and other trace evidence from the victim's body. She places each article in its own plastic bag and then labels the bag. The six-two Cochrane towers over the stocky Reynolds.

"Get this, Bill," Reynolds says, pointing to the headless body. "The ID we found on the body indicates that he was Rafael Herrera." A prime suspect in the murder of Luisa's aunt, Rosa Gonzalez, Herrera allegedly shot her and three others execution-style. "If it's him, the sonofabitch got what he deserved."

"I'd appreciate it if you'd send me the results of the fingerprint test," Cochrane says.

"You bet."

Cochrane watches as Battista examines the second corpse. She is kneeling before the body with her back to him. Her blue nitrile gloves are splotched with red. A large pool of blood surrounds the second corpse, and the face is chalk-white.

"What happened to this guy?" Cochrane asks.

Battista rises to her feet and says, "The cause of death appears to be blood loss and asphyxiation resulting from a deep cut across the victim's throat."

"What kind of weapon?" Cochrane asks.

"I'd say a large knife," Battista replies, "or maybe a machete."

"And the injuries?"

"Punctured trachea, severed jugular vein, torn right and left common carotid arteries. The victim probably died within a few minutes of the injury."

"What happened to the third victim?" Cochrane points to yet another corpse lying a few yards from the second.

"Cause of death appears to be evisceration," Battista answers. "The wound runs across the entire abdomen."

"One of the victims survived the attack," Reynolds tells Cochrane.

"Where is he?" Cochrane asks. "I want to ask him some questions."

"The EMS just took him to the hospital. He's going into surgery to have his right hand reattached."

"Did any of our people go with him?"

Reynolds shakes his head. "We were too busy securing the crime scene. But the first responders got a statement."

"Okay," Cochrane says. "Where are they?"

Two uniformed police officers approach the detectives.

"We found the victim sitting over there," the older officer says, indicating a spot in front of Eva's, a Salvadoran restaurant on Fourteenth Street. "He was holding his severed hand and going into shock. I immediately began to administer first aid. I tied off the victim's wrist to stop the bleeding and had him lie down. "

"The victim said his name was Javier Rodriguez," the younger officer tells Cochrane. "I've got his statement right here," he says, taking a black notebook out of his jacket pocket. "I translated it from Spanish." The officer finds the page and starts reading: "'The killer appeared out of nowhere. He was dressed in black like a ninja. His eyes glowed bright red. He moved real fast, like a blur. In the blink of an eye, all four of us were down and he was gone.'"

"Are you sure you heard that right?" Cochrane asks.

"Absolutely," the officer insists. "I had him repeat the part about *los ojos rojos*. That's what he said—the attacker had red eyes."

"He was probably wearing red contact lenses," Cochrane says.

"Or maybe he's the Terminator," Reynolds says.

"Do we have any other witnesses?" Cochrane asks. "Anyone who can ID the assailant or assailants?"

"Nobody inside the restaurant saw the attack," Reynolds answers. "One of the waitresses said she heard yelling but thought it was just some teenage boys fooling around."

Cochrane and Reynolds resume their crime scene walk-through. They follow Battista to the third victim's body.

"We need to start questioning bystanders," Cochrane says. "Let's find out what they know."

"Right," Reynolds says. "I sure as hell don't buy the gangbanger's statement."

Cochrane says nothing. He intently watches Battista collect evidence.

"One thing is certain," Reynolds says. "The Escorpiones took out Herrera to avenge two of their own."

"A lot of people wanted Herrera dead," Cochrane says. "But gangbangers didn't do it."

"Why not?"

"Going up against four guys, they would've used fire-arms, not edged weapons. And there would've been more of 'em. According to our eyewitness, we're searching for a lone assailant."

"That's bullshit," Reynolds says. "But it might be useful to let the Camazotzas believe that a one-man killing machine is after them. Won't *that* give 'em nightmares!"

Cochrane turns to Reynolds and smiles. "Maybe, but I can think of one person who'll sleep better tonight."

It is 11:05 p.m., and Cochrane is back in his office. Stacks of police reports cover his desk, and yellow sticky notes bearing names, phone numbers, and messages hang like banners from his computer monitor. The one photo on Cochrane's desk depicts three soldiers in full battle gear posing before a Bradley Fighting Vehicle. A youthful-looking Cochrane stands in the middle, his arms draped around the shoulders of the man on either side. The walls are bare save for his degree from James Madison—a Bachelor of Arts in History—and a commendation for valor from the Metropolitan Police Department.

Cochrane retrieves his report for the Gonzalez case and begins reading. The story is familiar by now . . . *too* familiar. This leaves him with the nagging sense that he must be overlooking something. At about 4:30 p.m. on April Fools' Day, Rosa Gonzalez, sixty-five, picked up eight-year-old Maria Sandoval at the local child care center. Ms. Gonzalez was retired and walked the Sandoval girl home whenever her mother, a next-door neighbor, had to work late. They stopped at Dos Gringos Café for ice cream and spent about twenty minutes there. As they descended the steep steps of the entrance, two youths named Eduardo Reyes and Carlos Arias approached from the direction of the Columbia Heights Metro station. Reyes was on his way to meet his *chica* and had promised to hook Arias up with one of her friends. They were members of the Takoma Park clique of the Escorpiones.

As the two pairs of pedestrians converged, a white, late-model Lincoln Navigator screeched to a stop on Mount Pleasant Street about fifty feet away. Four Latino males were inside the vehicle. All were members of the Mara Camazotza gang under orders to kill Reyes and Arias for trespassing on their turf. The hit men jumped out of the vehicle and opened fire on the four pedestrians. The shooters were armed with large-caliber handguns. In the ensuing hail of bullets, Reyes and Arias were hit but managed to crawl behind a parked delivery truck. One of the youths was shot in the thigh and shoulder, and the other in the abdomen. Using her body to shield Maria Sandoval, Ms. Gonzalez crumpled to the sidewalk with five bullet wounds in the chest, arms, and abdomen. Although unhurt, the Sandoval girl was trapped under the Gonzalez woman's body. On emptying their clips, three of the assailants returned to the Navigator. The fourth assailant, probably the leader, shot each of the victims in the head at close range. Then he returned to the Navigator and the assailants sped off. Soon afterward, the four shooting victims were rushed to the Emergency Department of the George Washington University Hospital. They were pronounced dead on arrival.

As the case's lead detective, Cochrane had to notify the next of kin and meet them at the chief medical examiner's office to identify the bodies. It's the part of his job he hates most. Maria Sandoval's mother arrived in hysterics and had to be calmed down before she could identify her daughter's body. She was too upset to answer Cochrane's questions. About an hour later, Luisa Santiago arrived in a state of shock. She identified her aunt and then muttered some unintelligible responses to Cochrane's questions. Since then, Cochrane has talked to the two women several times. Both have had a rough time of it, but Cochrane believes that the Santiago woman's grief has developed a sharp edge bordering on rage.

Cochrane's office phone rings. He picks up the receiver. "Detective Sergeant Cochrane here. What can I do for you?"

"Hello Sergeant Cochrane. This is Luisa Santiago. I'm so glad you're in."

"And I'm glad you called, Ms. Santiago. There's been a major development in your aunt's case. One of the suspects, Rafael Herrera, has been murdered. I was planning to call you in the morning."

"Well, I just heard about it on the news. Are you sure it's him? I mean, the reporter said his head was missing."

"That's true, but there's still plenty of evidence that it was Herrera."

"What about the other three shooters? Are you any closer to finding them?"

"Nothing much has changed since the last time we talked. They're still at large. The word on the street is they've skipped town and gone to LA or El Salvador. But I'm convinced they're still around. We'll keep looking until we find them."

Cochrane pauses to let Luisa respond, but there is only silence on the other end.

"Ms. Santiago, are you still there?"

"Somebody else had to kill Herrera for you," she blurts. "If you'd done your job, the rest of the killers would be dead or in jail by now. I should've listened to my roommate and hired a private detective."

"Ms. Santiago, I've done everything humanly possible to bring the suspects to justice. And I'm still very much on the case." Cochrane leaves unsaid the fact that he doesn't know how much longer that will be.

Luisa begins to cry. "I'm sorry," she says between sobs. "I shouldn't have called. I just want this nightmare to be over."

"I know," Cochrane says. "Believe me, I know."

Chapter Six

METAMORPHOSIS

L uisa hangs up the phone and reaches for a Kleenex. *Well, it's done*, she thinks, blowing her nose. *One down, three to go.*

There's no use denying it any longer. The death of her Aunt Rosa has left a huge void that neither her friends nor even her dancing can fill. The success of her ballet has exceeded all her expectations, yet she feels utterly unsatisfied because her aunt wasn't there to share it with her. All the joy and inspiration have fled out of her life as if someone had doused the fire that nourished them. She wonders how long she can go on before others will start to notice.

The only thing keeping her afloat these days is the thought of avenging her aunt.

Luisa is tired of feeling helpless—she wants to feel strong and in control again. She is ready to place her fate in Miguel's hands.

The kitchen clock reads 11:25. Luisa leaves out plenty of dry food and fresh water for Mauricio and cleans his litter box. She sticks a note on the fridge asking Karen to feed the cat for the next few days. Then she goes into the bedroom, peels off her sweats, and slips on a little black dress and high heels à la Constance Bennett.

She also takes down a large, brown leather volume from the closet shelf. It is a scrapbook that her aunt compiled to trace Luisa's development as a dancer. The album is titled, "*La Mariposa*." Luisa's eyes fill with tears as she comes to her aunt's favorite photo. It is Luisa's first publicity shot, taken when she was twenty. Luisa is wearing a filmy, white silk dress with a ruffled top. She is posing *en pointe*, the knee-length dress clinging to her fully extended left leg. Her dark hair is pulled back in a bun. She gazes downward, displaying her long eyelashes to full effect. Her bare right leg is folded like a jackknife across her midsection, while her elbows point outward like wings, her right hand touching her right thigh just below the buttocks, and her left hand pressing against her right shin. Luisa's aunt said that the image reminded her of a butterfly emerging from a chrysalis.

Sensing that she is being watched, Luisa lifts the scrapbook and finds Mauricio seated at her feet, his pale blue eyes staring up at her. Much to her amazement, the cat hops onto the bed, curls up in her lap, and starts to purr. This is Mauricio's first show of affection outside the kitchen. Once upon a time, he was her aunt's pampered brat and, until tonight, honored her memory by snubbing his stepmother. Luisa is unsure of his motive—perhaps her tears have aroused his sympathy, or maybe he is just tired of being lonely. In any event, she is grateful for his company and rewards him by stroking the fur behind his ears. Mauricio blinks his eyes and purrs contentedly, but his contentment is short-lived. The sudden realization that she is holding Mauricio for the first and probably the last time causes Luisa to break down. She takes the cat into her arms, embraces him, and showers him with tear-soaked kisses. Mauricio seems to find Luisa's emotional display more than he can bear and struggles to free himself. She releases the writhing cat, but in making his escape, he rakes her forearms with sharp claws badly in need of trimming. The result is a less than fond farewell, with Luisa hurling a high-heeled shoe and a torrent of abuse at the fleeing feline.

While she is in the bathroom dressing her wounds, the doorbell rings. *That's gotta be the other fanged predator in my life.* As Luisa walks to the door, she notices that the kitchen clock reads 12:00. *He's right on time.*

She opens the door and says, "Come in,"—not because he needs permission to enter (he doesn't), but because it's the polite thing to do.

His eyes widen and his nostrils flare. "I smell fresh blood. Are you all right?"

"Just a little farewell gift from my goddamn cat." She holds out her bandaged forearms.

"Did you watch the news?"

"Of course." She nods toward the black duffel bag in his right hand. "Is that what I think it is?"

"Would you care to take a peek?" He reaches for the zipper.

"Absolutely not!"

"You look ravishing," Miguel says, extending his arm. "Shall we?"

"I need to pack a few things, first."

"All right, but leave your cell phone."

"Why?" she shouts from the bedroom.

"The police will use it to track you down."

Luisa returns to the living room carrying her handbag and an overnight bag. "Okay, let's go."

Miguel holds out his hand. "Your phone, please."

She reluctantly hands it over, and he crushes it in his right hand.

"You owe me two hundred bucks," she says.

He smiles. "Relax. I'll buy you another one. I can get the same model for a tenth of what you paid."

"I'll bet somebody's hand is still attached to it."

In the doorway, Luisa says goodbye to Mauricio, who is still in hiding. As she closes the door, Luisa feels as though a part of her has already died. Miguel opens the front passenger door of his Mercedes for her, but she stops to gaze up at the sky. Then she looks at him and says, "Before you change me, I want to visit my aunt's church."

"It's after midnight," he says. "The doors will be locked."

"Okay, so unlock them."

Miguel parks the car a few blocks from the church. It is a cool, crisp autumn night. A gentle breeze caresses Luisa's hair and rustles some fallen leaves under her feet. They walk in silence through the gloom. As they approach the church, the moon appears from behind a cloud. A sliver of pale moonlight illuminates the façade, revealing a tall porch fronted by a colonnade. Miguel simply pushes on the massive, horseshoe-shaped door, and it swings open.

"Hurry, Luisa."

Once inside, she looks behind the door, but no one is there. It's been years since her last visit. She stuffs some crumpled bills into the poor box in atonement for their trespass. They walk side-by-side up the center aisle, their footsteps echoing against the great stone walls. Darkness has transformed the magnificent Byzantine cathedral into a haunted castle.

"This place is creeping me out," she says with a shudder. "I get the feeling we're not alone."

"I think it's perfect!" Miguel says. "Let's do it right here." He vanishes into the shadows and then reappears beside the altar. "Come here, my little lamb!"

"No way!"

"Why not?"

"I need to clear it with my aunt, first."

Luisa slides into a pew near the front and sits down. Bowing her head and closing her eyes, she begins to pray to her Aunt Rosa.

"*Mamá*," she whispers, "*perdóname por lo que voy a hacer. Lo haga porque se lo debo todo a usted. Yo le vengaré si es la última cosa que hago.*"

Luisa rises from the pew, walks over to Miguel, and grasps his right hand. She studies the fanged monster on his ring finger and then looks into his eyes. "I'm ready now."

As Miguel undresses, he explains, "This can be a little messy."

Luisa kicks off her shoes and slips out of her dress, revealing a matching black lace bra and bikini panties. "It's kind of chilly in here," she says. "How long is this going to take?"

"Not long." He beckons her to the altar. "I need your help."

As they remove the devotional candles, communion chalices, and floral garlands from the altar, Luisa glimpses a pair of red eyes in the shadows.

"Who's there?" she calls out.

"I asked a few friends to join us," Miguel says.

"Why?" She folds her arms over her breasts.

"They're our lookouts."

"Oh, God, it's a fucking peep show." She starts to shiver. "Let's do this before I change my mind."

Miguel unfolds a large red velvet coverlet which he found on a nearby chair and spreads it over the white linen altar cloth. He tells Luisa to lie down on the altar. Lying there on her back, she feels a sudden urge to bolt for the exit.

"Don't worry" Miguel says as he strokes her hair. "I'll protect you." Then he smiles. "Are you ready?"

"I think so."

Miguel bends over and kisses Luisa on the lips. Moving lower, he briefly nibbles on her soft brown flesh before plunging his fangs into her throat. She feels a searing pain and then sinks into oblivion. Her last conscious thought is, *Ohmigod, I'm dying.*

She is suspended in absolute darkness. Then she becomes aware of a distant, faint luminosity. The light grows nearer and brighter until it blinds her, and then *poof*, it vanishes. Luisa realizes that she is in bed and Aunt Rosa is reading to her. The scene is somewhat out of focus—her aunt looks twenty years younger.

"*Y vivieron felices para siempre.*"

"*Mami,*" little Luisa asks, "*¿me va a leer otra cuento?*"

"*Sí, pero entonces debes ir a dormir.*"

Aunt Rosa begins to read the story of *Caperucita Roja*—Little Red Riding Hood. Luisa becomes conscious of a scene shift—she is now clad in a red, hooded cloak and is skipping down a woodland path with a basket of food in her hand. Aside from her scarlet cloak, everything is in grainy black-and-white, like an old movie. A Big, Bad Wolf on two legs appears and asks her where she's going.

To Grandma's, Luisa replies. *She's sick and I'm bringing her some goodies.*

That's very sweet! the Wolf says. He suggests that she stop along the way to pick some pretty flowers for her sick grandma.

What a wonderful idea! Luisa says. And she proceeds to collect flowers. Meanwhile, the Wolf scampers ahead to Grandma's house. Peering through an open window, he sees the old woman in bed, buried beneath the covers, looking just like Aunt Rosa. The Wolf leaps through the window and devours her in one gulp. Then he climbs into bed and pulls up the covers until only his head is visible. When Luisa knocks on the door, the Wolf affects a sick, old woman's rasping voice and tells her to come inside. Luisa cannot believe her eyes. Her grandmother looks so different!

Grandma! Luisa cries. *What big eyes you have.*

The better to see you with, *my dear*, the Wolf cackles.

My, what big ears you have!

The better to hear you with, snarls the Wolf.

My, what big teeth you have!

The better to eat you with!

The Wolf throws off the covers and springs at Luisa. As he opens his jaws to swallow her whole, Luisa opens wide her own mouth, revealing a pair of gleaming white fangs. She seizes the Wolf by the shoulders and plunges her fangs into his throat. The Wolf howls with pain and terror—the cries sound human. She opens her eyes and discovers that the creature she's feeding on isn't a Big, Bad Wolf, but only a man. To her horror, she realizes that it isn't even a man—*it's Miguel.*

"Luisa!" Miguel exclaims, a look of relief on his face. "For a moment, I thought I'd lost you."

"What happened?" She notices that the red coverlet is wrapped like a shroud around her body.

"I had trouble reviving your heart. Here, this will make you feel better." Using a sharp fingernail, Miguel makes an incision in the vein protruding from the crook of his right arm. The blood bubbles up, fresh and inviting. Like a pair of leeches, Luisa's eager lips fasten onto his forearm, and she begins to drink. The metallic saltiness is intoxicating. In her excitement, she nearly chokes.

"Take your time," he says. "Learn to savor it."

Luisa manages to restrain the urge to gorge by settling into a slow, steady rhythm. She maintains this languid pace for a long time. At last, she pauses to catch her breath. Opening her eyes, she gazes around the church in amazement. It's as if a veil has been lifted. The interior no longer appears dark and menacing, and even distant objects come into sharp focus.

"How are you feeling, my dear?" Miguel asks.

"I think I'm okay," Luisa answers.

"You can go now!" Miguel shouts to the unseen sentinels.

As the great door swings open, two shadowy figures appear before it and then vanish without a trace. Had Luisa blinked twice, she would have missed Miguel's two guardians.

"Do you feel strong enough to move?" Miguel asks.

"I think so." No sooner does Luisa stand up than her head starts to spin. As the blood rushes downward, she faints, but Miguel is there to catch her. She leans against him for support. "Wow, was that Constance ever wrong! I feel weak as a kitten."

"You must be patient," Miguel says. "The transformation doesn't happen overnight."

Miguel has Luisa drink some more from his arm. The fresh supply of blood invigorates her. But when she removes the coverlet, she makes a startling discovery. "Jesus Christ, Miguel! I'm bleached."

"Relax," Miguel says. "You will become less pale over time."

"So what do I do in the meantime?"

"I would suggest getting used to it."

They dress in silence; Luisa notes that the altar cloth is spattered with blood. Though upset over her ghostly complexion, she is pleased that the scratches on her arms have already vanished.

As they head for the door, Luisa becomes aware of strange noises emanating from the dark corners of the church. She holds up her hand. "Wait a minute. What is that scratching noise?"

"Rats," Miguel says. "They're everywhere."

They walk hand-in-hand into the early-morning still-ness, the heavy wooden door closing behind them. Luisa steals one last backward glance at the church. She smiles. *Now it's time to turn the tables on the Big, Bad Wolf.*

Chapter Seven

BACK IN BLACK

Miguel drives Luisa from the church to a restored eighteenth-century townhouse in Old Town Alexandria. He gives her the grand tour, saying that this will be home for the next few weeks. She assumes that he means *their* home. When they come to the master bedroom, she wraps her arms around his waist and kisses him on the mouth. "I don't know about you," she says, "but I'm feeling kinda frisky." But when she tries to maneuver him onto the Queen Anne four-poster, he doesn't budge. "What's wrong?" she asks.

"Luisa, I have to leave town on business."

"You mean right now?"

"I'm afraid so."

"Why don't you take me with you?"

"It's too risky. You might be recognized."

"I'll take my chances."

"No, it's out of the question."

She releases him and takes a few steps back. "Look, Miguel. You can fuck whoever you want whenever you want for all I care. Just don't lie to me."

Miguel stares at her in astonishment. "Luisa, I'm a businessman! When I say I have to go out of town on business, I'm simply stating a fact."

"How many vampire brides do you keep on the side?"

"What a ridiculous question!"

"I have a right to know."

"The answer is zero." He takes her by the shoulders and looks intently into her eyes. "That's why I made you, my dear."

"You always say the right thing." She flops down on the bed. "Now show me you mean it."

"I just told you. I have a plane to catch."

"You're making me work too goddamn hard at this!"

He shrugs and begins to unbutton his shirt. "I suppose I could delay my flight."

"That's more like it!" Luisa sits up and unbuckles his pants for him. Then she slips out of her black dress and pulls him down on the bed beside her. "Just lie back and enjoy the ride."

No sooner does Luisa roll off Miguel than he springs out of bed and jumps into the shower.

"Hey!" she yells from the bedroom. "When are we going after the gangbangers?"

"When I say you're ready."

"I'm ready now."

"We'll discuss it when I get back."

As he dresses, Miguel lays down some ground rules for Luisa. "You are a creature of the night now," he says. "Darkness is your friend. Avoid going out during the day. Sunlight will only hurt your eyes and skin and dull your senses."

"Not to worry," Luisa says. "With this complexion, I'd get a second degree burn just picking up the morning paper."

"When you feed," he continues, "don't overdo it. Dead bodies are trouble. And be discreet. Too many people know your face. Above all, trust your instincts. They won't let you down." He kisses her on the lips. "I'll be back before you know it. Ciao."

"And I'll be gone by then!" she calls to him, but he is already out the door.

Overcome with fatigue, Luisa lies down and soon falls asleep. When she awakens, the room is dark and the clock reads 11:00 p.m. She rolls over, picks up the remote, and switches on the TV. The local news is on. Scrolling down the channel guide, she notices that the date is Sunday, October 30, two full days ahead of schedule. She presses the appropriate button but is unable to return the guide to the current date. Glancing at her watch, she is astonished to discover that it also reads Sunday the thirtieth. Then it dawns on her: *I've been asleep for three fucking days! Why didn't the sonofabitch warn me!*

Luisa is about to turn off the TV when she hears her name mentioned and then sees Amanda Donovan—the same reporter who interviewed her on *Top o' the Mornin'*.

Amanda is standing outside Luisa's apartment building. Luisa's publicity photo fills the screen as Amanda provides the voiceover: "The Capital Ballet is stunned by the recent disappearance of one of its leading members, dancer-choreographer Luisa Santiago, who missed a Friday morning rehearsal and her weekend performances at the Kennedy Center. The twenty-six-year-old Santiago had just premiered her first ballet, *The Offering*, about a Mayan queen who sacrifices herself to save her people."

The next sound bite is a taped interview with John Mitchell, the executive director of the Capital Ballet. "Luisa dedicated the ballet to her aunt, who died while she was working on it. It was like losing her mother. Luisa's artistry gave her the ability to transform her grief into something beautiful and noble." A photo of Luisa in her college graduation robes standing beside an elderly woman appears. Amanda's voiceover states that Santiago's aunt, Rosa Gonzalez, was shot to death during a gang-related killing six months ago, and that Santiago disappeared just a day after the brutal slaying of a suspect in her aunt's murder.

The camera cuts back to Amanda. "Santiago was last seen in the company of Miguel Maldonado, a wealthy businessman from El Salvador and one of the Capital Ballet's newest patrons. Maldonado could not be reached for comment. A recorded message at his business number states that he is currently on vacation." Luisa gasps as the camera pans to her best friend. "Standing beside me is Luisa Santiago's longtime roommate, Karen Silber. What do you think happened to her, Karen?"

"Well, Amanda, I believe Luisa was abducted or lured away by this Maldonado character. I tried to warn her about him, but she wouldn't listen." With tear-filled eyes, Karen faces the camera. "Luisa, if you're watching, please let me know you're okay. I'm really scared for you."

Luisa switches off the TV and cries herself to sleep.

For the first time in four days, Luisa steps outside. It's a cool, damp, and dreary late afternoon on Halloween—in short, a perfect day for a vampire to venture outdoors. A patchwork of red, yellow, brown, and orange leaves hangs from the trees and covers parked cars, streets, and side-walks. Loud honking heralds the passing of Canada geese overhead. Here and there, little monsters, witches, wiz-ards, superheroes, and vampires are already making their rounds. She walks down to the neighborhood supermarket and scans the outdoor newspaper vending machines. One of the headlines reads, *LOCAL BALLERINA REPORTED MISSING*. Her eyes also fall on a handbill announcing a Halloween party at Scalawags, an Alexandria nightclub. The event is billed as the "Rave to the Grave." Although self-conscious about her bleached complexion, she decides to go anyway, if only to get out of the house for a while.

Luisa cobbles together a costume from the detritus of a few secondhand stores in Old Town Alexandria: a black leotard that she adorns with a splash of silver glitter across the front, a black miniskirt, a crimson sash, black fishnet stockings, and a pair of black high heels.

As she stands before the bathroom mirror applying her black eyeliner and purple lipstick, Luisa can't help admiring her new physique. The lean muscle mass has added sexy contours to her lithe dancer's body without diminishing its suppleness. Even her pale skin takes on an alluring sheen when set off against all that black. After trying out some provocative poses while flashing her new fangs, she deems herself ready.

And then it hits her. She's just joined the ranks of the undead, and yet she's never felt more *alive*.

With a shiver of anticipation, she steals into the night, feeling feisty and in her element. As she walks down King Street, a silver BMW 750i with tinted windows pulls alongside her. She looks straight ahead and continues walking. The Bimmer follows her for a block or two and then speeds off.

When she reaches Scalawags, the waiting line wraps around the block. Two brawny bouncers stand guard on either side of the door. She catches the eye of the one on the right. He motions to her.

"Who . . . me?" she asks.

"Yeah, you," he says. "Let's go." He opens the door for her.

The people at the front of the line raise holy hell. As she steps inside, they surge forward, demanding to be let in. The bouncer holding the door orders the jostlers to move back, and they grudgingly yield. He turns to Luisa and says, "Have a good time."

The interior of the club reminds her of an old barn-turned-B-horror-movie set. Above the entrance, "RAVE TO THE GRAVE" appears in red letters that suggest dripping blood. There are fake headstones marked "RIP" propped up here and there. Giant cobwebs hang from the walls, and huge vampire bats dangle from the rafters. An open coffin occupied by an adult-size human skeleton stands in a dark corner near the bar. The flashing lights, loud music, and various scents given off by the crowd assault Luisa's senses. The glare bothers her so much that she asks James Dean if she can borrow his black Wayfarers.

"Keep 'em," he tells her. "They look better on you."

As she passes through the crowd, Luisa is relieved to see that some of the Goth girls are just as pale as she is. She heads down to the dance floor with the intention of losing herself in the ocean of gyrating bodies. But before she can take two steps, Sweeney Todd asks her to dance with him.

"Why not?" she says.

Not only is Sweeney good-looking, but he's also a pretty fair dancer. As she sways to the music, Luisa realizes that she's enjoying herself for the first time in a long while.

"Wow!" Sweeney shouts above the music. "Where did you learn to dance like that?"

"I studied ballet," Luisa yells back.

"Awesome!"

Luisa soon tires of Sweeney. His good looks cannot overcome a vocabulary that consists of "Wow," "Awesome," and half a dozen similar exclamations. After their third dance, she excuses herself to powder her nose. Sweeney offers to buy her a drink, which she declines. He then asks her to go home with him.

"I just got here," Luisa says.

"You don't know what you're missing."

"Oh, yes I do."

Realizing that he has just been shot down, Sweeney retreats to the bar for some liquid solace.

No sooner does she disentangle herself from one serial killer than she's approached by Jason Voorhees and Freddy Krueger.

"Hi," Freddy says with a friendly wave of his metal-clawed hand.

"Hi," Luisa answers. She eyes him warily.

"Love your costume," Freddy says. "Did you make it yourself?"

"Um, sort of." *There's something weirdly familiar about these guys . . .*

"So whaddya think of ours?" Freddy asks.

Jason's costume appears a few sizes too small while Freddy's calls to mind a little boy trying on his father's clothes. "You look like a couple of *mendigos*," Luisa laughs. Then she whispers into Freddy's ear, "I know what you guys are."

"We're not gay, if that's what you mean."

Luisa laughs again. "Show me yours and I'll show you mine." Grinning, she flashes her fangs.

"Wow! They look terrific!" Freddy says.

Having made her point, Luisa steers the conversation in another direction. Nodding toward Jason, she asks, "What's with your friend? Is he autistic?"

"Not really," Freddy says. "He's more into sports."

"Very funny."

Freddy gives her a nonplussed look, indicating that he's perfectly serious.

Just then, the DJ announces a ladies' pole dancing contest. First prize consists of 500 dollars in cash and a large trophy featuring a buxom lass twirling on a vertical pole. As the crowd roars in approval, Luisa tells Freddy and Jason, "Well, guys, it's been nice talking to you, but I've got a contest to enter." She walks over to the registration table and identifies herself as Vampira, a 1950s TV character she saw in the Johnny Depp film, *Ed Wood*.

Six women have already entered the contest, making Luisa the seventh and final contestant. The first contestant is a Jessica Simpson lookalike who's wearing a red bikini and a Miss Universe banner. Though drop-dead gorgeous, she's not much of a dancer. The blonde bombshell is easily outclassed by contestant number two, a statuesque redhead masquerading as a porno-movie-nurse whose skimpy uniform leaves little to the imagination. The contestant standing next to Luisa says, "That slut oughtta be disqualified! Anyone can see she's a pro." The redhead's suggestive undulations elicit a raucous crowd response that contestants three through six cannot match. Thus far, the second contestant is the clear crowd favorite.

The DJ announces that contestant number seven is Vampira. For her dance number, Luisa has chosen the Santana cover of the AC-DC classic, "Back in Black." As the music begins, she removes the Wayfarers and tosses them into the crowd. "I'M BACK IN BLACK . . . BEEN GONE TOO LONG . . . LET LOOSE FROM THE NOOSE . . . GLAD TO BE BACK." Straddling the pole, she bumps and grinds as if riding a mechanical bull on a merry-go-round. "FORGET THE HEARSE 'CAUSE I NEVER DIE . . . GOT NINE LIVES . . . USIN' EVERY ONE OF 'EM . . . 'CAUSE I'M RUNNIN' WILD." The shouts and wolf whistles that accompany her sinuous gyrations nearly drown out the vocal track. She leans back, kicks her right leg high into the air, and shakes her mane of wavy, raven hair. "YES I'M B-A-A-A-ACK . . . I'M B-A-A-A-ACK . . . I'M BACK IN BLACK!" Thighs wrapped snugly around the pole, she shimmies to the top, executes several rapid spins, and then glides down into a squatting position. She rises slowly, writhing serpent-like and flicking her tongue at the spectators crowding the stage. Then, as she sashays around the pole, she notices that the audience has fallen silent. At first she thinks, *Dammit, I've lost them*. But as Luisa gazes at the crowd, she realizes that they're mesmerized. Their hungry stares trigger a terrifying vision: for an instant, she's being attacked by soldiers armed with knives and spears.

When the music stops, she clings to the pole like a pale vine, utterly spent. A moment of stunned silence follows, and then the audience begins to applaud. As the clamor increases, she bows and walks offstage. The crowd takes up the chant, "More, more." As the DJ pleads for quiet, the chanting and clapping only grow louder and drown out his appeals. He waits in the hope that the audience will soon tire. In the meantime, he has the seven contestants join him onstage. Before the DJ can begin the voting, a second chant begins: "Vampira, Vampira."

The DJ sees no point in going through the motions of a vote. "The people have spoken," he announces. "The winner by acclamation is Vampira!" He gives her a congratulatory hug and presents her with the trophy and 500 dollars. Luisa waves to the crowd, which applauds and whistles in appreciation. Five of Luisa's fellow contestants congratulate her. The redhead, however, calls Luisa a "goddamn ringer" and is booed off the stage.

Luisa decides that she's had enough excitement for one night. On her way out the door, she waves to the bouncer who let her in.

"Need some help with that trophy?" he asks. "It's damn near big as you."

Luisa smiles and says that she's okay. She walks past Freddy and Jason, who are getting into a candy-apple red '69 Ford Mustang. They offer her a ride.

"No, thanks," she says, "I'd rather walk."

A few blocks from the club, Luisa senses that she is being followed. The scent is familiar. As she turns, a lean figure emerges from the shadows. It's Sweeney Todd.

"Hi," he says. "I thought you could use a hand."

"Thanks," she answers, "but it's really not a problem. I'm a lot stronger than I look."

"I'll walk you home, then. You shouldn't be out all alone."

"I can take care of myself."

"Oh, is that a fact?" Sweeney reaches into his breast pocket and pulls out a straight razor. "There's no telling who or what you might run into at this hour."

"You damn fool," Luisa says. "Put that thing away."

"Just keep your pretty little mouth shut," Sweeney says, "and you won't get hurt." He lunges at her, but she eludes him easily. "You leave me no choice," he says, flipping open the blade.

"For the last time," Luisa says, "just walk away." Her eyes flash red, but the color change passes unnoticed in the darkness.

"So you want to play rough." Sweeney laughs. "This is gonna be fun."

He lunges at Luisa a second time, thrusting the blade at her face. With her free hand, she grabs his forearm and snaps it like a twig. Crying out, Sweeney drops the razor and falls to his knees. As he clutches his shattered limb, she grabs his collar and drags him behind a nearby dumpster. Then she sets down the trophy and straddles him like a hobbyhorse. Her taut skin tingles with anticipation.

"My arm!" he moans. As Luisa leans forward, she sees the terror in his cold blue-gray eyes. "I'm sorry," he whimpers. "I only wanted to scare you. You've got to believe me."

"Too late for apologies, lover," she whispers into his ear. "I tried to warn you. And now it's time to pay."

As she lies on top of Sweeney, Luisa feels the rapid pounding of his heart against her breasts. She sinks her fangs into his throat, and a stream of thick, warm blood fills her mouth. With each swallow, she experiences a delicious thrill, while Sweeney's breathing becomes slower and shallower. Her thirst is overpowering, and she drains him quickly. He manages one last gasp, briefly shudders, and then goes still. In death, Sweeney's eyes remain wide open. His handsome face reminds her of a marble sculpture—alabaster white, smooth, frozen.

As she rises to her feet, a car screeches to a stop about fifty feet away. Two figures jump out and converge on her without a sound. As she prepares to strike, another familiar scent greets her nostrils. It's Freddy and Jason. Both have removed their masks. Their faces are youthful, but neither one is as handsome as Sweeney.

"What are you two doing here?"

Freddy kneels down to examine the corpse. "This guy looks familiar." He picks up the razor. "Wasn't he the dancer?"

"Yeah, that's him all right," says Jason, breaking his long silence. "What happened?"

"He came at me with a straight razor," Luisa says, "so I made a meal out of him."

"Jesus!" Jason exclaims. "Miguel is going to be royally pissed."

"Do you mean Miguel Maldonado?"

"He ordered us to keep an eye on you," Freddy replies.

"So what took you so long?"

"Blame it on motorhead over there," Jason says, pointing an accusatory finger at Freddy. "First he floods the carburetor, and then he almost crashes into a brick wall."

"Stop exaggerating," Freddy retorts. "I didn't even come close."

"Did so!"

"Did not!"

"Excuse me, guys," Luisa says. "But shouldn't we be going?"

"She's right," Freddy tells Jason. "Dump the body in the trunk while I start the car."

"Why do I always end up doing the grunt work?" Jason says, hoisting Sweeney's corpse onto his shoulder as if it were an oversize rag doll.

"Because you're built like King Kong, that's why." Freddy turns to Luisa and asks, "Was he your first human?"

"Yeah."

"Welcome to the club."

"Thanks."

As they shake hands, Freddy pulls out the razor and slashes Luisa's wrist. "Gotcha!"

"What the—" Breaking free, she is relieved to find her wrist uncut. But she is incensed at Freddy. "*¡Pendejo!*"

"C'mon, it was only a joke," Freddy says with a chuckle. "That blade couldn't cut butter."

"Well, I'm not amused!"

So Sweeney had attacked her with a dull blade. Maybe, like Freddy, he had intended it as a joke. Well, she had seen to it that he would never make *that* mistake again.

They all climb into the Mustang—Freddy in the driver's seat, Luisa in the middle, and Jason riding shotgun. On the way to Miguel's townhouse, Freddy tells Luisa that he and Jason were the lookouts in the church the night Miguel changed her.

"So you guys were the Peeping Toms!" she says. "I'd better not catch either one of you looking into my windows."

"What are you talking about?" Freddy juts out his chin. "We're perfect gentlemen."

Luisa smiles. "Did you two gentleman happen to steal your costumes off a couple of crackheads?"

"We bought 'em off two guys outside Scalawags," Freddy says. "I also bribed one of the bouncers to let us in. We've got a lot invested in you."

"I could've taken care of the bouncers," Jason says, "and saved you the fifty bucks."

"Okay, genius, what were you planning to do when the cops arrived? The idea was to remain inconspicuous."

"What is it with you guys?" Luisa says. "Do you ever stop fighting?"

"Can't help it," Freddy shrugs. "We're brothers."

When they pull up to the townhouse, Freddy tells Luisa that he and Jason will dispose of Sweeney's body.

"Miguel's gonna want a full report when he gets back," Freddy says. "We'll have to tell him about your coming-out party at Scalawags. But let's keep the dead guy our little secret, okay?"

Luisa says that that's fine with her. Then she slides out of the car.

"Here, I want you to have this." She hands the trophy to Jason, who's holding the car door for her.

"Are you sure?" Jason says, casting an appreciative eye on it. "It's one fine-looking piece of hardware."

"I'd rather give it to you than keep it around for Miguel to find. It would only upset him."

"Okay. I'll hold onto it for you. Who knows? You might want it back."

At the door, Luisa hugs Jason and waves to Freddy, who's waiting in the car.

"See ya, kid," Freddy says with a tip of his brown fedora. "We'll be back in about an hour. Think you can stay out of trouble that long?"

Luisa yawns. "Are you kidding? I'm going straight to bed." She shuts the door and then peers out the window. After the Mustang speeds away, she heads out into the night to find her aunt's killers.

Chapter Eight

CONFRONTATION

"Professor Brower, thank you for coming here on such short notice," says Denise Johnson, a special agent for US Customs and Border Protection. They are standing in the lobby of the US Customs House in Baltimore.

"Call me Andy," he says as they shake hands. "Glad to help out."

On the way to the elevators, Denise explains the reason for the call. "One of our agents spotted a couple of suspicious-looking crates from El Salvador. They're marked 'handicrafts,' but the pieces we checked appear to be very old. I'm hoping you can tell us exactly how old."

"Okay. Let's have a look."

Andy Brower is a part-time consultant for US Customs in cases involving smuggled pre-Columbian artifacts. Andy is recuperating from a concussion and some cracked ribs he suffered in the fall at Ciudad Antigua. Aside from an occasional headache, the concussion hasn't been a problem, but the sore ribs make getting in and out of cars a challenge and laughing or coughing excruciatingly painful. When Denise called, he was hurrying to finish a paper on the tomb mural that he had recently discovered. But he set the paper aside when she told him that the situation was urgent.

They pass through a security checkpoint and take an elevator to a restricted area where they are required to sign in. Then they enter a large storage room that contains two large wooden crates on a long table. The crates are sealed with yellow tape. Andy cuts the tape, gently unpacks the contents (which are individually wrapped in towels and newspaper), and places them on the table. As he removes the wrapping, it becomes clear that the agent's hunch was spot-on. Save for a few excellent forgeries, the items are indeed ancient artifacts.

"There's no way the shipper could legally transport the authentic pieces to the United States," Andy tells Denise. "Our Memorandum of Agreement with El Salvador forbids it."

Denise informs the US Customs legal department of Andy's findings; it orders her to seize the artifacts and catalog them. Andy and Denise spend several hours taking pictures and writing detailed descriptions of each piece. At one point, Denise points to a ferocious-looking fanged creature with cape-like wings and huge male genitalia.

"What's that?" she asks.

"That's Camazotz, the bat god," Andy replies. "Bringer of death and destruction and decapitator of one of the Hero Twins."

"Looks like a horny vampire to me."

Andy starts to set her straight but then decides that he'd better stay focused on the job at hand. As he catalogs the Camazotz statue, word arrives that the Salvadoran embassy has been notified of the seizure. The repatriation process is under way. Instead of landing in private collections, the artifacts will one day reside in the National Museum of Anthropology in San Salvador.

When they're finished, Andy asks Denise who the shipper is. She has a copy of the bill of lading in her laptop bag. It reads, *Maldonado and Company*.

"Isn't that the guy who's linked to the missing ballerina?" she asks.

"Yeah, that's him."

Although Andy has never met Miguel Maldonado, he has long known of him as a dealer in pre-Columbian artifacts. During the drive home, Andy decides to call a few of his Salvadoran colleagues and see what they know about their elusive fellow countryman.

It's dark when Andy pulls into the driveway of his College Park home. He unlocks the front door and steps into the foyer. Switching on a lamp in the living room, Andy is shocked to find Miguel Maldonado sitting in an armchair about ten feet from where he is standing.

"Good evening, Professor," Maldonado says with a smile. "Pardon the intrusion."

"Maldonado. What the hell are you doing here?" Andy is shaking in his boots, but he is doing his best to appear in control. "Get out, or I'll call the police." He pulls out his cell phone and dials 911.

"Turn off that phone now, or you're going to need it to call an ambulance."

Andy shuts off the phone and puts it back in his pocket. "All right, what do you want?"

"You know very well why I'm here. Some valuable artifacts of mine were seized on the strength of your expert opinion. Because this is our first encounter, I'm going to let you off with a warning. Don't give me a reason to pay you a second visit. Do I make myself clear?"

Andy glares at Maldonado. "How dare you! Get out of my house!"

Before Andy can react, Maldonado is out of the chair and lifting him off the floor by his lapels. There is an eerie reddish glint in Maldonado's eyes. "Don't be a fool, Brower."

Maldonado lowers Andy onto his own two feet. Andy is amazed to discover that he stands almost a head taller than Maldonado. He straightens his sport coat and swallows hard.

"I said, *get out.*"

The lamp blinks off, plunging the room into darkness. When it switches on again a few seconds later, Maldonado is gone. Andy curses himself for not asking about Luisa. Once his hands stop shaking, he picks up the phone and calls Carlos Espinoza, an anthropology professor at the University of El Salvador. After Carlos spends a minute or two talking about his latest project, Andy asks if he knows Miguel Maldonado.

"Not personally, if that's what you mean," Carlos says. "Why do you ask?"

Andy tells Carlos about his confrontation with Maldonado.

"I suggest you do exactly as he says. He's bad news."

"But he threatened me in my own home, Carlos. I won't stand for it."

There is a pause on the other end. "Andy, you don't know what you're dealing with. Maldonado is dangerous. People who cross him disappear and are never heard from again."

"But that's down there. Things are different up here."

"I wouldn't bet my life on it if I were you."

Andy calls a few other Salvadoran colleagues, and they repeat more or less what Carlos told him. Believing that the search for Luisa Santiago will lead to Maldonado, Andy decides to learn as much about his new enemy as he can.

He begins his search on the Internet and gets a few pages' worth of good hits. It soon becomes clear that Maldonado's birth date is unknown. Or to put it another way, if Maldonado knows his age, he's not saying. "Let's just say I'm older than I look," he recently told a *People Magazine* reporter. While no one seems to know when he was born, he's been around for as long as anyone can remember.

Until recently, Maldonado has kept a low profile. A few years ago, *60 Minutes* did a piece on him called "In Search of the Latino Howard Hughes." But that was before he popped up in Washington, DC, and became the prime suspect in the Luisa Santiago missing person case.

Maldonado is the CEO of Maldonado and Company, an international shipping firm that has made him one of the wealthiest men in Central America. But he considers the discovery of pre-Columbian artifacts his true vocation.

A legendary figure in El Salvador, Maldonado is revered by some and reviled by others. Rumor has it that he peddled weapons to both the government and the guerrillas during the Salvadoran Civil War, earning him the nickname, the "Merchant of Death." People began calling him the "Guardian Angel" after the FMLN reported that he singlehandedly saved a remote village from a government death squad. After the war, Maldonado became a patron of the arts and a benefactor of hospitals, orphanages, and churches.

As interesting as these factoids are, Andy believes that they reveal far less about Maldonado than what he learned during that brief encounter in his living room. Andy must somehow rescue Luisa from this monster, but he hasn't a clue how to go about it.

He only knows that he can never forget that bright October afternoon when she walked into his office to discuss her idea for a Maya ballet. She was decked out in brown leather boots, designer jeans, a silky white V-neck blouse, and a beige suede jacket. And the way she moved! God, it was sheer poetry. Then he caught a whiff of her perfume, redolent of honeysuckle on a warm summer evening. All it took was one look into those dark eyes, and he was hers—only he couldn't muster the courage to tell her.

One year later, he gazed into those haunting eyes again as they looked down from that cave wall at Ciudad Antigua.

Now Andy wonders if he will ever see her again.

Chapter Nine

REVELATION

Cochrane is roused from a sound sleep by the ringing of his phone. The alarm clock reads 4:47 a.m. He fumbles for the receiver. "Cochrane here. What is it?"

"Bill, this is Steve." The caller, Lt. Steve Alonzo, is Cochrane's boss and onetime partner. "How soon can you get out to Langley Park?"

"That's outside our jurisdiction."

"I know, but two suspects from the Gonzalez case just turned up there . . . what's left of them, anyway. I want you and Reynolds to ID the victims." Alonzo gives Cochrane the address. It's an apartment building on a rough stretch of Fourteenth Avenue.

"I'm on my way."

When Cochrane arrives at the crime scene, a TV news van is already there. A dozen or so people—the victims' neighbors, he assumes—are gathered just outside the building. At the barrier tape, Cochrane shows his ID to a uniformed cop. "Go through that door," he says, pointing over his shoulder. "It's the last unit on the left."

Cochrane walks down the hall. Jack Reynolds is waiting for him in the apartment doorway.

"How'd you get here so fast?" Cochrane asks.

"I live in the PRTP."

"The what?"

"The People's Republic of Takoma Park."

"So what do we have?"

"Two corpses that used to be Eduardo Melendez and Hector Rivera—better known as 'Daredevil' and 'Rogue.' Remember them?"

"How could I forget? They've been dodging us for months. Did they both live here?"

Reynolds shrugs. "The apartment belongs to a cousin of Rivera's—Lisa Suarez. She apparently gave him a key."

"Is she here?" Cochrane pulls out his notebook.

"One of the neighbors said that she's visiting her mother in El Salvador."

"Who's the neighbor?"

"Name's Lupe Delgado. She's outside talking to the first responders. You probably passed her on the way in."

"I want to ask her some questions after the walk-through."

"You got it."

Reynolds and Cochrane step into the living room. The air is heavy with the pungent odor of pot. Cochrane's eyes are drawn to the glass-top coffee table, which is littered with six empty Corona bottles, a bong, and some seeds and stems. He notices a pair of black high-heeled shoes lying on the floor in front of the sofa.

"Looks like the boys had company," Cochrane says. "She may have been the last one to see them alive."

"Wait, there's more . . ." Reynolds points up to a pair of black fishnet stockings hanging from the ceiling fan.

"Where are the bodies?"

"Down the hall. Rivera's in the bathroom, and Melendez is in the bedroom. The forensic team's still working on them." Reynolds shakes his head. "Y'know, I've been doing this for twenty years, and this has gotta be the weirdest crime scene I've ever investigated."

"C'mon, Jack. Just last week, you said the same thing about the Herrera crime scene."

"Well, that was then, and this is now."

Cochrane walks past the bedroom on the left and peers into the bathroom at the end of the hall. The first thing that meets his eye is the shapely backside of the forensic tech, Cheryl Lucas. She is bent over the tub snapping photos of the crime scene, the flashes popping every few seconds and filling the room with bright light.

"Hi there," Cochrane is standing with his arms folded and his head cocked to one side. "Don't mind me. I'm just admiring your work."

"Can you give me a minute?" Cheryl says between shutter clicks. "I'm almost done."

"Take your time. I've got nothing better to do."

She takes a few more shots and then steps back, revealing a pale, thin figure in the bathtub. Rivera's upright torso is leaning against the front of the tub; his head is tilted sideways and turned to the right. The almond-shaped eyes are shut, and the lips are slightly parted. Rivera's right arm hangs out of the tub, the hand touching the floor. A kitchen knife lies on the floor to the left of the hand. The victim's body rests against a white shower curtain draped over the tub. Cochrane assumes that the curtain landed there after being torn from the curtain rod. Rivera's left hand rests on the front of the tub. Clasped between the thumb and forefinger is a crumpled sheet of paper that bears a terse warning: *YOU'RE NEXT, RUIZ!* Tony "Batman" Ruiz is the fourth suspect in the Gonzalez murder case and the only one still breathing.

"Take a look at this." Cheryl raises the camera, and Cochrane squints into the viewfinder. "What do you think?"

"Looks like a dead guy in a bathtub," he says.

"No shit, Sherlock. Ever hear of *The Death of Marat*?"

"The death of who?"

"You know, the famous painting by Dah-veed."

"Still doesn't ring any bells."

"You really ought to broaden your horizons."

"Is that a proposition?"

"You wish, Detective. Marat was a leader of the French Revolution. The David painting shows him just after he was murdered in his bathtub."

Cochrane gestures toward the bathtub with his pen. "So you think this was staged?"

"Absolutely! Every detail is right out of the David painting—with one exception."

"What's that?"

"In the painting, Marat has a stab wound in the chest just below the right clavicle." She leans forward and points to the corresponding wound on Rivera's body. "Now take a look at the throat."

Cochrane moves a couple of steps closer to the tub and kneels down. He finds a pair of deep puncture wounds in Rivera's throat. "Jesus Christ . . . who or what did that?"

"I have no idea. There's nothing like it in the Marat painting."

"What was the cause of death?"

"I'd say it was exsanguination caused by the severing of the right common carotid artery. The victim was already dead when he was stabbed in the chest."

"Where did all the blood go?"

"That's pretty obvious—down the drain."

"Obvious to you maybe, but I'm a skeptic by nature. Where are the bloodstains?"

"Maybe the killer left the water running."

"Or maybe not. Now let's have a look at Melendez."

Cheryl and Cochrane enter the bedroom. Two other forensic techs, Dev Rendall and Ron Graham, are already there. Rendall is dusting for fingerprints, and Graham is collecting trace evidence in small plastic bags. Melendez's pale, naked body is lying on the bed. The head is detached from the body and lying on the floor to the right of the bed. The sheets are soaked with blood. A message is pinned to the dead man's chest: *JUDITH WAS HERE.*

Cochrane notices a pair of blue jeans and a black-and-silver number three football jersey lying on the floor at the foot of the bed. "What can you guys tell me?"

"Well," Graham says, "I can tell you the victim was killed by decapitation."

"Are there any puncture marks on the throat?"

Graham shakes his head. "I can't say—there's too much tissue damage."

"What about the murder weapon?"

"It was a machete . . . There it is," Rendall says, pointing to the floor where the head is lying. The bed blocks Cochrane's view of the murder weapon. "I couldn't find any prints or blood on it. The perpetrator probably wiped it clean."

After the walk-through, Cochrane heads outside to question Lupe Delgado. She says that she awoke around 4:00 a.m. and heard music in the Suarez apartment next door. This aroused her suspicion because she knew that her neighbor was out of the country. She knocked on Suarez's door and discovered that it was unlocked. Fearing that someone had broken into the apartment, she dialed 911 from her home phone. The other residents Cochrane questions say that they didn't hear any noise coming from the Suarez apartment and didn't see anyone enter or leave it.

When Cochrane returns to the station, Alonzo informs him that he will be leading the investigation of the Melendez-Rivera case. Alonzo also says that Luisa Santiago's driver's license and some other personal effects were found in a handbag on the Wilson Bridge that morning. Has she taken a swan dive off the bridge, or is the handbag just a smokescreen? Cochrane calls several of Luisa's friends and asks their opinion. Not one of them believes that she jumped. Luisa's roommate is convinced that Miguel Maldonado abducted her. Cochrane wants to believe that Luisa is still alive, but experience warns against being too hopeful.

The day is full of surprises. That afternoon, Tony Ruiz walks into the Third District station and turns himself in. Ruiz wants to cut a deal. In exchange for police protection, he will make a full confession. He also wants to talk to the detective in charge of the Melendez-Rivera case. When Cochrane arrives, Ruiz insists that everyone else—including the attorney representing him—leave the interrogation room. Cochrane sits down opposite Ruiz.

"You're lookin' at a dead man," Ruiz tells Cochrane.

"Why do you say that?"

"Not even this place is safe, man. My own clique will whack me for talkin' to you if the fuckin' Terminator don't get me first."

"You mean the guy who killed your friends?"

"Who else?"

"What makes you think it was one person?"

"That's the word on the street."

"So who's the killer?"

"How the hell should I know?" Ruiz rubs his eyes. "I've heard all kinds of crazy shit."

"Such as?"

"Like it's some kinda killing machine—once it targets you, you're as good as fucking dead."

"You're wrong, Tony. One man survived the first attack."

"Yeah . . . if you call being locked away in a prison psycho ward survival."

"Relax. We're putting you in solitary. Nobody can get to you there."

"That won't save me." Ruiz's eyes fill with tears. He blinks several times and looks up at Cochrane with pleading eyes. "Hey, I could really use a smoke."

Cochrane opens a desk drawer and pulls out a fresh pack of Marlboro Reds and a book of matches. The detectives keep a carton each of Marlboros and Newport 100s on hand for such occasions. He tosses the pack and the matches to Ruiz. "Okay, Tony. So what have you got for me?"

Ruiz lights up, takes a long drag, and exhales. "I talked to Melendez and Rivera just before they got whacked."

"When and where did this conversation take place?"

"The Club Inferno around one in the morning. They had just picked up this hot little *chica* and were heading over to Langley Park. Rivera said his cousin had a place where they could party."

"Did you meet the woman?"

Ruiz smiles. "Like I said, the girl was really hot. She had on this sexy little Halloween costume. I won't lie to you. I tried to hit on her, but the boys hustled her out of there before I could even get her name."

"Can you describe her appearance?"

"Sure."

Cochrane goes to the door and asks the guard to tell Alonzo that he needs someone who can do a facial composite. The detective then begins to pace back and forth.

Ruiz leans back and blows a series of perfect smoke rings. He looks over at Cochrane and says, "Do you think she had something to do with the killings?"

"I don't know," Cochrane says. "But I'm going to find out."

"Just put her alone in a cell with me," Ruiz says as he stubs out his cigarette. "She'll be singin' in no time."

Cochrane walks around the right side of the table, grabs a chair, and sits down beside Ruiz. "You're one bad hombre, Tony. Only a tough guy like you would have the *cojones* to gun down a little girl and an old lady."

"Don't pin that on me," Ruiz says, avoiding Cochrane's stare. "That was Herrera."

"Herrera's dead. I don't care about him. I want the guy who ordered the hit."

"Herrera said the order came straight from El Salvador. That's all I know."

"Why are you covering for him, Tony? He threw you and your pals under the bus. Who is he?"

Before Ruiz can answer, his lawyer bursts into the interrogation room, closely followed by one of the guards and a bespectacled young man with a laptop bag slung over his shoulder.

"What's going on here?" Cochrane asks no one in particular.

"The lawyer said he had to talk to you," the guard says by way of explanation.

"Before you proceed any further," the lawyer tells Cochrane as he opens his briefcase, "I must insist—"

"I can speak for myself, *pendejo*," Ruiz interrupts. "You're fired."

"You'd better reconsider," the lawyer says, "because I'm all that's standing between you and life without parole."

"Get the fuck out of here."

"Have it your way," the lawyer says as he snaps his briefcase shut. "Goodbye, my friend, and good luck." With that, he exits the room, slamming the door shut.

"Asshole!" Ruiz yells after him.

"Take it easy," Cochrane says. "He was just trying to help you." He nods toward the door, signaling the guard to leave.

"Well, I don't need his fuckin' help."

"What can I do for you?" Cochrane says to the young man with the laptop bag.

"Lieutenant Alonzo said you needed a facial composite. Where do you want me to set up?"

"Over there is good." Cochrane points to the chair next to his.

It takes the artist less than a minute to unpack and power up his laptop. "All set," he says.

"Okay, Tony, describe the woman you saw with Melendez and Rivera."

Cochrane watches the woman's face take shape on the laptop screen: oval face . . . long, dark, wavy hair . . . large round eyes . . . button nose . . . high cheekbones . . . full lips . . . large ears.

"Yeah, that's her," Ruiz says.

Cochrane can't believe his eyes. He's looking at Luisa Santiago. "Are you sure?"

Ruiz glances at the screen and then looks up at Cochrane. "Abso-fuckin'-lutely."

Cochrane tells the artist to print a dozen copies of the composite. After he leaves the room, Cochrane turns to Ruiz and says, "Okay, Tony. Who ordered the hit?"

"What the fuck, I'm already a dead man. Herrera told me it was *El Jefé* himself."

"I need a name, Tony."

"Vazquez . . . it was Tito Vazquez." Ruiz covers his face with his hands. "No more questions. I want to go to my cell now."

"All right, we'll call it a day." Cochrane summons the guards. As Ruiz is led away, Cochrane says, "See you tomorrow."

"No, you won't," Ruiz says just before he turns the corner and disappears.

At 5:15 the next morning, Cochrane is awakened by a phone call from Alonzo informing him that Ruiz was found dead in his cell, an apparent suicide despite being on suicide watch. When Cochrane arrives at the crime scene an hour later, Ruiz is still hanging from a bed sheet tied to the bars of his cell door. His eyes are bulging from their sockets, and his tongue is swollen and purple.

When Cochrane gets back to the station, he retrieves the file on the Luisa Santiago missing person case. Since her disappearance a week ago, the department has received reports of over a dozen sightings. A few are of the "I saw Luisa Santiago hanging out with Elvis and Jim Morrison at Ben's Chili Bowl" variety, while most of the others prove to be cases of mistaken identity. Two of the leads, however, merit further investigation. The first eyewitness Cochrane interviews is an exotic dancer named Aurora LeFleur who claims that she saw Ms. Santiago compete in a pole-dancing contest at Scalawags, an Alexandria nightclub, on Halloween night.

"I knew she was a ringer," Ms. LeFleur says, "from the way she carried herself." She demonstrates by throwing back her shoulders and holding her head perfectly erect. "The skank shoulda been disqualified." When Cochrane suggests that Ms. LeFleur's status as an exotic dancer might just as easily have disqualified her, she insists, "I wasn't trained at no dance academy, baby. I had to learn my moves on the job."

The statement of a second eyewitness, Dr. Donald S. Rossiter, supports Ms. LeFleur's affidavit. Dr. Rossiter saw Ms. Santiago a few blocks from Scalawags around 9:30 p.m.—a short time before Ms. LeFleur saw her. His credibility is buttressed by the fact that he was personally acquainted with Ms. Santiago, having served on the Capitol Ballet's board of directors for the past five years.

"I spotted Luisa as she was crossing King Street," Rossiter says. "She was dressed in this outrageous Halloween getup. At first I refused to believe it was her. She looked so . . . different." Cochrane asks him to elaborate. "Well, the Luisa I knew was a dark and slender little thing. The woman I saw was deathly pale and muscular. And there was a trashiness about her that was absolutely foreign to Luisa. But when I read the stripper's statement in the paper, I knew that it had to be her."

Both Ms. LeFleur and Dr. Rossiter confirm that Ruiz's facial composite matches the appearance of the woman they saw.

Cochrane stops by the Club Inferno and questions the employees who worked Halloween night. He also shows them Ruiz's composite. One of the bartenders recognizes the woman's face. "She ordered a Bloody Mary just before closing," he says. "Then she left with two guys. Never even touched her drink—left a nice tip, though."

"Did she appear nervous or under duress?" Cochrane asks.

The bartender shrugs. "She looked okay to me. But the guys she was with ended up dead, right?"

Cochrane nods.

"Do you think she's alive?"

"We're still looking for her."

Cochrane's next stop is Scalawags. Almost everyone on duty identifies the composite as the winner of the Halloween pole-dancing contest. One of the bouncers says that her entrance into the club nearly started a riot. Cochrane asks him to elaborate.

"Well, she comes struttin' up just as pretty as you please," the bouncer replies, "and I wave her inside. Next thing I know, me 'n' my partner have a major stampede on our hands."

"Sounds like you had only yourself to blame."

"Not exactly." A wry smile creases his craggy face. "She put me under some kinda spell."

Cochrane gives the bouncer a quizzical look. "What do you mean?"

"Well, she caught my eye, and the next thing I know, I'm holdin' the door for her."

"Does this happen often?"

"Nope—first time."

"She must be quite a woman."

"That's for damn sure."

When Cochrane returns to the station, he learns of a second missing person case that might be linked to the Santiago case—a twenty-five-year-old white male named Christopher Lawson who was last seen at Scalawags on Halloween night. That evening, Cochrane returns to Scalawags with Ruiz's facial composite and a photo of Lawson. Several patrons recall seeing the two dancing together, including a man who says that he gave the woman his Wayfarers because she said that the club's bright lights hurt her eyes.

"At first I thought she was putting me on," the man says. "I mean, it's like a cave in here."

Yet another promising lead takes Cochrane to yet another dead end.

Lacking suspects for the Herrera, Melendez, and Rivera murders, Alonzo decides to call in a criminal profiler. "I know you don't put much stock in this stuff," Alonzo tells Cochrane, "but I think we need to explore all our options." Cochrane has to admit that Alonzo is right. When the profiler's report lands on his desk, Cochrane eagerly scans the pages in hopes of finding some useful information, but he is sorely disappointed. Although he concedes that the murders could have been the work of a rival gang, he is not convinced that the Escorpiones are responsible. With nowhere else to turn, Cochrane calls Cheryl Lucas and asks her to lunch.

"Some other time," she says. "I'm really swamped."

"Look, this is about the Melendez-Rivera case," Cochrane says. "I've hit a dead end, and I need your help."

Cheryl reluctantly agrees to meet him at the Wok and Roll in Chinatown. When she arrives, he waves to her from a table in the back of the tiny, crowded restaurant.

"I'm not sure I can tell you anything you don't already know," she says, unbuttoning her beige wool coat and draping it over a chair, "but I'll do what I can."

When the waitress approaches, Cochrane says that they need a few minutes to look over the menu. She asks if they'd like something to drink. Cochrane orders iced tea, and Cheryl says that she'll have water.

"Do you remember what you said about Melendez's corpse being arranged to resemble that dead guy in the painting?"

"*The Death of Marat*?"

"Exactly! At first I thought you were way off base, but now I'm beginning to think you might be on to something."

"Oh, really?" Cheryl says with a smile. "Did you happen to notice that my theory didn't make it into my report?"

"That's why I asked you to lunch. I'd like you to study the photos of Melendez's corpse and see what you can make of them using the same methodology you applied to Rivera. Then I'd like you to work up a profile of the killer."

"Now wait a minute! You're asking me to take on something that's above my pay grade. Not to mention way outside my area of expertise."

Now it's Cochrane who smiles. "You're the only person who seems to have a clue about this case."

"Then I'd say you've got a problem."

The waitress returns with Cochrane's tea and refills Cheryl's water glass. "Are you ready to order?" Cheryl orders sweet and sour chicken, and Cochrane beef and broccoli.

"Okay, I'll take another look at the Melendez photos. But I can't promise anything."

"Thanks, you'll be doing me a huge favor."

"I know."

A few minutes later, the waitress places their orders on the table. "Enjoy," she says.

They eat quickly. As they get up to leave, Cochrane offers to give Cheryl a ride back to work.

"That would be great."

During the drive, Cochrane asks Cheryl how soon she can look at the photos.

"Is today soon enough?"

He nods sheepishly.

"That means I'll get back to you sometime tomorrow. So don't start calling me this afternoon, okay?"

"Fair enough."

The first thing that Cochrane does when he arrives at his office the next morning is play back his voicemails. There's a rapid-fire message from Cheryl that he has to repeat several times to decipher:

"Bill, this is Cheryl. It's o-dark-thirty. Just finished the report you requested. Gimme a call ASAP. Ciao."

Cochrane makes the call. She answers after the first ring. "Can you meet me at the Starbuck's on the corner of Seventh and H?"

"What, now?"

"No, next Thursday. I thought this couldn't wait."

"I'm due at a staff meeting in five minutes. Can we get together for lunch?"

"I can tell you what the killer is."

"Don't you mean *who*?"

"I meant just what I said. Meet me at Starbuck's in an hour, and I'll explain."

Chapter Ten

THE CAVE

Miguel finds himself back in Ciudad Antigua. He is in the royal tomb, putting the finishing touches on his full-length portrait of Lady Morningstar. He has labored on the mural for many months. Having lost all patience, the King has just ordered him to finish his wife's portrait by sundown or else. Miguel is so lost in his work that he scarcely notices the tumult overhead. But the noise becomes so loud that can no longer ignore it. Racing up the stone steps to the surface, he cannot believe his eyes—the city is in flames! Terrified men, women, and children are running in every direction. Enemy soldiers clad in jaguar skins and plumed helmets swarm into the acropolis through a breach in the palisade fence. Each of the warriors is carrying a spear in one hand and a torch in the other. Some of them mount the main temple-pyramid. They topple the huge, hourglass-shaped incense burners on the steps and set fire to the thatched roof of the shrine at the top.

Miguel sees a knot of women and children being pushed and prodded by a squad of soldiers coming his way. Judging from their finery, they are the King's wives, children, and servants. He withdraws into the tomb and douses his torches. Then he crawls under his workbench and crouches behind a large basket. As he looks on, the soldiers hustle their prisoners down the steps and into the darkness. In the flickering light cast by the guards' torches, Miguel counts twelve women and half as many children, including an infant.

He recognizes the regal figure of Lady Morningstar. She demands to know where her husband has been taken. The commander tells her not to worry, the King is safe, and she will soon join him. Just then a soldier points to a scene in one of Miguel's murals—three bound captives kneel before the King, who is seated on his double-headed jaguar throne. The commander says to his men, "Who is on his knees now?" The soldiers all share a good laugh at the fallen King's expense.

Lady Morningstar cannot bear to see her husband mocked. She grabs the knife of the guard standing on her right and plunges it into his back. He cries out, frantically gropes for the handle, and then collapses to the floor. One of his comrades kneels down and examines him. He raises his bloodied hands and says that the guard is dead. The soldiers converge on Lady Morningstar with spears and knives at the ready. Miguel springs from his hiding place and tries to shield her from their blows, but he succeeds only in mingling his blood with hers. As they lie dying on the cave floor, she whispers something into his ear. The last thing that Miguel hears before he passes out is the commander shouting, "Kill them! Kill them all!"

Miguel awakens with a start. He struggles to recall Lady Morningstar's last words but cannot. Blinking, he realizes that he is in the cabin of his private jet. A glance out the window reveals that the jet is somewhere over the Gulf of Mexico. There is a faint glow on the eastern horizon. Soon it will be dawn, his favorite time of day.

Since the downfall of Ciudad Antigua, Miguel has not returned there because the memories connected to the place remain too painful even after a thousand years. Then he made an extraordinary discovery. During his "visit" to Brower's house, Miguel found a paper in which Brower proclaims his mural "the greatest find in the realm of Mesoamerican pictorial art since the discovery of the Bonampak murals in 1946." By some miracle, the mural has survived! Viewing the picture through Brower's photos wasn't enough—Miguel has to see it again with his own eyes.

Miguel is en route to El Salvador, having made his getaway one step ahead of the law. After learning that US Customs had seized his artifacts, Miguel called Robert Butterfield, his lawyer in DC, and told him to obtain an injunction blocking their return to El Salvador. Butterfield said that he'd look into it and see what he could do. He called back an hour later.

"Miguel," Butterfield said, "I hate to break this to you, but those priceless antiquities of yours now belong to the government of El Salvador, and there ain't a damn thing we can do about it."

There was a lengthy pause. Miguel said at last, "How much do you think it will cost to get them back?"

"You're not listening! This thing is way past fixing. The FBI is taking a keen interest in you. Get out while you can. Spend some time in a country that doesn't have an extradition treaty with the US of A."

"Would you please remind me why I'm paying you a retainer?"

"Look, I'm just trying to talk sense to someone who's in a shitload of trouble and doesn't seem to know it."

When Miguel's jet touches down at Comalapa International Airport, a black Escalade is waiting for him on the tarmac. Miguel opens the front passenger door and climbs in. The driver is a bearded, five-hundred-year-old former conquistador named Enrique de los Santos. Miguel met Enrique long ago while they were stalking dockside prostitutes in Havana. Their first meeting proved less than cordial. In the course of conversation, the two vampires discovered that they had fought on opposing sides during the Conquest. This revelation sparked a duel over territorial rights, in the course of which the two swordsmen shed a copious amount of blood. Spying a comely young wench among the onlookers, the exhausted duelists abruptly broke off their swordplay, lured their prey into a dark alley, and shared a few pints of her blood. The pair thereupon swore an oath to let bygones be bygones. It is an oath that they have yet to break.

"Take my advice, Miguel," Enrique says between puffs on a Cuban cigar. "Get back on your plane and fly as far away from here as you can. You should've stayed in America. El Salvador is much too small. Tito will find you, and he will rip your heart out."

"What's the difference?" Miguel says. "He'll come after me no matter where I go. But he's not expecting me to come to him."

"Fuck that Sun Tzu shit." Enrique spits out the window. "I'll bet he already knows you're here."

"What does it matter to you? This is between Tito and me."

Enrique laughs hoarsely. "Are you crazy? Ever since the Civil War, he's been trying to take over the country. We'll all have to choose sides sooner or later."

"Which side will you choose?"

"I think you know the answer to that."

From Comalapa, Miguel and Enrique drive twenty-five miles north to San Salvador. On the outskirts of the city, they head west on the Carretera Panamericana, El Salvador's main highway. It is noon when they reach the rectangular brown sign indicating the turnoff to Ciudad Antigua, or "*Las Ruinas*," as the locals call it. The rugged dirt access road twists and turns for about half a mile. In the distance looms the Santa Ana volcano. As the Escalade pulls into the parking area, Miguel glimpses the pyramid. He is disappointed to find that it is now little more than a grassy mound.

"What the hell are we doing here?" Enrique says. "These old ruins all look the same."

"Show a little respect," Miguel replies. "I was born here."

"For God's sake, don't go weepy on me. I don't think I could fucking bear it."

"Shut up and follow me."

Miguel steps up to the ticket window and hands the young man three dollars for parking and admission. A uniformed security guard cradling a short-barreled, pump-action shotgun stands near the entrance. He eyes Miguel and Enrique as they pass through the turnstile.

"*Buenos*," Miguel says.

The security guard nods in reply.

Once inside, Miguel pauses to get his bearings. It's all so open and green and quiet, nothing like the bustling metropolis of his memory. He also wishes that it was dusk. The midday sun blazes overhead, and the air hangs hot and heavy. A young couple lounging in the shade of a huge amate tree appears to be the only tourist traffic.

Miguel and Enrique stride past the first two stops on the self-guided tour—the foundation of a small temple on the left and a ball court on the right—and head straight for the entrance to the royal tomb. It is surrounded by a tall chain-link fence. They pass a large, yellow sign with black lettering that reads, *Closed to the Public*. The tomb appears empty—the digging crew must be taking a siesta. The security guard hustles after the two vampires. He orders them to stop, but they keep walking.

Miguel turns to Enrique and says, "Don't kill him."

"No problem."

Miguel approaches the fence while Enrique turns to face the guard. He glances over his shoulder as Enrique bends down to pick up the shotgun. The guard is lying unconscious at his feet. As Miguel looks on, Enrique rips the gate off its hinges and tosses it aside. Miguel steps inside, removes his sunglasses, and climbs down the ladder into the cool shade of the tomb. And there it is. The mural consists of three panels. The first panel depicts a procession, the second a dance, and the third a bloodletting ritual featuring Lady Morningstar. Much to his surprise, the mural—like its creator—has survived the past millennium in pristine condition. He is struck by the naturalistic rendering of her lovely face and lithe form—and of her resemblance to Luisa. Tears of joy fill his eyes as he gazes on his masterpiece. He hears shouting overhead.

A woman's shrill voice cries, "Come on up, you thief. I know you're down there."

"Just a moment!" he yells, wiping away his tears. He hears arguing, followed by shouting and a piercing scream. A woman's flowered sunhat tumbles down into the cave. Miguel flies up the ladder and finds Enrique standing over four dead bodies. One of the corpses belongs to the woman who called down to Miguel. She's staring up at the sky in wide-eyed bewilderment.

"Why did you kill them?"

"I had no choice. They came at me with fucking machetes! And you know," Enrique jerks his hands as if he were snapping something—or someone—in two, "they break so easily."

"You should have spared the woman." Miguel presses her eyelids shut. "She posed no threat."

"The bitch jumped on my back and tried to gouge my eyes out. Look." He points to several deep scratches on his face.

"Serves you right."

"Did you find what you were looking for?"

"Yes."

They walk back to the Escalade and climb inside. Enrique turns the ignition key, shifts into drive, and steers onto the access road. "Why didn't you kill the Santiago woman?"

"I almost did." Miguel closes his eyes and recalls his first taste of Luisa Santiago. "But something stopped me."

Enrique lights another cigar. "You changed her, didn't you?"

"Don't be ridiculous!" Miguel's eyes blaze under his sunglasses. "Why would I do a thing like that?"

"Bullshit!" Enrique says between puffs on his cigar. "You're a worse liar than I am."

As the Escalade approaches the main road, he adds, "With luck we should reach the airport in a few hours."

"I have to see Tito first."

"I'm taking you back to the airport while you still have time."

"Enrique, I have to face him."

"All right, have it your way." Enrique tosses his cigar out the window. "But you'd better let me do the talking."

Miguel laughs. "Don't you think you've done enough damage for one day?"

"I have a bad feeling about this."

"You always say that."

"And I'm always right."

Chapter Eleven

TITO

David Arroyo lies wide awake on his bunk, too terrified to sleep. It's only his first day on the inside, yet several mean-looking homies have already claimed him as their girlfriend.

"Hey, Niña," a cellmate calls to him in the darkness. "You're a regular Salma Hayek. All the boys want to fuck you." This statement triggers a gale of raucous laughter and wolf whistles.

For the first time in his life, David regards his good looks as a curse. He knows that a scowl or a grimace on his pretty face merely looks "cute," for he has studied his facial expressions in the mirror countless times. He longs for a jagged scar across his cheek and a death's head tat on his forehead to make him look tough.

As dawn approaches, he weeps softly and prays for a miracle.

God must be listening, for his prayers are answered.

He drifts off to sleep and dreams that a huge black jaguar with gleaming red eyes is gliding toward him.

The creature stops just shy of his bunk, rises up on its haunches, and assumes a human shape. Amid the snoring and the coughing of David's cellmates, the mysterious stranger whispers, "Don't be afraid, my son. I have come to save you."

"Who are you?" David asks, blinking his eyes.

"I am your guardian angel." With that, the stranger kneels beside David's bunk and kisses him on the forehead.

"What are you going to do to me?"

"I'm going to make you stronger than you ever imagined. Just close your eyes and let sweet sleep wash over you. When you awaken, you will never have to be afraid again."

David does as he is told. He lets the stranger unbutton his shirt and pull his collar aside. He feels a sharp pain in his throat. But the pain soon gives way to a bliss he hasn't known since he was a babe suckling at his mother's breast. As he drifts off, the dull gray walls of his prison cell begin to crumble and fall, giving way to bright sunshine and endless green fields. His dying thought is, *I am coming home.*

"What do you mean, he can't see anyone?" Miguel asks. "Since when?"

"Since he was moved to solitary," the prison guard replies. "No visitors allowed."

"But this is an emergency," Miguel exclaims. "There has been a death in the family."

"Who died?"

"His sister. They were very close. I have a photo of them together. Here it is." Miguel opens his wallet and hands the guard a crisp hundred-dollar bill.

"Oh, yes," the guard says, stuffing the C-note into his shirt pocket. "She was lovely . . . *very* lovely." He rubs his chin. "I'll see what I can do." The guard knocks on the door of his supervisor's office and enters. A few minutes later, he emerges from the office and nods to Miguel. "Follow me," he says.

Above the cell block entrance, the words "MARA CAMAZOTZA" appear in red spray-painted letters. On either side of the long hallway, hundreds of eyes peer out of small, barred windows. The inmates' chatter subsides as Miguel passes and then resumes with his departure. The word spreads quickly: *Miguel Maldonado está aqui.*

At the end of the hall, Miguel waits as the guard speaks into a wall phone. A few seconds later, the door clicks. The guard opens the door and waves Miguel inside. They walk a short distance to a second door, which opens onto a small room with a rickety wooden table and a few chairs. Miguel looks up and finds himself staring into the lens of a security camera.

The door opens and in walks Tito Vazquez. He is flanked by a guard on either side. His wrists and ankles are shackled. His arms are covered with tattoos—Maya hieroglyphs that proclaim him to be the incarnation of

Camazotz the Bringer of Death. Tito is the same height as Miguel, but his broad shoulders and solid build make him appear taller.

Tito sits down at the table. He is smiling. "Miguel, my old friend, how kind of you to visit me."

Tito's guards file out of the room. "You have fifteen minutes," Miguel's escort tells him. "And remember," the guard nods toward the camera, "I'll be watching." The door slams shut behind him.

At first, Miguel and Tito say nothing. They sit poker-faced on opposite sides of the table, sizing each other up. Tito's swarthy, round head is freshly shaved, and he sports a reddish-brown Fu Manchu mustache and goatee. He keeps his shackled hands and feet under the table and his fierce hawk eyes on Miguel.

"What are you doing in here?" Miguel says at last.

"I'm looking for a few good men," Tito replies, "or boys, as the case may be. I assume you came here to beg my forgiveness."

"You assumed wrong," Miguel says. "I'm tendering my resignation, effective immediately."

Tito scowls. "You can't just walk away from unfinished business, Miguel."

"I did as you ordered. Herrera won't steal from you anymore, and the Santiago woman is now under my control."

"I ordered you to get rid of her!"

"You underestimate her usefulness."

"She's good for only one thing." Tito's scowl curls into a broad smile, revealing a pair of gleaming white fangs. "But I'm afraid I'll have to kill her before I can fuck her."

"You bastard!" Miguel lunges at Tito, who raises his hands in self-defense. The shackles are gone. Two of the guards rush into the room and try to Taser Miguel. Grabbing their hands, he turns the weapons on their users. The guards drop to the floor in a twitching heap. Miguel looks up: the door is open and Tito is gone. The guard who took the bribe is lying unconscious just outside the door, and half a dozen more guards are running toward him. He sits down at the table as the reinforcements arrive. The commander of the prison guard asks Miguel to recount what happened.

"I was hoping you could tell me," he says with a shrug.

Another guard retrieves Tito's shackles from under the table. He asks Miguel to explain how Vazquez managed to shed them.

"I'm as mystified as you are." Miguel is lying: he knows that no restraint built by human ingenuity could hold Tito for five minutes if he wanted out.

"A dangerous prisoner has just escaped," the commander says, "and I'm holding you responsible."

"I want to call my lawyer."

"You'll get your phone call. But first, I want some answers."

The commander asks Miguel how he managed to pick the locks on Tito's shackles without being seen. Miguel says that he didn't pick the locks and had no intention of helping Tito escape. "The purpose of my visit," he says, "was to tell Tito to leave me alone."

"What could Vazquez possibly do to you while he was locked away in solitary?"

"You have no idea. He runs his empire by cell phone."

"That's impossible! We kept him in complete isolation and searched both him and his cell three times a day."

"I'm just telling you what I know. He called me from here just a few days ago."

"Where do you think he's headed?"

"I don't know . . . Soyapango, maybe."

The commander and four guards escort Miguel to the prison director's office. The director asks him the same questions that the commander just asked, and Miguel gives him the same answers. Only then does the director allow Miguel to call his lawyer. A few minutes later, two plainclothes detectives enter the director's office and begin their interrogation. When Miguel's lawyer finally arrives, he threatens to sue the prison director for violating his client's rights. The attorney's name is Ricardo Alvarez. Impeccably dressed in a gray pinstripe suit, Alvarez has a swashbuckling air about him, thanks to a jet black handlebar mustache and an eye patch that he has worn since losing his right eye in the Civil War.

"My client has done nothing. I demand that you release him at once or face the consequences." Alvarez's booming voice fairly rattles the framed photos hanging on the director's office walls.

"All right, he is free to go," the director says with a dismissive wave of his hand. "Get him out of my sight."

"But he's still a suspect," the lead detective cuts in. "On no account is he to leave the country. He is your responsibility, Alvarez."

"Of course, of course, my client will cooperate fully." Alvarez turns to Miguel. "Won't you?"

It is dark when Miguel emerges from the prison. He tells Enrique, who has waited for him in the prison parking lot, that he is returning to San Salvador with Alvarez.

"You're making a big mistake," Enrique says. "Get out of the country while you can."

"Enrique," Miguel says, "I have nowhere else to go."

Shaking his head, Enrique guns the Escalade and zooms away, spitting gravel and leaving a dust cloud in his wake.

Alvarez is driving his faded black Nissan pickup. The proud owner of a small fleet of vintage sports cars, Alvarez drives his truck when he wants to avoid attention or, conversely, when he wants to be seen as a man of the people. During the Civil War, he served as an FMLN guerrilla, watching two older brothers and too many friends die. To justify outliving them, he vowed to help the poor and the oppressed if he survived the war. He kept his vow, but he still manages to earn enough from representing Miguel and other wealthy clients to indulge his car-collecting hobby.

Alvarez first heard about Miguel during the Civil War. Miguel was a shadowy figure in those days, an arms dealer who played both ends against the middle, selling Soviet-made weapons to the FMLN and American-made weapons to the Salvadoran army. Neither side seemed to care, though, just as long as he supplied them with the tools of the trade.

One morning, Alvarez was on patrol deep in the Guazapa jungle when his squad happened upon a village that didn't appear on their maps. The place seemed deserted. A few of the huts had burned down; the ashes were still smoldering. As the guerrillas searched the village, Alvarez made a startling discovery. He entered one of the huts and found a dozen or more bodies stacked in the middle like cordwood. They reeked of gasoline. Their uniforms indicated that they were government soldiers. As Alvarez stared in disbelief, he felt a tapping on his shoulder. It was a wizened old man with a face so craggy that it resembled the face of the Guazapa volcano. He was pointing upward and jabbering away in Nawat. Alvarez could make out a few words—something about an eagle warrior who swooped out of the sky and saved this heavenly place.

The old man was joined by a woman who said that she was his granddaughter. Standing barely five feet tall, she was a softer, somewhat less wizened version of her grandfather. "'Listen, it's Cuauhtli—the Eagle Warrior,'" she said, patting the old man's arm. "That's what he says when he hears the army helicopters overhead. He gets very confused these days. But why shouldn't he be confused? He's at least a hundred."

They stepped outside for some fresh air, the woman gently leading the old man by the arm. Alvarez pointed back at the hut with his thumb. "What happened to them?"

She looked at the hut and then at Alvarez. "I don't know. The soldiers came here yesterday. They herded all of us into the hut of the *tlatoani*. There were about fifty of us in there—mostly old men, women, and children. The officer in charge posted guards around the hut and told us that we would be shot if we tried to escape. A few minutes later, we began to smell smoke. Some of the children began to whimper and cry. The grown-ups told them to be brave, that everything would be all right, but I don't think any of us really believed we would survive the day."

"Then how did you escape?"

"That's just it. We didn't." The woman looked intently at Alvarez. "As we prayed, shouting and gunfire erupted outside the hut. We could see soldiers running this way and that and hear the officers barking orders. For what seemed a very long time, all was noise and confusion. Then it grew quiet and the birds started singing again. We were saved. It was a miracle." She crossed herself and kissed the crucifix that hung around her neck. "We spent the rest of the day dragging the bodies into our huts and dousing everything with gasoline. That's what the stranger told us to do. He told us to burn everything. We must leave behind no trace of what happened here."

"Where will you go?"

"There's a village not far from here where we can rebuild. We'll manage. Our people always have."

"What about the stranger?"

"He said his name was Miguel—like the archangel."

"*El Viejo!*" the old man shouted.

She smiled. "'The Old One.' That's what he calls the stranger. But he looks very young."

"Atlacatl *nemi!*"

"He thinks the stranger is the spirit of Atlacatl."

"The warrior chief who fought the conquistadors." Alvarez had heard the legend of Atlacatl when he was a boy.

"Exactly. It is said that our ancestors followed Atlacatl to Guazapa. They refused to surrender to Alvarado. They hid out here and fought the Spaniards for many years. Our village still bears the name they gave it: *Ilhuicatli*, The Heavenly Place."

After the war, Alvarez returned to the site but could find no trace of the village. It was as if the jungle had swallowed it up. Only later did he make the connection between the stranger and Miguel Maldonado. He had always known that Miguel was "different," but he was astonished when his long-time friend and client told him one day that he was a vampire.

"Why are you telling me this?"

"Because you're crazy enough to believe me," Miguel said with a straight face, "and because I happen to know that everyone else thinks you're crazy. So I'll never have to worry about you giving away my secret."

Sometimes it upsets Alvarez that Miguel doesn't seem to take him seriously, but then he reminds himself that whenever his friend gets fang-deep in legal trouble—

which is pretty much all the time these days—it is Ricardo Alvarez to whom he turns for help.

Alvarez once asked Miguel why he had gone to the trouble of saving the villagers. Miguel muttered something about being sick and tired of the soldiers killing off his favorite food source—the *campesinos* of Cuscatlán.

"I think you're just getting sentimental in your old age. How old *are* you anyway?"

"It's none of your business."

"Don't be so touchy about it."

"How would you like to end up on tonight's menu?"

End of conversation.

"As your attorney, I advise you to keep out of sight for awhile," Alvarez says as he passes a dilapidated pickup truck piled high with baskets of produce.

"As your client, I will take your advice under consideration." Miguel notices the St. Christopher medal dangling from the rearview mirror and smiles. "Still clinging to the old superstitions, I see."

Alvarez points to his chest. "And I'm still wearing my Ché Guevara T-shirt. Some things never fall out of fashion."

"You're truly hopeless."

"Thank you for noticing."

"*De nada.*"

Alvarez waves to a passing white Toyota 4x4 filled with police. "Why did you pay a visit to Vazquez?"

"To submit my resignation."

Alvarez shakes his head. "You should have e-mailed him."

"We have too much history for that."

"An American detective by the name of Cochrane is looking for you. Do you know him?"

Miguel shrugs. "Let me guess. He wants to ask me some questions about Luisa Santiago."

"He says you haven't returned his phone calls. He also says that your cooperation will help to allay any suspicion about your involvement in her disappearance."

"The police always say that. But they never mean it. They can remove the gun and badge but never their suspicion."

"Maybe you should stop giving them reason to be suspicious."

It is almost midnight when they roll into Soyapango on the east end of San Salvador. Aside from some parked cars, the streets are empty.

"So what have you done with Señorita Santiago?"

"She's in hiding."

"And you left her alone?"

"Not exactly. I asked a couple of friends to keep an eye on her."

"Aren't you even a little concerned for her safety?"

"No," Miguel lies. "She can take care of herself. I changed her."

The ancient hunger begins to gnaw at Miguel's insides. There is no putting it off. He tells Alvarez to pull over.

"You're not going after Vazquez, are you?"

Miguel laughs. "Don't be ridiculous. I'm just going for a walk."

"In Soyapango at midnight? Why don't you let me drive you home."

"No thanks. I want to sniff the breeze."

Alvarez shrugs. "Suit yourself."

Miguel climbs out of the truck and shuts the door. As Alvarez starts to drive away, Miguel remembers something and taps on the window. "Oh, I almost forgot. You're probably going to get a call from the police about an incident that occurred at Ciudad Antigua today."

"What else have you done?"

"It wasn't me. It was Enrique. Just turn on the news. You'll learn all about it."

"I'm tired," Alvarez says, "and I'm going home to bed. For God's sake, try not to get into any more trouble." He drives off into the night.

In this part of town, there are few streetlights, but that is fine with Miguel. He is on the prowl. To appease his late-night cravings, he seeks out vagrants or prostitutes much as a hungry teen heads to the local McDonald's or Burger King. The downside is that the blood of this particular class of victim is even more polluted than a Big Mac or a Whopper. Luckily, his immune system has become adept at purging the toxins before they can do much harm. He walks a few blocks and happens upon three *putas* plying their trade. One of them waves to him and asks if he'd like some company. She is the tallest of the trio. On closer inspection, he discovers that under the blonde wig, the pancake makeup, the fishnet stockings, and the fuck-me pumps, there lurks a sweet, young girl of sixteen who should be at home with her parents rather than on a dark street corner soliciting strange men. If Miguel weren't so ravenous and it weren't so late, he'd take the *chica* off the street and buy her a decent meal. Instead, he asks her if there's a dark alley nearby.

"Are you too cheap to get a room or something?" She turns to her two smirking companions and says, "What is it with this guy?"

"I'll double your usual price."

"Okay, lover. Have it your way. Take my hand."

They walk down a side street, passing some sleeping vagrants curled up inside their cardboard boxes. They come to a narrow alleyway so dark that even Miguel has difficulty penetrating it. "Well, here we are." She names her price, and he pays her that plus a little extra, which she stuffs inside her shoe. He backs her up against the wall and kisses her on the mouth. She begins to unbuckle his trousers, but he stops her.

"I prefer to lead," he says.

"Whatever. It's your money, honey."

Miguel slowly nibbles his way from her mouth down to her neck. As he sinks his fangs into her throat, her firm, young body goes taut, but when the venom enters her bloodstream, she begins to relax. Holding her limp form in his arms, Miguel drinks until he is satiated. He then hoists her onto his shoulder and carries her back to where her companions were, but they are gone. So he finds a cheap hotel a few blocks away and rents her a room, telling the clerk that she's dead drunk and needs a place to sleep it off.

"How many times have I heard that one," the clerk says as he hands over the key.

"Second floor. Last door on the right."

Miguel carries the girl up to her room and gently lowers her onto the bed. Standing in the doorway, he blows her a kiss and whispers, "Adios, Dulcinea." It's his nickname for ladies of the night, courtesy of his hero, Don Quixote.

Miguel spends the rest of the long night wandering the barrios of La Campanera, a suburb of Soyapango. "MC·· ·" graffiti pops up everywhere, marking this part of town as Mara Camazotza turf. The dots are Maya symbols for the number three, which represent "C," the third letter in the alphabet and the first letter in Camazotz. In short, this is Tito Vazquez's turf. Which is why Miguel isn't surprised to encounter a poster with Tito's face emblazoned on it Ché Guevara style. What *does* surprise him is the announcement that Tito is sponsoring a free concert at the Estadio Cuscatlán on Friday night. Headlining the event is the British rock group, Majesty of Despair—not the sort of music one would associate with Salvadoran *pandilleros*, yet it is quite a coup for Tito to book both the Estadio and MOD on such short notice. Miguel can scarcely believe his eyes: *Viene uno vienen todos los!* Perhaps Tito has truly lost it this time. Or maybe he knows exactly what he's doing.

Miguel walks down a section of abandoned railroad track that divides Mara Camazotza territory from that of a rival gang. It is 4:00 a.m., and the homies are all fast asleep. Lining each side of the tracks is a long row of one-room houses. Made of concrete block walls and corrugated tin roofs, they're called "microwave ovens" for good reason. The clouds suddenly part, and the light of the full moon suffuses the squalid scene with a pale luminosity. He wonders, *How many of these poor bastards will still be sleeping aboveground a year from now?*

Miguel comes to a street that is dominated by a high cement wall covered with graffiti. It is an MC · · · memorial to fallen comrades. A row of painted headstones bearing the legend *RIP* and the names of deceased gangbangers occupies a fifty-foot section of the wall. Out of the corner of his eye, Miguel spots a huge poster at the far end of the wall. At first, he thinks that it's one of Tito's concert handbills, but a closer look reveals the subject to be female. The photo is so grainy that it takes a second or two for him to realize that it is a blown-up, black-and-white image of Luisa Santiago. Above her likeness appear the words:

SE BUSCA

LA MARIPOSA.

Using red paint (or blood?) someone has drawn a pair of dripping fangs over the mouth and scribbled *MUERTO VIVIENTE* across the poster. Miguel could recognize that childish scrawl anywhere—it belongs to Tito Vazquez.

Chapter Twelve

SPECTACLE

At nightfall, Miguel walks out of the Hilton Princess in the Zona Rosa and hails a taxi. He tells the driver to take him to the Estadio Cuscatlán. As the cab speeds down the Autopista Sur, Miguel glances to the right and sees the stadium's three light towers glowing above the city skyline. The traffic soon slows to a crawl; Tito's free concert has drawn a large crowd. When the cab at last reaches the stadium, Miguel pays the driver and joins the procession to the gate. The crowd is buzzing with excitement. Many in the throng sport Majesty of Despair's trademark black T-shirt: a blood-red moon in the center flanked by the letter M on the left and by the letter D on the right in white Gothic script. The design appears on the cover of *Apocalypse Boogie*, their previous album. The words on the back of the shirt are from the Book of Revelation: "The sun became as dark as black cloth, and the moon became as red as blood."

At the entrance, Miguel flashes a yellow plastic badge marked MOD ACCESS to a uniformed security guard.

The badge arrived at his hotel suite that morning in a FedEx envelope, which also contained a brief note. The elegant handwriting looked vaguely familiar: *See you at the show tonight. An Old Friend.* In the end, Miguel's curiosity overcame his suspicion.

The guard asks to see Miguel's photo ID. An usher leads Miguel down a long, winding corridor that feeds into an opening behind the stage at one end of the stadium. Miguel walks down an aisle, crosses a short expanse of football field, climbs some metal stairs, and steps onto the stage. He passes a long row of loudspeakers and a circular riser that supports a mammoth drum kit backed by a pair of Chinese gongs. Glancing overhead, he sees several rows of lights mounted on trusses and ten large video screens suspended from a hundred-foot-tall steel frame that surrounds the stage. A brilliant white light suddenly flashes into Miguel's eyes, momentarily blinding him. He slips on his sunglasses to prevent another such mishap. A dozen roadies are onstage setting up guitars and keyboards and testing monitors and amplifiers. Miguel notices a tall, rough-hewn man with thinning gray hair tied back in a ponytail. Brandishing a Bonzo-size drumstick and issuing orders in a booming baritone fit for the Shakespearean stage, he has the unmistakable air of a man who knows what he's about.

Miguel approaches the tall man and says, "Could you tell me where I might find Tito Vazquez?"

The man turns to Miguel and says, "Who the fuck are you?"

"My name is Miguel Maldonado."

"Congratulations. How in bloody hell did you get past security?"

Miguel's eyes flash bright red behind his sunglasses. "You don't have to be so rude, my friend."

"Christ, man! Can't you see I'm busy? Bobby!"

A wiry, blonde man in his early twenties appears at the tall fellow's side. "What is it, Patrick?"

"How many times do I have to tell you? *Only authorized personnel onstage.*"

"Sorry. It won't happen again."

"You're goddamn right it won't! Next time it'll be your *arse.*"

"Follow me," Bobby says to Miguel. "I'll take you to the VIP tent."

"Your employer is a real asshole," Miguel says.

Bobby manages a smile. "That's just Patrick. He always freaks out on opening night."

Once inside the VIP tent, Miguel searches in vain for Tito. Among the guests he recognizes an assortment of high-powered lawyers, businessmen, and politicians—not the sort of company that Tito has been in the habit of keeping . . . until now. Some of the high rollers come up and introduce themselves and their wives. Miguel is a few steps shy of leaving the tent when he feels a tap on his shoulder. He turns and beholds a pretty young Salvadoreña in a red evening dress carrying a glass of champagne in her right hand.

"Where ya' goin'?" she says in perfect Middle American English. "You're gonna miss 'em."

"Miss who?"

"You're joking, right?"

At that instant, a phalanx of six bodyguards wearing earpieces and dark suits enters the VIP tent. They are closely followed by the five members of MOD and their entourage: a motley assortment of wives, girlfriends, lawyers, accountants, press agents, personal assistants, and hangers-on. The band gathers at one end of the tent, and the lead singer, John Keats (real name George Kettering), steps forward to say a few words to the assemblage. Keats is slender, dark-haired, fair-skinned, and good-looking. He pauses at the end of each sentence to allow the interpreter to translate his English into Spanish:

"*Buenas noches, mis amigos.* It is an honor to open our world tour in the great city of San Salvador. Tonight, we'll be performing our new album live for the very first time. We hope you enjoy it. *Muchas gracias.*"

The crowd responds with polite applause. A man sporting a diamond earring (Miguel later learns that he is Frank Di Lorenzo, MOD's tour manager) takes the microphone and says in a thick New Yawk accent, "Now we've come to the reason why you're all here. Here's your chance to meet and greet the band. Please form a line, and try not to jostle your neighbor."

"This is so cool!" the Salvadoreña says. "I've got all their albums, but *Pandemonium Point* is my favorite. What about you?"

"I couldn't say," Miguel replies, never having heard a note of MOD's music.

"I know what you mean! They're all great!"

As the line inches forward, the Salvadoreña says, "My name is Eva. What's yours?"

"I'm Miguel." They shake hands. "Where did you learn to speak English?"

"I went to school in the States. Got my degree in poli sci at UCLA last spring. Graduated with honors. Woo-hoo! I've been living here with my folks ever since. My father says I'd better find a husband or a job *pronto*, 'cause he's not gonna support me forever."

"And why not? He has only himself to blame."

"How's that?"

"He's the one who spoiled you."

Eva laughs. "Would you mind telling him that? I've never been able to stand up to my dad. He can be pretty intimidating."

"Who is he? I might know him."

"He's the president of El Salvador."

Miguel senses the sharp stare of unseen eyes. "Where's your security?"

"Over there." She nods toward the tent opening, where a pair of hulking, well-dressed young men stand sentinel. "And there's a few more floating around that I'm not supposed to know about."

"So why haven't I seen you on TV?"

"My father tries to keep me out of the spotlight. He says I should live a normal life, whatever that means. That's why he shipped me off to America."

A waiter bearing a tray of champagne glasses walks by. Eva takes one and puts her empty in its place. "Want some?" she says. "It's Veuve Clicquot."

"No, thanks. What can you tell me about the band?"

"Well, they're all from London, and they've been together since they were like teenagers. One minute they're borrowing money from their parents to record their first album, and the next," she snaps her fingers, "they're megastars. There's a rumor they're all Satan-worshippers, but John Keats says that's total bullshit, he just likes writing songs about demons and monsters."

"Who is the fellow with the shoulder-length platinum hair and eye makeup?"

"That's Jackson Ripley, better known as 'Jack the Ripper.' He's the lead guitarist."

"And the pale one with the tall hat and braids?"

"Colin Moorcroft, the keyboard player."

"What about the brawny fellow with the shaved head and tattoos?"

"He's the drummer, 'Mad Max' Aspeth."

"And the short one with the spiked hair and muscle shirt?"

"That's the bass player, Nick Montague. He's sooo hot!"

At last, Eva and Miguel find themselves standing face-to-face with the band members, who start hitting on Eva. After a minute or two, Di Lorenzo intervenes. He suggests that the group give the rest of the line a chance to meet them.

The moment they step outside the tent, Eva grabs Miguel's arm. "Ohmigod I don't believe it!" she cries, holding out a business card for his inspection. "Nick Montague gave me his cell phone number!"

"Miguel! I have a surprise for you."

Removing his sunglasses, Miguel looks up and sees Tito Vazquez, decked out in a gray business suit and tie, walking toward him. Tito is accompanied by two other vampires: a handsome youth whom Miguel has never met and a beautiful female whom he thought he'd never see again. The youth's dark, wavy hair hangs about his shoulders. The female's long, blonde hair is put up in a bun. He wears a tight-fitting, tie-dyed T-shirt and faded blue jeans. She is clad in a dark business suit and high heels.

"Anna," Miguel whispers. "Is it really you?"

"Miguel," Anna Schiller says, her pale blue eyes staring straight through him. "I've missed you terribly!" She embraces him and kisses both of his cheeks.

"I thought you were . . . dead."

"As you can see," she twirls around once, "the reports of my demise were greatly exaggerated."

"Um, you guys obviously have some catching up to do," Eva says. "Goodbye, Miguel. It was nice meeting you."

"The pleasure was all mine, Eva Sanchez," Miguel says. "Tell your father that Miguel Maldonado sends his regards."

Eva turns and walks back into the VIP tent, the bodyguards clearing a path for her.

Once Eva is out of earshot, Tito says, "Was that President Sanchez's daughter?"

"I'd love to sink my fangs into *that*," the youth says, his red eyes flashing.

"Leave her alone, David!" Tito growls. "One misstep at this point could ruin everything."

"What are you up to, now?" Miguel asks. "On second thought, I don't want to know."

"I'll fill you in later. As I was just telling Anna, I want to patch things up with you, Miguel. We said some things the other day we shouldn't have."

"I take nothing back. I meant every word."

Tito laughs a hollow, mirthless laugh. "You see what I'm talking about, Anna? He defies me at every turn. Maybe you can reason with him."

Anna takes Miguel's hand. "Tito is your maker, Miguel. You should treat him with more respect."

"Respect must be earned." Miguel pulls away from her. "Are you working for him?"

"As a matter of fact, I've agreed to serve as his press secretary."

"And I have a job for you, Miguel."

"I won't go back to being your enforcer."

"That position has already been filled." Tito claps David on the back. "Don't let his pretty face fool you. David reminds me a lot of you . . . before you went soft."

"I don't work for you anymore."

"Now, just hear me out, Miguel."

"Aren't you a fugitive from justice?"

"Haven't you heard? I just received a presidential pardon! Cost me a million in campaign contributions to *el presidente*. Here's the best part—I'm going to run against the sonofabitch in the next election! And I want you to manage my campaign."

"Why me? I don't know anything about politics."

"That doesn't matter. You've been a soldier, painter, pirate, priest, planter, and businessman, and you've been damn good at all of them. During the Civil War, you made quite a name for yourself. The poor people came to respect you, and the rich learned to fear you. Hell, *you* should be the one running for president."

"And if you're elected, how long do you think you can hide what you are?"

"That's the beauty of it!" Tito grins. "Once I'm president, I won't have to."

The climactic, surging strains of the "Liebestod" from Wagner's *Tristan und Isolde* blast over the PA system, signaling the start of the concert.

Tito looks around. "Where's David? The little bastard! I told him not to run off."

"He'll be fine," Anna says. "Let's find our seats."

"Come on, Miguel," Tito says. "Why don't you join Anna and me in our private box?"

"I'll catch up with you later. I'm going to watch from backstage."

"Enjoy the show. I think you'll find the subject very much to your liking."

Miguel takes up his station in the wings. He looks around for Patrick, but Patrick is too revved-up to watch. He's gone behind the stage to chain-smoke and walk off his nervous energy.

The "Liebestod" fades out and is replaced by a dissonant orchestral prelude titled "In Memoriam Vlad Drakulya" that opens MOD's latest release, *Dracula's Revenge*. Above the music, a shrill male voice announces, "Ladies and gentlemen, direct from London, it's M . . . O . . . D!" The audience erupts in a frenzy of clapping, shouting, stomping, whistling, and cheering. The groundlings at the back surge forward to get a closer look at the band, shoving the people in front into the cordon of security guards ringing the stage.

And yet nobody can see anything because the stage is still dark. Then a massive fireball shoots out of the blackness straight at the audience, bathing the stadium in brilliant orange, yellow, and red light before bursting into a million pieces.

Propelled by the hard-driving rhythm section of Aspeth and Montague, Jack the Ripper and Moorcroft launch into a heavy-metal rendition of the prelude. But where is John Keats? Ten thousand hands point heavenward: a huge spotlight follows Keats as he soars high above the crowd and then lands softly onstage, his full-length black cloak flapping like a pair of giant bat wings.

"*Hola*, San Salvador!" he shouts above the tumult.

"*Hola!*" the audience roars back in unison.

Like a man possessed, Keats dashes from one side of the stage to the other, sometimes venturing onto the narrow gangway that juts far into the audience, slapping outstretched hands and strutting in time with the music. Throughout the *Dracula* set, the stage is cloaked in somber red and purple hues. The video screens display close-ups of the band members interspersed with clips from *Nosferatu*, *Dracula*, and other classic vampire movies.

The band is in top form. This is their first live gig in over a year, and they're eager to show off the new material. The first song, "Sundown," recounts the pursuit and slaying of Dracula as told in the Bram Stoker novel. The rest of the album, as John Keats writes in the liner notes, is presented from the vampire's point of view. After he is resurrected by gypsies, Dracula tracks down his surviving killers—Arthur Holmwood, Dr. Seward, and Jonathan Harker—and eliminates them one by one. The last to go is Dracula's nemesis, Professor Van Helsing, who is impaled with one of his own wooden stakes in the ironic "This One's for You." The album's finale, "Forever Yours," is Dracula's honeymoon serenade to Mina Harker, his vampire bride. "I thus gave *Dracula's Revenge* the happy ending that the Bram Stoker novel lacks," Keats writes, "although I leave room for a possible sequel involving the Harkers' young son, Quincey, should he choose to seek vengeance against the slayer of his father and the seducer of his mother."

As the final chord fades away, the audience gives MOD a thunderous ovation. Keats waves to the crowd and yells, "We're gonna take a short break. Don't go anywhere!"

The five band members, glistening with sweat and glowing with opening-night euphoria, sweep past Miguel and head back to their dressing areas. Seconds later, Tito and Anna materialize at Miguel's side.

"Now it's my turn," Tito says with a wink. "Watch this." Wireless mic in hand, Tito strides onto the stage and addresses the multitude in Spanish: "Good evening, my friends. Are you all enjoying the show?" He pauses to let them answer in the affirmative. "Good! This is only the first of many free concerts I'll be bringing to you in the coming months. My name is Tito Vazquez, and I'm announcing my candidacy for the presidency of El Salvador. And as of tonight, I'm cutting my ties to the organization known as Mara Camazotza." Tito's announcement is met with stunned silence. But a few shouts of "Liar" and "Murderer" soon swell into a chorus of boos, jeers, and catcalls, which Tito's large cheering section cannot suppress. Undaunted, Tito waves his arm toward stage right. "And now, I'd like to introduce my campaign manager, Miguel Maldonado."

Miguel grits his teeth. "*That bastard.*"

"Go ahead, Miguel," Anna says, giving him a gentle push. "A chance like this comes only once every hundred years."

Miguel steps into the glare and joins Tito onstage. He is greeted with loud applause and chants of "Mi-guel, Miguel!" from Tito's throng. Tito seizes Miguel's right hand and raises it above his head in a gesture of solidarity. Smiling at the crowd, Miguel whispers, "*I'll get you for this.*"

"My friends," Tito says, "I solemnly swear to you that, if elected, my first task will be to end the gang violence that has plagued El Salvador for so many years. Why, our own president is so fearful that he sent his only daughter to school in the United States, far from her family and friends. What have we come to when we cannot protect our children? Our country desperately needs a strong leader who can bring peace and prosperity to her suffering people. I am that leader! But I must have your support. Thank you and enjoy the rest of the show!"

Once again, the applause of Tito's supporters fails to drown out the hecklers.

Tito is beaming and waving to the crowd as he and Miguel exit stage right. "All in all, I'd say that went rather well," he tells Anna.

"You were superb!" she gushes. "Wasn't he, Miguel?"

"Let's get one thing straight," Miguel says. "I don't care what you just told the crowd. I'm not your campaign manager."

"But they loved you!" Tito says. "How can you turn your back on them?"

"You're the one running for president, not me."

"All right, Miguel. Have it your way. But my offer still stands. Take a few days to think it over."

"I hope you'll change your mind," Anna says. "We'd make a great team." She and Tito return to their box for the second half of the concert.

Miguel resumes his place in the wings. The remaining songs consist of MOD favorites dating back to *Goblin Market*, the group's first album. For the final encore, Jack the Ripper shreds a guitar solo on his white double-neck Gibson based on the revolutionary anthem, "The People United Will Never Be Defeated." As the rest of the group joins in, the audience rises to its feet, the stadium suddenly glimmers with innumerable points of light, and the people begin to sing along with John Keats:

"Arise and fight! The people are going to win! The life to come will be better . . . And now the people . . . with a giant voice cry out—Forward! The people united will never be defeated!"

The concert closes with a magnificent fireworks display high above the stadium, courtesy of Tito Vazquez. The band members link arms center stage and take their final bows. The applause is deafening. All eyes are locked on the group, so no one sees Patrick reappear backstage, carrying the body of Bobby, the blonde-haired roadie.

"He's dead!" Patrick bellows. "Some heartless bastard killed him!" He gently lays the corpse down on a long table, buries his face in his hands, and starts to weep. Miguel is the first one to notice. As he examines the body, a roadie wanders over.

Thinking that Bobby is playing a prank, the roadie says, "Yo, Bobby, stop fuckin' with us, bro. This shit ain't funny."

"The man's neck is broken, you fool," Miguel says.

Just then, Eva Sanchez's bodyguards arrive on the scene, but Eva is not with them. "Have you seen Señorita Sanchez?" the one in charge asks Miguel. "She was supposed to meet the bass player backstage after the concert."

Miguel shakes his head.

"We were following her, and then she just melted into the crowd. I think she was trying to lose us."

"Well, she apparently succeeded," Miguel says. "Have you notified stadium security and the police?"

"I was expecting to find her here," the head bodyguard says. He turns to one of his men and orders him to call stadium security. Then he calls the San Salvador police.

"I think I know where to start looking," Miguel says. He turns to Patrick, who is blowing his nose with a faded purple bandana. "Can you show us where you found Bobby's body?"

"Sure. Why?"

"His death may be connected to Eva Sanchez's disappearance."

Patrick takes Miguel, Eva's bodyguards, and several roadies to the place where the band's empty equipment cases are stacked.

"This is the spot," Patrick says.

Some security personnel arrive with flashlights, and everyone begins to search the area.

"I think I found one of her shoes," Miguel calls out. Bending over to pick up the Jimmy Choo high-heel sandal, Miguel notices that he's standing before a case that's nearly as tall as he is. Resting lengthwise on the ground, it calls to mind a metal coffin. He raps on it a few times—something large and solid is in there. He flips the clasps, raises the lid, and finds Eva Sanchez stuffed inside. One look at her throat tells him all he needs to know. Miguel supposes that Bobby blundered onto the scene as David was disposing of Eva's body, and that Patrick discovered the young roadie's corpse shortly after he was killed.

The police arrive looking a bit worse for wear, no doubt the result of pushing upstream against the departing crowd. They question Miguel, Patrick, and anyone else who might have seen or spoken to either of the victims that night. Miguel says nothing to the police about his theory, because they would ask too many questions. In any event, it soon becomes clear that they consider Patrick a prime suspect. Miguel is not surprised, for he knows that the lead detective is under considerable pressure to make an arrest—after all, one of the murder victims is the president's daughter.

While the police handcuff Patrick, Di Lorenzo, the tour manager, whispers something into Miguel's ear. Miguel nods his head and addresses the lead detective in Spanish. "Would you be willing to keep this man under house arrest in his hotel room?"

"That's out of the question," the detective says. "He's being charged with two counts of murder."

"Then could you put him in a cell by himself? He won't last five minutes in a holding tank."

"I'll see what I can do."

Tito and Anna arrive as the police lead Patrick away. Running a hand through his mane of wavy brown hair, Di Lorenzo says, "Jesus fucking Christ. What am I gonna do?"

"Stop whining," Tito says. "We've been through far worse than this, haven't we, Miguel?"

"Don't hand me that bullshit," Di Lorenzo snaps. "One of my best roadies is dead, and my stage manager's been busted for murder. And it's all because we had to come to this third-world shithole."

"Watch your mouth." Tito warns. "You're insulting my homeland."

"I'll say whatever I damn well please."

Quick as lightning, Tito is in Di Lorenzo's face, red eyes glaring and fangs at the ready. "Don't tempt me."

"Back off, you crazy fuck!" Di Lorenzo barks. But it is Di Lorenzo who backs away, stumbling as he does so. "You'll be hearing from my lawyers, Vazquez."

"My lawyers will be glad to hear from your lawyers," Tito shouts back. "They're always looking for an excuse to pick my pocket." He watches Di Lorenzo hustle back to the stage, which is already being broken down. "That's gratitude for you. I paid those bastards a fucking fortune to play here, and now they want to sue me. Well, they can go to hell! I'll countersue for breach of contract."

"What are you talking about?" Miguel says. "They put on a fantastic show."

"That's your opinion," Tito says. "Things looked very different from where I was sitting."

"I agree with Miguel," Anna says. "The concert was a great success, Tito. You're obsessing on a few minor problems and overlooking the many positive things that happened here tonight. Why, you could even use the Sanchez girl's death to your advantage." She pauses to let the idea sink in.

"Go on—I'm listening."

"Tomorrow, you should call a press conference to condemn the senseless murder of Eva Sanchez. Close your statement with an appeal to the Salvadoran people to join with you in declaring war on gang violence: 'Let us take back our schools and our barrios and make them safe again.'"

Miguel claps his hands three times, very slowly. "Bravo, Anna. Those are stirring words indeed. There's just one problem. Something must be done about Eva's murderer."

"Of course," Tito says. "But it appears the police already have the killer."

"You know damn well who I'm talking about. David must be destroyed."

"Are you crazy? I *need* him."

"He's out of control."

"What about you, Miguel? You've defied me time and again, and yet I keep hoping you'll come around."

"Well, I can never be like David, if that's what you want. I won't kill humans for sport."

"No, what you do is far worse—you fall in love with them. When will you learn? They're just food."

"Miguel," Anna says, "you seem to forget that humans are our inferiors."

"I don't need a lecture from you," Miguel says, "on humans or any other subject."

"You should thank Anna for convincing me to give you another chance," Tito says, wrapping his steely right arm around Miguel's shoulders. "You see, I have big plans for you."

Miguel struggles to break free, but Tito's grip proves too strong. "I don't work for you anymore, remember?"

"You owe me, Miguel," Tito says, tightening his grip. "I want you to be my campaign manager."

"And if I refuse?"

"I'm confident you'll do the right thing." Tito glances at his watch. "My God! It's almost midnight. Looks like I'm going to be late for my own meeting."

"What meeting?" Miguel asks.

"I've arranged a truce with my competition. We're getting together for a late supper. I'll be laying down some new ground rules."

"What makes you think they'll agree to them?"

"Believe me, they won't have a choice."

Tito offers Miguel a ride to the Hilton Princess. Anna says that she is also staying there.

"How convenient," Tito says. "You can talk over old times."

It is midnight when Anna and Miguel step out of Tito's black Jaguar XJ in front of the hotel.

"*Liebchen*," Anna whispers into Miguel's ear. "Take me dancing."

"I'd love to, darling, but I'm exhausted."

"I'll make it worth your while." She kisses him on the mouth and squeezes his crotch. Miguel knows that it is useless to protest. He takes her by the hand, and together they cross the Boulevard del Hipódromo to Club Code, the biggest disco in San Salvador. When they walk in, the place is packed and pulsing with trance music. Overhead, strobe lights and lasers flash in sync with the rapid-fire beat. On the way to the dance floor, Anna sheds her jacket and lets her blonde hair fall down on her shoulders. She soon vanishes into the swirling crowd, and Miguel finds himself dancing with a stunning Salvadoreña about the same age as Eva. A few minutes later, Anna reappears with none other than Nick Montague, the bass player for MOD. After they've danced for about half an hour, Montague suggests that they head over to the bar.

On the way, Anna shouts into Miguel's ear, "I want him."

"Be my guest," Miguel shouts back.

She nods toward the Salvadoreña. "I see you've made a new friend."

At the bar, the young woman introduces herself as Elena Lopez. In Spanish, she tells Miguel that Montague danced with her for a few minutes and then veered off toward Anna like a shark catching the scent of fresh blood—an analogy he finds deliciously ironic.

"Don't take it personally," Miguel says. "He's a rock star."

After a few mojitos and some small talk, Montague suggests that the four of them continue the party back at his suite in the Hilton Princess. Anna readily agrees, but Elena needs some coaxing. It is 2:00 a.m. when they reach Montague's penthouse suite. The three guests sit down in the living room while Montague mixes himself a nightcap at the mini-bar. Drink in hand, he asks Anna if she'd care to inspect the marble bathtub. They enter the master bedroom together, and the door closes behind them.

Elena and Miguel are left sitting on the sofa. She reaches for the remote, flips on the TV, and turns up the sound to mask the noise from next door. Miguel caresses her hair and tells her that she's very lovely. Elena tells him that she wants to be an actress and a model. He says that she should move to New York or LA. She agrees, but says that her English is not so good.

"Don't let that stop you," he says. "I'll help you get started."

"You would do that for me?"

Miguel gazes into her brown eyes and says, "Of course, my dear. Now, let's make love."

"I don't know if that's such a good idea," she says. "The last vampire I slept with almost drained me."

Miguel laughs. "What a strange girl you are! Is this some kind of weird fantasy of yours?"

144

"It was no fantasy," she says. "He was much better than that. You might know him. His name is David Arroyo."

The mere mention of the name fills Miguel with hatred. "How did you get mixed up with him? You're lucky he didn't kill you."

"I couldn't help myself." Elena leans back, closes her eyes, and waits for Miguel to make his move. Nothing happens. She opens her eyes, only to find him *staring at the fucking TV screen*. "Hey, do you need an engraved invitation or something?"

Miguel grabs Elena by the shoulders and sinks his fangs into her throat. Even as the venom does its work, his feeding arouses her. She involuntarily wraps her legs around his ass and rocks her hips until she comes with a violent shudder. She awakens soon afterward, feeling randy and ready to try just about anything. Having satisfied his hunger, Miguel takes Elena into his arms and carries her down to his room for more fun and games.

Miguel is awakened by a loud knocking at the door. He is lying in bed. Elena is fast asleep beside him, her arm draped across his chest. He rises and puts on a hotel bathrobe. His path is littered with Elena's shoes, stockings, dress, bra, and panties. He peers into the peephole and sees Anna in a hotel robe just like his, standing there with her shoes in one hand and her clothes in the other. He opens the door for her. As she steps inside, he says, "What happened?"

"It's a long story."

"I'm all ears."

Anna tells Miguel that she and Montague were making love in the bathtub when someone started pounding on the door. It was Di Lorenzo. He said that Montague's wife had just called him. She had heard about the murders on the news and was frantically trying to reach her husband. Montague said he was going back to sleep. *Call her* now *goddammit,* Di Lorenzo shouted, *or I'll tell her why you're not answering your fucking phone!* Montague made the call and assured his wife that he was okay. Then Di Lorenzo told Montague, *pack your shit and be down in the lobby in fifteen minutes, 'cause we're gettin' the fuck outta Dodge.*

"Even as I speak," Anna says, "Montague the Magnificent is on his way to the airport, and I didn't even get a taste. Where is your lovely Señorita?"

"She's asleep."

"Mind if I look in on her?"

"I don't think—"

Anna sweeps past Miguel and enters the bedroom. She removes her robe and slips into bed beside the sleeping Elena. Noting the bite marks on Elena's throat, Anna says:

"How is it?"

"I've had better."

Brushing aside Elena's long, dark hair, Anna bites into the soft brown flesh of her throat and takes a drink. With childlike glee, she licks the blood from her lips and says, "Hmm, not bad . . ."

Elena chooses this moment to awaken. She opens her eyes and beholds a red-eyed Aryan demon leering at her. She screams.

"*Halt den Mund!*" Anna slaps Elena across the face, but that only makes her scream louder. She gives the young woman's neck a violent twist, and *snap!* The screaming stops.

Miguel lunges onto the bed in a desperate attempt to save Elena. By the time he lands on top of Anna, the young woman is already dead. He wraps his fingers around Anna's neck and begins to squeeze.

"Stop!" she gasps. "You're hurting me!"

Anna struggles with all her might but cannot break Miguel's death grip. Then Miguel tosses her aside. "You had no right. She was *mine*, damn you!"

He races into the bathroom, slams the door, and turns on the shower to hide his tears of rage. As the hot water splashes over him, the tension starts to drain from his body. By the time he has dried off, he is ready to face her again. When he steps out of the bathroom, she is sitting naked on the edge of the bed, one leg draped over the other, watching *CNN en Español*. Just a few feet away, Elena is lying on the bed, her lifeless eyes staring at Anna's rear end.

"We're the day's top story," Anna says, her back to Miguel. "You know what they say. Any press is good press." She turns to face him, revealing several large bruises on either side of her slender neck. "Miguel, how much real estate do you own in San Salvador?"

"More than I can keep track of."

"So why are you staying here?"

"I happen to like it."

"Let's dump her body out the window and say she killed herself."

"Do you know why she jumped?"

"She was distraught over losing Nick Montague."

"Is that the best you can do?"

"Do you have a better plan?"

"No."

Miguel looks out the window and sees a faint glow above the horizon. "If we're going to do it, we'd better do it now." Seizing the floor lamp, he slams it into the window, breaking the glass. He lifts Elena's body off the bed, carries it to the window, and tosses it through the opening. The corpse plummets seven stories and strikes the pavement with a thud.

"The police will be here soon," Anna says. "I'd better jump in the shower."

After she disappears into the bathroom, Miguel casts one last, lingering look down at the body and then dresses. Tito calls and says that he wants to announce a press conference for two o'clock.

"Can I count on you to be there?" he asks.

"I doubt it," Miguel says.

"What's the problem?"

"Let's just say it concerns the death of a young woman."

"Okay, I'll make a few phone calls. In the meantime, sit tight and deny everything."

As soon as Miguel gets off the phone with Tito, he calls Alvarez.

"What have you done now?" the attorney asks between yawns.

Miguel explains the situation. Alvarez says that he's due in court that morning but will request a continuance. "I'll get back to you as soon as I can."

Anna emerges from the bathroom and begins to dress. As she slips on her pantyhose, Miguel tells her about Tito's press conference.

"It can wait," she says. "We have to come up with a story."

Their story unfolds something like this: heartbroken over losing Montague to Anna, Elena spent the night with Miguel to salve her wounded pride—or so she tearfully confessed to him after they made love. After Montague checked out, Anna came down to Miguel's suite. While the pair talked in the living room, they heard the sound of shattering glass in the bedroom. They rushed in, only to see Elena leap out of the window to her death.

To conceal the bruises on her throat, Anna drapes a white pashmina over her hair, crosses the ends under her chin, and ties them off at the nape of her neck á la Grace Kelly.

"How do I look?" she asks.

"Enchanting."

There is a knock at the door.

"That must be the police," Miguel says.

"So soon?"

He shrugs. "The desk clerk must have seen Elena come in with us."

As Miguel heads to the door, Anna says, "Admit it, *Liebchen*. You're never bored when I'm around."

Chapter Thirteen

MYOPIA

In accordance with her wishes, Susan Stanley's memorial service is held at the foot of the main pyramid at Ciudad Antigua. Over a hundred people—including many of the world's leading pre-Columbian scholars—have gathered to pay their last respects. Among the dignitaries are the US ambassador and the Salvadoran Secretary of Culture. The congregation is seated on folding chairs under a large canopy. It's a typical hot and humid afternoon, so there is much fanning and mopping of faces. One by one, those who wish to do so step up to the podium and say a few words about Susan, and then Andy Brower, soggy in coat and tie, delivers the eulogy. He recounts his first meeting with her—"the beginning of a lifelong friendship." When Andy reaches the end of the anecdote, his voice catches, and he is unable to go on. The gathering sits in awkward silence until Chad Wilkinson stands up and delivers the punch line for him: "Congratulations, kid! I think you nailed it." The ensuing laughter breaks the tension, and Andy manages to regain his composure.

"As cruel and senseless as Susan's death seemed when the news first reached me," he continues, "I can now take solace from the knowledge that she died defending the ground she loved so much. And it is only fitting that this be her final resting place."

Andy doesn't mention that he has already fulfilled Susan's request to scatter her ashes on the acropolis. Instead, he points to a small marble tablet at the foot of the pyramid, which was his idea. He reads the epitaph:

SUSAN B. STANLEY
BORN MAY 2, 1948 DIED OCTOBER 29, 2010
FRIEND, COLLEAGUE, MENTOR.

Andy concludes with the promise to continue Susan's work at Ciudad Antigua and to organize a conference in her memory for the following year. The service ends with the singing of "Amazing Grace" in both English and Spanish, accompanied by acoustic guitar, violin, and cello.

After the service, Andy climbs to the top of the pyramid. With a pang of regret, he looks across the acropolis to the excavation marking the royal tomb. The thought crosses his mind that if he hadn't tumbled down that goddamn rabbit-hole, she would probably still be alive. All he can do now is carry on. With hard work and persistence, perhaps the tomb will divulge its ancient secrets: who died there and who did the killing and why. In the meantime, he can only hope that Susan's killers are brought to justice.

Andy walks over to the museum, where the gathering has adjourned for some refreshments and air-conditioned solace. It is a modest A-frame building with smooth, cream-colored concrete walls, a tile floor, and a stucco roof. It contains a dozen bilingual exhibits that tell the story of the birth, life, and death of Ciudad Antigua. The reception gives Andy a chance to reconnect with some old friends he hasn't seen in years. The person he is most eager to talk to is Carlos Espinoza, but Espinoza doesn't show up until the end of the reception without so much as an explanation or an apology. Andy notes that his friend's glasses are held together by electrical tape.

After Andy has said goodbye to the last of the guests, Espinoza offers him a ride back to San Salvador. "Maria is expecting you for dinner," he says.

"Thanks," Andy says. "I can't stay long, though. I've got a plane to catch in the morning."

"No problem. I'll drive you to the airport."

"But I've reserved a room."

"Cancel it," Espinoza tells him. "You're staying with us."

They get into Espinoza's vintage white Honda Civic and drive off. Andy has removed his coat and tie and tossed them on the back seat. Just before they reach the highway, their path is blocked by a herd of cattle lumbering along from right to left. Three men and a young boy are urging the herd on and looking over their shoulders as if they're being followed. Espinoza climbs out of the car and tells the men that they are trespassing on park land. In reply, they point in the direction whence they have come. One of the men spreads his arms wide to suggest something very large.

Another says, "Hahg-WAHRR NAY-grroe."

The third cries, "El Diablo!"

Shielding his eyes, Espinoza looks off in the direction they are pointing, directly into the rays of the setting sun. Then he walks back to the car and gets in. He sits in silence, waiting for the stragglers to pass.

"There haven't been any jaguars in El Salvador for a long time," Espinoza says at last, "at least not in the wild."

"Whatever they saw, it sure scared the hell out of them."

"Probably just a big feral cat lurking in the shadows."

As Espinoza speaks, something catches Andy's eye. Looking to his right, he sees a pair of gleaming red eyes in the fading light. They are the same red eyes that haunted his dream after the fall into the tomb. The creature is standing so close that the faint spots on its black coat are visible. It is staring straight into Andy's eyes.

"Carlos, do you see what I see?"

Espinoza follows Andy's gaze. "*Jesucristo!*" He shoves the Civic into gear, floors it, and shoots into the highway, swerving just in time to avoid a head-on collision with an oncoming El Camino.

"Holy shit!" Andy yells. "You almost killed us."

"Did you see those eyes?"

"You can slow down now, Carlos."

"Are you sure?" Espinoza peers into the rearview mirror, as though half expecting to see the jaguar in hot pursuit. "I could use a drink. What about you?"

"I don't think that's such a good idea." Andy knows that Espinoza has been clean and sober for the past five years. He also knows that his friend quit drinking only after his wife had threatened to leave him if he didn't. "Wasn't Maria expecting us for dinner?"

"I'll give her a call. She'll understand. There's something I've been meaning to talk to you about."

"Can't we discuss it on the way?"

"It requires my full attention."

"Maria's gonna kill me for letting you fall off the wagon."

"My friend, the only person she will kill is me."

Espinoza pulls over at a roadside cantina. He reaches into the glove box and retrieves a manila envelope lying under a black .38 Special.

"So when did you start packing heat?"

Espinoza gives him a puzzled look and then smiles. "Oh, you mean the gun. I bought it a few weeks ago."

"Why?"

"In case you haven't heard, this is a very dangerous country."

He gets out of the car and walks inside, closely followed by Andy. They sit down at a small table in a dark corner. "Limón y Sal" is playing on the jukebox. The only people in evidence are the bartender and a solitary customer at the bar. Espinoza orders a bottle of José Cuervo and Andy orders a Pilsener.

"So what's in the envelope?" Andy takes a swig from his beer.

"Evidence." Espinoza downs a shot of tequila and grimaces. "You remember that conversation we had about Miguel Maldonado?"

"How could I forget?"

"Well, I told you only part of Maldonado's story—a very small part. Had I told you everything I know, you would've said I was crazy." He knocks back another shot. "I can hardly believe it myself."

Espinoza pulls several old black-and-white photographs out of the envelope. He hands one to Andy. "This is a group portrait of Maximiliano Hernandez Martinez and some of his cronies. It was taken in 1931, just after he became president of El Salvador. *El Presidente* is the one standing in the middle. Now check out the second fellow on the right. Look familiar?"

At first, the close-cropped hair and handlebar mustache throw Andy off. But on taking another look, it dawns on him. "That's Maldonado!"

"Correct. Only he went by a different name back then."

"No way."

"It's him, Andy. That's how Maldonado looked eighty years ago. As you can see, he hasn't aged a day. Do you recognize this fellow?" Espinoza points to the man standing on Miguel's left.

"Should I?"

"He currently goes by the name of Tito Vazquez."

"You mean the gangster who's running for president?"

"The very same."

Noting the epaulettes and the gold braid on Tito's uniform, Andy quips, "Kinda looks like Harpo Marx in *Duck Soup*."

"Don't let his appearance fool you. Tito Vazquez was . . . is . . . a cold-blooded killer. And so is Maldonado." Espinoza takes another shot of tequila. "They served Martinez as spies and assassins. In 1932, they uncovered a plot by Faribundo Martí to lead a peasant revolt against the Martinez regime. So Martinez arrested Martí and most of the other ringleaders, cutting off the head of the revolt."

"But the revolt took place anyway."

"And the rebels never stood a chance. The uprising was badly organized and never spread beyond a few departments in the west. Martinez crushed all resistance by slaughtering thousands of peasants. He almost wiped out the Pipil Indians. No one knows exactly how many thousands died in *La Matanza*. Most of the victims weren't even involved in the revolt. It's no surprise that Martinez was an admirer of Hitler and Mussolini." Espinoza takes a jolt straight from the bottle. "And this is the guy Vazquez and Maldonado worked for."

"Don't you think you've had enough?" Andy says.

Espinoza ignores Andy's question and pulls out another photo. "This is a still taken from the Leni Riefenstahl film, *Triumph of the Will*."

The photo shows Adolf Hitler in an open car returning the Nazi salute to a cheering throng lining the roadside. Two of the bystanders are surrounded by a halo of red ink. Andy points to them and says, "Um, let me guess. Our two heroes."

Espinoza nods his head. "In the summer of 1935, Martinez sent Vazquez and Maldonado to Germany to observe the annual Nazi Party rally at Nuremberg. At some point, they had a private audience with *Der Führer*. Maldonado apparently found Hitler to be a pompous bore and returned to El Salvador a few weeks later. But Vazquez became a fanatical follower and remained in Germany for over a year. He later repudiated Martinez for betraying Hitler when Nazi Germany declared war on the United States."

"What's your source for all this?"

"My grandfather was an official in the Martinez government and an amateur historian. At great personal risk, he compiled a secret history of the regime. Most of the photos in this envelope belonged to him."

"Why didn't he publish it?"

"Come on, Andy. Do you think Vazquez and Maldonado would have let him do that? My grandfather was no fool. He kept the manuscript hidden away. Just before he died, he gave it to me. But he made me swear that I would never attempt to publish it as long as the *vampiros* were still around."

"Vampires? What in the hell are you talking about?"

"How else can you explain their longevity?"

"You're putting me on, right?"

"I only wish I was." With his index finger, Espinoza pushes his broken glasses up the bridge of his nose. "The person who arranged the meeting with Hitler was Hitler's mistress, Eva Braun. She did it as a favor for a close friend named Anna Schiller, a young actress and singer who apparently fell for Maldonado at first sight—or first bite, as the case may be."

Espinoza places a snapshot of an archetypal Aryan female—fair-skinned, blonde, and beautiful—in front of Andy. "Not long after Maldonado left Germany, Fräulein Schiller dropped out of sight. She resurfaced about a year later as private secretary to Ribbentrop when he was the German ambassador to Britain. Her mission was to foster good will toward Nazi Germany among the British ruling class. She threw herself into her work and became the *femme fatale* of Whitehall. Legend has it that King Edward VIII numbered among her conquests. But Ribbentrop proved to be such a tactless buffoon that her success between the sheets came to nothing."

"What happened to her?"

"She was recalled to Berlin and assigned to the Propaganda Ministry. Her ambition was to become a movie star. But Dr. Goebbels put her on the radio instead. She adopted the stage name Viktoria Jungblut, or "Vickie Young Slut," as the GIs called her. During the war, she had her own nightly program, "The Dear John Hour," which targeted American soldiers fighting in Western Europe. She sang sad songs filled with homesickness and longing for lost loves, and read Dear John letters taken from dead or captured GIs. She also portrayed fallen American women in plays like "I Was a Teenage Jezebel" and "Victory Girls Never Say No." She ended every program with, "That's all she wrote, boys," a tagline used by GIs on the receiving end of Dear John letters. She remained on the air until the end of the war and then vanished. I assumed she was dead until she turned up a few weeks ago in San Salvador."

Espinoza places a recent color photo of Anna next to the old black-and-white snapshot. Andy studies the two images and then looks up at Espinoza. "I admit there's a strong resemblance, but she can't be Vickie Young Slut, any more than these two guys," he points to the pair in the Hitler photo, "can be Maldonado and Vazquez."

"My friend," Espinoza says, "what must I do to convince you?"

"Give it a rest, Carlos."

"How can I give it a rest," Espinoza's voice is quavering with emotion, "when I know what Vazquez and Maldonado are up to and what they are capable of?"

"You don't have to tell me about Maldonado."

"Well, Vazquez is much worse. During the Civil War, he was D'Aubuisson's secret weapon. The guerrillas called him the One-Man Death Squad. And he could be our next president."

"Keep it down. Everyone can hear you."

"This is not the time for keeping quiet, Andy. The bodies are starting to pile up. Did you hear about the two gang leaders who were recently found in a Soyapango dumpster? Rumor has it they told Vazquez to fuck off. Good riddance, you might say, but there's also President Sanchez's daughter and the young model that allegedly jumped out of a hotel window. They were both seen with Maldonado shortly before they died. And then there's the young man who found the Sanchez girl's body and the guy who was arrested for killing her. One was found with a broken neck and the other was hanging from a light fixture in his jail cell."

"Okay, you've made your point. Can we go now?"

"I'm not finished." Espinoza downs the last of his tequila. "I have a theory. I believe Vazquez and Maldonado have existed on the dark fringes of human society for God knows how long, content to prey on their victims in perfect anonymity. But for the past eighty years, they have become more and more ambitious. Now Vazquez wants to take over the country. And he'll do it, unless somebody stops him." Espinoza slams his fist down on the table, knocking over his empty José Cuervo bottle. "Mark my words, Andy. I will kill Vazquez or die trying!"

Espinoza's declaration captures the attention of the bartender and the now-sizeable clientele inside the cantina. Andy hustles over to the bar and pays both his and Espinoza's tab.

"All right, Carlos, time to go."

Espinoza rises unsteadily to his feet and staggers to the door, waving off Andy's attempt to help him.

Unknown to Andy and Espinoza, a pale, handsome youth standing next to the jukebox watches them as they leave. He smiles as Andy wrests the car keys from his drunken friend and then pushes him into the front passenger seat. The youth waits until the Civic has turned onto the highway before venturing out into the night. Though on foot, he is confident of overtaking his quarry, for he intends to steal the first good car that comes to hand.

Espinoza is fast asleep when Andy pulls into his driveway. His mouth is agape and he is snoring loudly. As Andy gets out of the car, the light bulb above the front door flashes on.

Espinoza's wife opens the door and says, "Where have you been?"

"*Hola*, Maria," Andy says as he opens the passenger door. "I know we should've called. But Carlos had something on his mind that couldn't wait. You know how he is."

Maria is standing on the stoop with her arms crossed, her face hidden in shadow. She is just thirty-one—a dozen years younger than Espinoza—but has always been more than a match for her husband. "I don't blame *you*, Andy. Carlos is a grown man. He should be able to take care of himself."

Andy shakes Espinoza in a vain attempt to rouse him. "Come on, Carlos. Time to wake up."

"He's drunk, isn't he?"

"I'm afraid so." Andy tries to lift Espinoza out of the seat, but he is too heavy. "I think I'm going to need your help. He must weigh a ton."

She walks over to the car, bends down to within six inches of Espinoza's head, and yells, "*¡Ándale! ¡Despertarse!*"

Blinking his eyes, Espinoza says, "*¿Qué pasa?*"

"*Estás borracho,*" she says. "*Ahora venga adentro.*"

Espinoza struggles to his feet. He sways from side to side like a landlubber aboard a storm-tossed ship. After she removes his glasses, Maria takes him by the arm and leads him up the steps and through the doorway. "Sit down at the table," she calls from the bedroom. "I'll fix you something to eat as soon as I put this big baby to bed."

A minute or two later, Maria emerges from the bedroom. She opens the refrigerator, pulls out a plate of *arroz con pollo*, and puts it in the microwave. Then she takes a pitcher out of the fridge, pours some *horchata* into a glass, and puts it on the table in front of Andy. When the dinner is cooked, she removes the plate from the microwave and sets it down beside the glass.

As Andy eats, she tidies up the kitchen. When he is finished, she asks, "Do you want some more?"

"No thanks," he says.

"What about dessert?"

He smiles. "I can't eat another bite."

She laughs. "No wonder you're so skinny! Why, even little Tomás can put away more than you do." Tomás, six, is the younger of Maria and Carlos's two sons. Both he and his older brother, nine-year-old Carlito, are asleep in their bedroom just down the hall.

For the first time that evening, Andy takes a close look at Maria. She appears haggard and careworn. A few strands of white hair have taken up residence atop her head. She collects Andy's plate and glass. As she places them in the sink, she bursts into tears. To avoid waking the boys, she sobs into a dish towel. After a minute or so, Andy rises to take her into his arms and tell her that everything will be all right. But by the time he's out of his chair, she's already drying her eyes.

"Sit down," she says between sniffles. "I'm okay now."

Andy returns to his chair, but he remains standing.

"This isn't the first time he's been drinking and staying out." She wipes her nose with a tissue. "He hasn't been going to work, either. The department chair called the other day and said that Carlos hasn't taught class in over a week."

"What brought this on?"

"Ever since Tito Vazquez announced that he was running for president," Maria brushes a ringlet of hair off her forehead, "Carlos has acted like it's the end of the world. You should see what he's collected out in the shed."

"I can just imagine."

"He's filled it with all kinds of sharp things—spears, machetes, and wooden stakes. He says bullets only slow them down. Slow who down, I asked. Then he told me. Vampires." She giggles in spite of herself. "It's weird. The funnier he acts, the scarier he gets." She turns away and stares out the window. "I think he's losing it." When she turns to face him, the tears are falling again. "What am I going to do, Andy?"

This time, Andy takes her into his arms and says that everything will be all right. The words ring hollow, but it's all he can think of. In any event, Maria soon ceases her crying.

"Thank you for being such a good friend," she says, kissing him on the cheek. "I'm glad you're here."

Andy pulls the sleeper sofa out while Maria gets some sheets from the closet. She makes the bed, says goodnight, and then disappears into the bedroom.

That night, Andy dreams that he is back in the royal tomb at Ciudad Antigua. As he scans the walls, his flashlight quits working. He flips the switch off and on and shakes the flashlight a few times . . . nothing. The tomb is so dark that he has to feel his way around it. A pair of gleaming red eyes comes hurtling at him. The creature knocks him down. He can feel its hot breath on his face and its paws on his chest. It is staring intently into his eyes. Then it goes for his throat . . .

Andy awakens with a start. He scans the room. *Nothing.* But the window is open, and a soft breeze is rustling the curtains. Andy gets up and closes the window. Then he returns to bed and soon drifts back to sleep.

"Wake up, sleepyhead." Maria shakes Andy's shoulder, but he is slow to respond. "*Vámonos.* You've got a plane to catch."

He opens his eyes at last. "That's strange."

"What?"

"Did you open the window?"

"No. I thought you did." She closes and locks it.

Maria and Andy head out the door before sunrise. Espinoza is still asleep when they leave. She drops off Carlito and Tomás at the neighbors' and then drives Andy to Comalapa Airport. They exchange barely a dozen words on the way.

As Maria pulls into the kiss and ride area, Andy says, "I don't feel right about leaving you."

"I'll be okay."

"I can cancel my flight."

"Don't be ridiculous."

"Are you sure?"

"Look, this isn't the first time I've had to babysit Carlos."

"Give me a call tonight."

Maria nods her head. They hug, and she says, "Now go catch your plane." There are tears in her eyes.

Andy climbs out of the car and heads for the terminal. Just outside the entrance, he turns to wave goodbye, but she is already gone.

After his plane touches down in Houston, Andy checks his voicemail. There's one from Maria. She's worried because Carlos was gone when she got back, and his glasses were still on the nightstand.

"He's lost without them," she says. "He can't even find his way to the bathroom."

During the stopover, Andy calls Maria. She's just driven around the neighborhood looking for Carlos and turned up nothing. Andy suggests that he may have taken a bus or a cab to work.

"I just called. They haven't seen him."

That evening, there's another message from Maria waiting for him when he lands at BWI: "Andy, I still haven't heard from Carlos. I'm afraid something's happened to him. Do you think I should call the police?"

Before calling Maria back, Andy decides to contact the detective who recently stopped by to ask him some questions about Luisa Santiago. The guy seemed to be a straight shooter. And his card is still in Andy's wallet: WILLIAM COCHRANE.

Chapter Fourteen

PROFILING VAMPIRA

Dripping wet after a mad dash through a sudden downpour, Cochrane enters the Seventh Street Starbucks and heads upstairs, where he finds Cheryl Lucas seated at a window table. She is flipping through the pages of a legal pad and sipping espresso. He peels off his raincoat and sits down opposite her.

"You're late," she says, looking up from her pad. The first things that Cochrane notices are the dark circles under her eyes.

"Sorry. I got here as fast as I could." He takes out a notebook and pen. "So, what have you got for me?"

"Before we go any further, I want to remind you that this was your idea. So don't blame me if you don't like what you hear."

Cochrane holds up his right hand. "Whoa. Let's start over . . . Hi, Cheryl, how are you today?"

"I've been better. How the hell are you?"

"I guess that all depends on how good a profiler you turn out to be."

"All right, smartass. Consider yourself warned." Cheryl flips back to the top page of her legal pad. "Okay, let's start with Rivera. We know that his murder was staged to look like *The Death of Marat*. And then there's Melendez."

"The headless guy. What's the deal with him?"

"Well, the head wasn't carried off as a trophy, as in the Herrera case. But I was pretty sure the decapitation carried some symbolic value. I just wasn't able to decode the symbolism until I saw the connection between the two murders through the perpetrator's eyes."

As Cheryl speaks, Cochrane takes notes using his own shorthand—a series of zigzag lines and dots interspersed with capital letters that another detective once described as "a meth head's alphabet soup."

"It occurred to me that the perpetrator also staged Melendez's crime scene after a famous picture. But after spending so much time on Rivera, she had to make fast work of Melendez. I Googled "beheading paintings" and turned up some hits with John the Baptist and a few other guys who lost their heads. But far and away the most hits were for *Judith Beheading Holofernes*. I found dozens of paintings by that title. That's where the message, 'JUDITH WAS HERE,' comes in.

"So you're sure the murderer is female?"

"Yep."

"And who is Judith?"

"She was an Old Testament heroine who killed the Assyrian general Holofernes. To save her people, Judith charmed her way into Holofernes' tent and got him so drunk that he passed out. Then she cut off his head and sneaked it out to prove that he was dead. Judith's bravery inspired the Israelites to defeat the Assyrians in battle."

"So what does that have to do with *The Death of Marat*?"

"Well, Marat was murdered by a woman named Charlotte Corday, who gained access to his chambers by a similar trick. Mademoiselle Corday believed she was saving France from a bloodthirsty fiend responsible for some of the worst excesses of the French Revolution. She was found guilty of murder and executed by guillotine. In his painting, David depicted Marat as a martyr to the French Republic, but over the years, French attitudes toward Marat and Corday flip-flopped. A painter named Baudry portrayed Corday as a martyr and Marat as a monster, and the writer Lamartine nicknamed her the Angel of Assassination."

"So you think our killer believes she's some kind of hero?"

"Absolutely. She sees herself as a modern-day Judith or Charlotte Corday. Vengeance was her motive, but she's not a gang member."

"How do you know that?"

"Call me elitist, but I just don't see a gangbanger having this level of sophistication. Our perpetrator's a free-lance vigilante with a fine arts degree."

"What else can you tell me about her?"

"She's very organized and very confident. The murders of Rivera and Melendez were carefully planned and executed, and the staging of the crime scene took a lot of time at great risk. The effort the perpetrator put into arranging Rivera's death scene suggests that she wanted to get it just right. I'd say she's an artist of some kind."

"The elaborate staging might indicate that the perpetrator left behind a bunch of false clues to throw us off."

"No. I'd say the killer was sending a message that she wanted us to decode. I'm also pretty sure that Rivera and Melendez were unconscious when they were killed. They both had quite a bit to drink and smoke. And there was no evidence of a struggle. I believe that Melendez was already dead when he was beheaded, like Rivera when he was stabbed. The autopsy reveals that they lost over eighty percent of their blood supply."

"So what happened to all that blood?"

"That's the million-dollar question. There were no incisions or needle marks on either of the bodies—just the two deep puncture wounds on the throat, which appear to have been made by a pair of oversize human eye teeth. So I did some reading on serial killers with a blood-drinking fixation. A clinical psychologist named the condition Renfield Syndrome, after Count Dracula's insect-eating henchman. The best-known cases are John Brennan Crutchley, known as the 'Vampire Rapist,' and Richard Trenton Chase, 'The Vampire of Sacramento.' They were blood drinkers all right, but compared to our perpetrator, they were rank amateurs. Whoever killed Rivera and Melendez isn't a Dracula wannabe, but an honest-to-God vampire."

Cochrane drops his pen. "Come again?"

"Take a good look at this." She shows him a photo of Rivera's throat. "That's the mark of the vampire."

"You're joking, right?"

"Do I look like I'm joking?"

"Okay, just for the sake of argument, let's say the murderer is a vampire—correction—a *female* vampire. How much blood would she have to drink to drain two adult males?"

"To leave Rivera and Melendez in the condition we found them, I'd say she had to drink at least two gallons, assuming she was working alone. But I think she had help."

"You mean there was more than one vampire?"

"Well, she couldn't have drunk all that blood by herself. Unless, of course, vampires are like vampire bats. They have the ability to excrete blood plasma almost as quickly as they ingest it. But that seems a bit far-fetched, doesn't it?"

Cochrane holds up his hands. "Come on, Cheryl. Give me something I can use."

"I tried to warn you, didn't I?" Cheryl touches his forearm. "There's one more thing you should know. Our perpetrator's just getting started. But look on the bright side."

"What's that?"

"At the rate she's going, she could fix DC's gang problem by Christmas."

On the Metro ride back to the station, Cochrane becomes so absorbed in his notes that he misses his stop. As he waits for the return train, it dawns on him that the prime suspect (discounting the vampire crap, of course) is Luisa Santiago. Not only does an eyewitness place her with Rivera and Melendez just before their murder, but she also closely matches Cheryl's profile.

That evening, Cochrane calls several of Luisa's friends and colleagues, asking if she has tried to contact them since her disappearance. Each one answers in the negative and then asks if he has reason to believe that she is alive. Cochrane invariably responds that he's just making a routine follow-up. Luisa's former roommate, Karen Silber, begins to cry and scolds him for tormenting her. Cochrane apologizes, hangs up, and calls Amanda Donovan, the morning show host who recently interviewed Luisa. They've been playing phone tag for several days, but this time, he reaches her. During their conversation, she mentions that the station videotapes its morning-show interviews.

Cochrane runs down to the TV station the next morning to watch Luisa's interview. The tape begins with Luisa staring straight into the camera lens during a close-up. Somebody off-camera tells her to look at Amanda instead. Cochrane asks the engineer to pause the tape.

"Is this live?" Cochrane asks.

"No it's not, thank God," the engineer replies. "This happened before the interview. The tapes roll during the commercial breaks. More often than not, the off-air chitchat turns out to be more interesting than the actual interview. But don't tell Mandy I said that."

The engineer resumes playback. Just before airtime, Amanda Donovan engages her nervous guest in conversation: "Luisa, I see that you enjoy visiting art museums. Well, that also happens to be a passion of mine. I've always been partial to Monet. Who's your favorite artist?"

"Degas," Luisa replies.

"I should've guessed! His ballerina pictures are so lovely, and he did so many of them."

"Over a thousand," Luisa says.

"Really? I had no idea."

"Ballet was his obsession."

"So I guess I'll be seeing you at the opening of the Degas exhibition next month."

"Oh, yeah! I wouldn't miss it for the world."

Cochrane borrows the engineer's laptop. He Googles "degas exhibit" and finds a traveling exhibition called "Degas's Dancers" scheduled to open at the National Gallery of Art in five days. He checks his Blackberry and sees that he's off-duty that evening. Once he's back on the street, Cochrane calls Cheryl and asks if she'd like to go to the opening of the Degas show.

"Are you asking me on a date?" she says.

"I'm just following your advice."

"What advice?"

"You told me to broaden my horizons."

She laughs. "Oh, yeah, I remember now." There's a brief pause. "Okay. I'll go on one condition."

"What's that?"

"Don't rush me, and if you're bored, keep it to yourself."

"I believe that's two conditions."

"That's the deal. Take it or leave it."

"All right, I'll pick you up at six."

Chapter Fifteen

THE MIRROR

Luisa is back in the studio where she took her first ballet lessons. The room is smaller and shabbier than she remembers. As she does her *pliés* and other leg stretches at the barre, two figures emerge from a dark mist and stand behind her in the mirror. It's her parents, dressed in their Sunday best. She recognizes them from the wedding photo in Aunt Rosa's album. Beaming with pride, they watch their little girl perform a *port de bras* routine. They applaud the arm-moving exercise as if it were a bravura performance. Luisa feels a hand on her shoulder. Looking into the mirror, she sees the birdlike Señora Chavez, her first teacher, telling her parents, "*La Mariposa es mi mejor estudiante.*" Luisa's mother's eyes fill with tears. Her father pulls out a handkerchief and blows his nose to hide the fact that he is also crying.

Yet another figure emerges from the mist. It is Aunt Rosa. Arms folded across her chest, she stands apart from the others. Luisa notes the stern expression on her aunt's face; she has never seen her so angry. Rosa waves her hand, causing a mist to envelop Luisa's parents and Señora Chavez. The trio barely has time to wave goodbye before they vanish into thin air.

"The visit was your parents' idea," Rosa says. "I had to cut it short to prevent them from seeing the monster you've become."

"What are you talking about?" Luisa says. "I'll always be their little girl."

"Their little girl didn't have red eyes and razor-sharp fangs. Their little girl is *dead*."

"I became what I am to punish your killers."

"I never wanted revenge, Luisa. I only wanted you to be happy."

"So this is the thanks I get. I gave up *everything* for you!"

"Don't try to fill me with guilt. I feel only remorse— remorse for raising a barracuda instead of a butterfly."

Luisa reaches into the mirror and grabs her aunt by the throat.

"You can't kill me," Rosa says with a laugh. "I'm already dead!"

The harder Luisa squeezes, the louder her aunt laughs.

"My, what big teeth you have," Rosa cackles.

As Luisa gazes into the mirror, her aunt becomes the Big Bad Wolf. Luisa has the beast firmly by the throat. Another look into the mirror reveals that she is choking herself.

Luisa awakens in the throes of a violent coughing fit and assumes that it's the reason for the bloodstains on her pillow. Then she recalls that the blood belongs to her latest victim—the brawny and heavily tattooed gangbanger lying beside her. Despite the buzz on TV, the radio, and the Internet about DC's mysterious femme fatale, the gangbangers flock to her like lambs to the slaughter. So, what's her secret? As the old whore told the young virgin:

"Use the right bait, and you'll catch a man every time, honey."

Chapter Sixteen

SHOWDOWN IN CHINATOWN

I t's dusk when Cochrane and Cheryl Lucas reach the entrance of the East Building. The twin towers of the H-shaped façade loom a hundred feet above them, as does the giant wedge that juts out from the right side, the once-rough edge rubbed smooth over the years by thousands of curious hands. They enter the museum. At the security checkpoint, Cochrane signs the log for his handgun while a female guard examines Cheryl's handbag.

As they walk into the atrium, Cheryl asks Cochrane, "So, what do you think?"

He takes in the acres of pink marble, the multi-level maze of stairs, mezzanines, and catwalks, and the huge, steel-ribbed skylight. Then he says, "Kinda reminds me of the Hyatt Regency in Crystal City."

Cheryl laughs. "You're in good company. A famous art critic once said this place reminded him of an airport terminal or a hotel lobby. But I don't care what the two of you think. I love it."

"I never said I didn't like it."

After she points out the Calder mobile hanging from the ceiling, they make a quick circuit around the crowded museum. The first artwork she takes him to is Dalí's *Sacrament of the Last Supper*.

Cochrane stares at the painting and says, "Is this the guy who painted the soft watches?"

"Uh-huh."

"I like it."

"I had a feeling you would."

"Modern art for dummies, right?"

She smiles. "You said it, not me."

Cochrane is less enamored of the elongated Giacometti sculptures and the Pollock drip paintings, but he finds the Rothko color field canvases strangely hypnotic. Then the inner detective takes over, reminding him that he's on the lookout for Luisa Santiago. Not that he expects her to show. After all, she's maintained a low profile since her "disappearance." But she's been keeping busy. In addition to the Melendez and Rivera murders, Cochrane believes that Luisa is involved in the recent killing of four more gangbangers, even though the evidence indicates otherwise. Unlike Melendez and Rivera, the most recent victims looked like they were attacked by wild animals—their throats torn out and their blood freely spilled. They also belonged to the Escorpiones and had nothing to do with the murder of Rosa Gonzalez. But those seemingly unrelated facts are precisely what convince Cochrane that Luisa is responsible.

He believes that, for all its flakiness, Cheryl's Vampire/ Vigilante Theory is right in at least one respect: the perpetrator *is* trying to exterminate the gangbangers, but not singlehandedly, as Cheryl supposes. Instead, the killer is trying to spark an all-out war between the Escorpiones and Mara Camazotza in order to make the bad guys kill each other off. Of course the "VV" exists only in Cheryl's hyperactive imagination. Since their meeting at Starbucks, Cochrane and Cheryl have discussed the Melendez-Rivera case a few times, but they have danced around the "VV Theory." Cheryl apparently has decided to say nothing more about it, and Cochrane has been only too happy to oblige. But he's decided that it's high time she face facts. Tonight, he's going to tell her who the *real* perpetrator is.

They return to the atrium and walk over to the entrance to "Degas's Dancers." A shiny black Steinway concert grand stands off to one side. The pianist, a slender Asian woman, is playing Debussy's "Clair de Lune." Cheryl and Cochrane pause to listen. The pretty young pianist steals a glance at Cochrane and smiles, and Cochrane smiles back.

Noting the exchange, Cheryl takes Cochrane by the hand and leads him into the Degas exhibition. Truth is, Cochrane scarcely noticed the pianist, because he can't get over how lovely Cheryl looks in her purple evening dress. He pretends to study the pictures while admiring her graceful architecture out of the corner of his eye.

For all her charm, Cheryl's leisurely pace taxes Cochrane's patience to the limit. The Degas exhibition occupies seven large galleries, and she lingers over each artwork and reads each interpretive text. By the time they reach the sixth gallery, he's had enough Degas to last a lifetime. As she examines a colorful pastel titled *Russian Dancers*, Cochrane tells her that he's going to scout ahead.

"Okay," she says without taking her eyes off the picture. "I won't be long."

Cochrane climbs a spiral metal staircase to reach the seventh and last gallery, a room devoted to Degas sculptures. He is drawn to a large sculpture under a glass case in the center of the room. The piece is called *Little Dancer of Fourteen Years*.

The interpretive text states that the figure is made from yellow wax and is almost life-size. The dancer wears actual clothing—a linen bodice, muslin tutu, and satin shoes—and stands on a wooden base that suggests the floor of a rehearsal studio. The model was Marie van Goethem, a dance student at the Paris Opera Ballet when she posed for Degas in 1880.

The *petit rat* (as Marie and her classmates were known) stands at ease, awaiting instructions from the ballet master: head cocked back, eyes closed, chin up, tummy pushed out, hands clasped behind derrière, right leg in front of left leg, feet turned out in fourth position.

"I just love that pose—so defiant and yet so vulnerable."

Cochrane cannot believe his ears. He turns around. Luisa Santiago is standing there, pale as death but absolutely stunning in a black satin dress.

"You look like you just saw a ghost, Detective."

"Maybe I have."

She smiles. "I'm guessing you're not here for the Degas."

"You guessed right."

"Well, here I am," she says, holding out her hands in token of surrender.

Cochrane frowns. "Put 'em down. I'm not going to cuff you. But I would like you to come down to the station and answer some questions."

"How can I refuse an invitation from you, Detective?" She leans forward and whispers into his ear, "Don't look now, but I think we're being followed."

"Can you point 'em out?"

"That's easier said than done in this crowd. He's really good at blending in."

Just then, Amanda Donovan and her cameraman enter the gallery. The reporter spots Cochrane and waves to him. He turns to Luisa, but she's gone.

"Hi, Bill," Amanda says. "Any sign of you-know-who?"

Cochrane shakes his head.

"Too bad. It would've made a great story."

Cheryl appears and asks Cochrane, "What have I missed?"

"Nothing," he says. "Amanda, this is Cheryl Lucas. Cheryl, Amanda Donovan."

The two women shake hands.

"Love your show," Cheryl says.

"Thank you. And this is Mitch Andrews, the guy who makes me look good."

"Could I get a shot of you two looking at the ballerina sculpture?" Mitch asks.

"Sure," Cochrane says.

Arms folded, he stares at the sculpture while Cheryl walks around it.

"That's great," Mitch says. "Thanks."

"Are we going to be on TV?" Cheryl asks.

"Tune in tomorrow morning at seven and find out," Amanda says.

Just then, Cochrane's cell phone buzzes. The display reads, *UNKNOWN CALLER*. He answers the call.

"Hello?"

"It's you-know-who. We have to talk. I'm outside the main entrance. Come alone. Ciao."

"Who was that?" Cheryl asks.

"Something's come up," Cochrane replies. "Gotta run. I'll explain later."

He hurries out of the exhibition and heads for the main entrance. A security guard tells him to slow down as he dashes past. He hits the door and bolts into the night, looking for Luisa.

"Hey."

She's right at his elbow.

"Jesus! You've gotta stop doing that."

"Sorry, I can't help it."

Cochrane brushes his hand against her bare arm. It feels like ice. "You're freezing. Here, take my coat." He starts to remove his sport coat, but Luisa stops him.

"I'm fine," she says. "Really."

"So what did you want to tell me?"

"I thought you'd like to know what's going on at the Verizon Center tonight."

"The Lakers are in town. What of it?"

"The *jefés* of four of DC's biggest gangs are meeting there."

"How do you know this?"

"Let's just say I have my sources."

Cochrane notices that Luisa's eyes are different. They're cold, hard, fierce . . . the eyes of a killer.

"Are the Escorpiones and Mara Camazotza involved?"

Luisa nods.

"Jesus."

Cochrane takes out his cell phone. He calls Lieutenant Alonzo and relates what Luisa has just told him. Alonzo wants to know the identity of Cochrane's source, but Cochrane won't divulge it, explaining that his informant insists on strict confidentiality.

"Your source better be right," Alonzo says, "or we're both gonna be in deep shit."

"It's going down," Cochrane says as he pockets his phone.

"Thanks for keeping my name out of it," Luisa says.

"I had to. The lieutenant wouldn't have believed me."

They walk from the portico down to Fourth Street. Cochrane hails a taxi.

"Here's your cab."

"Why don't you ride with me? The driver can drop you off at the Verizon Center."

Cochrane climbs into the cab. As the taxi pulls away from the curb, she points across the street.

"See that guy sitting by the fountain? That's the stalker."

Cochrane looks out the side window. He sees a handsome, long-haired Latino in a leather jacket and blue denims walking briskly toward the cab. When the taxi turns left onto Pennsylvania Avenue, the youth breaks into a run. He keeps to the sidewalk, effortlessly matching the cab's speed as it cruises down Pennsylvania Avenue.

"How fast are you going?" Cochrane asks the driver.

"I'm doing thirty-five," he says.

"That's ridiculous!" Cochrane says to no one in particular. "No human can run that fast."

"Exactly," Luisa says.

When the cab turns right onto Sixth Street, the runner stops in his tracks.

Cochrane watches the youth recede into the distance. He turns around to speak to the driver, unaware that the Latino has resumed the chase. Luisa watches him sprint across Pennsylvania Avenue, sidestepping cars and trucks like a running back eluding would-be tacklers. When the taxi reaches the Verizon Center, the youth melts into the crowd outside the building. Located within the Chinatown restaurant-entertainment district and perched atop the

Gallery Place Metro station, the Verizon Center occupies one of the busiest blocks in the city.

The taxi stops in front of the F Street entrance. Cochrane hands the driver fifty dollars. "That should also cover the lady's fare."

In a blur, Luisa snatches the money out of the driver's hand.

"Not so fast," she tells Cochrane. "I want to see how this goes down."

"No way in hell. It could get dangerous."

"I can take care of myself." She hands him the cash.

"Have it your way." Cochrane pays the driver, sending him off with the fifty dollars that Luisa just snatched out of his hand.

For the second time that evening, Luisa vanishes without a word.

"Hey, Bill. Over here!" Cochrane looks up and sees Lieutenant Alonzo standing in front of the Verizon Center. He is surrounded by plainclothes detectives, Verizon Center security personnel, and FBI agents.

"We just got here ourselves," Alonzo says. He introduces Cochrane to his FBI counterpart, Supervisory Special Agent Sam McDonough, and to Rodney Marshall, the Verizon Center security director. "The fourth quarter's already underway, so we're a little pressed for time."

"How many gangbangers?" Cochrane asks.

"I counted eight," Marshall replies. "They're unarmed, and they're all sitting together. Judging from their gear, I'd say they're Lakers fans."

"So, what's the plan?"

"We've got all the exits covered," Alonzo says. "We'll arrest 'em as they leave the building."

"Sounds easy enough," says McDonough, "but there's just one problem. One slip and you could end up with major collateral damage on your hands."

"What do you suggest?" Alonzo asks.

"We know they're parked in an alley off of H Street. My SWAT team will set up a perimeter around their vehicles. We'll let them enter the trap and then slam it shut. It's much better than trying to arrest them here in the middle of all this."

"Your plan sounds even riskier than mine," Alonzo says. "What if they spot one of your SWAT guys? We could find ourselves in a hostage situation or worse."

"Not to worry," says McDonough. "My people will take 'em down so fast, they won't know what hit 'em."

Against his better judgment, Alonzo defers to McDonough. The police detectives will watch the exits and keep the SWAT team informed of the gangbangers' movements. Meanwhile, the SWAT team will establish a perimeter around the gangbangers' vehicles that includes a pair of rooftop snipers.

Alonzo, Cochrane, and two other detectives, Heath and Williams, stand watch over the F Street exit. Each of them is wearing a miniature earpiece and microphone.

The time passes slowly. Cochrane paces back and forth while Alonzo follows the game on his Blackberry.

"Two minutes to go," he announces. "Lakers up by two."

Cochrane reaches inside his sport coat and checks his Glock pistol.

"One minute left. Score tied. Time out Wizards."

Cochrane takes a deep breath and exhales. *Please, God, don't let the game go into overtime . . .*

The arena erupts, indicating that the Wizards have scored. Seconds later, a hush falls on the crowd, suggesting that the Lakers have returned the favor.

"Five, four, three, two, one. Game over. All right, people. Stay sharp."

"Aren't you going to tell us who won?"

Cochrane notes that the speaker has a German accent.

"Cut the chatter," Alonzo says. "Here they come!"

The gangbangers are moving toward the F Street doors in a group. Just as the Verizon Center security chief said, all eight are decked out in purple-and-gold Lakers gear instead of their gang colors in an apparent show of solidarity. Cochrane recognizes the homies' tattoos—"MC · · ·" and a fanged bat for Mara Camazotza, a scorpion for Los Escorpiones, a death's head with a halo for Los Apóstoles de la Muerte, and a machete dripping blood for Los Carniceros Locos. They're all laughing and carrying on as if they were *compañeros*.

"Kicking team to receiving team," Alonzo says. "Suspects have exited the building at the F Street doors and are walking toward Sixth Street, over." Alonzo then addresses his three detectives. "Bill, you and I will tail them. Heath and Williams, you'll back us up."

Cochrane and Alonzo have a tough time keeping track of the gangbangers as they move through the postgame crowd. When the boys turn left onto H Street, it appears to Cochrane that they've picked up an escort—two men in black trench coats walking in front and a Latino youth in a leather jacket bringing up the rear—the same guy who chased Cochrane's taxi down Pennsylvania Avenue.

"Suspects are on H Street and heading your way, over." Alonzo says to McDonough. He pauses, waiting for a reply. "Do you copy? Over."

Still no reply.

"Does anybody on the receiving team copy? Over."

"They cannot answer you." Cochrane recognizes the voice. It belongs to the guy with the German accent.

"Identify yourself!" Alonzo demands.

"Consider this fair warning," the stranger replies. "Do not attempt to arrest the eight young men in our care. It would end just as badly for you as it did for your FBI colleagues."

"Who are you?"

"You need only know that we are not to be trifled with."

At the corner of Sixth and H, Alonzo and Cochrane watch the gangbangers and their escort disappear into the alley. Alonzo turns to Cochrane and says, "Bill, I'm gonna call for backup. In the meantime, I want you, Heath, and Williams to keep 'em penned up in the alley till the cavalry gets here. Whatever you do, don't try to take 'em down yourselves."

Leaving Alonzo on the corner talking to headquarters, the detectives proceed down H Street, using parked vehicles for cover and telling pedestrians to leave the area. When they reach the alley, Cochrane tells Heath and Williams, "I'm gonna try to talk 'em into surrendering."

"You cannot be serious," Heath says. "They just took out a fuckin' FBI SWAT team."

"You heard the lieutenant," Cochrane says. "He wants us to stall for time. That's what I'm gonna do."

Using his radio, Cochrane tells the gangbangers that they're surrounded and orders them to come out with their hands up.

The German laughs. "Run along to the nearest Dunkin Donuts and you won't get hurt."

"You arrogant prick!" Heath yells into the mic. "Who the hell do you think you are?"

Heath feels a tap on his shoulder. He swivels his head and beholds a tall man in a trench coat standing behind him.

"No need to shout," the German says. "I'm right here."

Heath manages to squeeze off a shot just as the big German snaps his neck, but the bullet misses its mark. Williams is next. He is crouching behind a car just a few yards in front of Heath. The German knocks his pistol loose with one hand and smashes his head into the driver's side window with the other, shattering the glass. Cochrane spins around in time to see Williams's body tumble to the pavement, his brains oozing from a deep gash across his forehead. Cochrane fires three rounds into the German's midsection at point-blank range, but the bullets have no apparent affect on him. The German slaps Cochrane's gun away and then lifts the detective off the ground by his lapels. Dangling helplessly in the German's powerful grip, Cochrane notices a long dueling scar on his left cheek.

"You just ruined my new suit," the German sneers. "Time to pay up."

His cruel mouth curls into a hideous grin, revealing a pair of large fangs. There's a reddish glint in his eyes.

"What the fuck are you?"

"Hold it right there." Alonzo is pointing his pistol at the German's back. "Set him down gently. And let me see your hands."

"Of course," the German says. He lowers Cochrane to the ground and releases him. Then, raising his hands, he turns to face Alonzo.

"Don't take your eyes off him," Cochrane warns the lieutenant. "He's a goddamn killing machine."

As Cochrane speaks, talons spring from the fingertips of the German's right hand. In a blur he slashes Alonzo's throat.

"Steve!" Cochrane shouts as a jet of his friend's blood spatters his white shirt. Coughing and gasping for air, Alonzo staggers toward Cochrane and collapses into his arms. Within a minute or so, he is dead. Cochrane closes his eyes and gently lowers him to the pavement.

Meanwhile, a second tall figure in a trench coat emerges from the alley. "Dieter," he says, "*was ist los*?" As German Number Two steps into the street, Cochrane gets a good look at his face and notes that he is Dieter's twin.

"The detectives proved more troublesome than I anticipated," Dieter replies. "Especially this one," he adds, pointing to Cochrane.

"They're coming!" the Latino shouts. "And they have an armored vehicle."

"Peter, break out the RPG," Dieter tells his twin brother. "It's time to show the police we mean business." He turns to Cochrane. "I'll deal with you later."

Peter rests the RPG-29 on his shoulder, takes careful aim, and fires a rocket-propelled grenade at the armored car rolling toward them. The German scores a direct hit. The explosion destroys the front end of the vehicle and brings it to a screeching halt under the Friendship Archway, an ornate, blue-and-gold Chinese gate that towers sixty feet above H Street. He fires a second RPG at one of the arch's two supporting columns, causing the mammoth structure to collapse onto the crippled armored car. The burning wreckage blocks the Seventh Street intersection.

Back in the alley, Dieter opens the gate of a BMW X5 and distributes AK-47 assault rifles and ammunition clips to the gangbangers. As he does so, the police set up a barricade at the Sixth Street intersection by parking half a dozen squad cars end-to-end across H Street. The gangbangers dash out of the alley and take position along H Street behind a row of parked vehicles. In a booming voice, Dieter warns the police to hold their fire, or he'll be forced to use the RPG on them.

Cochrane has crawled underneath a Chevy Silverado Z-71 that two of the gangbangers are using for cover. They open fire on the police barricade. Empty shell casings rain down on the pavement as they riddle the squad cars with bullets, blasting holes in the metal skin and shattering glass and plastic. The rapid-fire reports of AK-47s seem to come from everywhere. Ignoring Dieter's warning, the police return fire with handguns and shotguns. Muzzle flashes light up the night like fireflies on steroids. One stray round blows out a tire about a foot from Cochrane's head.

"Jesus Christ," he mutters to himself. "It's just like Fallujah."

Amid the gunfire, a woman emerges from the shadows across the street. She is accompanied by two men. Cochrane recognizes the lithe form of Luisa Santiago. He wonders why she is acting so rashly, but then it dawns on him: *she's risking her life to save me.*

Dieter orders the gangbangers to hold their fire, and the police follow suit to give the bad guys a chance to surrender. Up and down H Street, pedestrians who've been hugging the sidewalk since the lead started to fly duck inside Tony Cheng's or any other convenient safe haven.

Luisa walks to within fifty feet of the gangbangers' position and stops. "Here I am, boys," she says, hands on hips. "Come and get me." She is flanked by her two male companions. One stands as tall as the Germans while the other is a head shorter, about the same height as the Latino.

"David, take the Santiago woman," Dieter tells the Latino. "Peter and I will put the two buffoons out of their misery." Dieter opens his trench coat and unsheathes a saber, as does his brother.

Freddy turns to Jason and says, "These Aryan assholes think they're so cool, bro."

Jason nods, a look of grim determination on his face. "Let's chop 'em up!"

Each brother produces a retractable sword that opens with the touch of a button. Raising a barbaric cry, Dieter and Peter charge their two adversaries. The clang of tempered steel resonates on H Street as Freddy and Jason struggle to hold their own against the Germans. After slashing Freddy about the arms and torso, Peter at last lops off his wounded antagonist's head. Distracted by his brother's decapitation, Jason momentarily drops his guard, enabling Dieter to run his sword through his opponent's heart.

Luisa is too intent on trying to hack David to pieces with a machete to notice the killing of her two friends. David has just shot her above the left breast with a poisoned dart, or so she assumes. In her pain and fury, she flails at David again and again, but he eludes the blade effortlessly. With each swing she grows weaker and weaker until she can barely lift the weapon.

"You're very sexy when you're angry," he tells her.

"You make me sick," she hisses back. Overcome by the poison, Luisa drops the machete and faints dead away.

"Careful," David warns Dieter, "the bitch might be faking."

Dieter gives her a hard slap across each cheek; she doesn't move. "I think not."

Down the street at the police barricade, a Spanish-speaking cop with a bullhorn calls on the gangbangers to surrender.

"*Hablamos Inglés, Puerco!*" yells Martin "the Beast" Fuentes, the *jefé* for the Langley Park clique of MC · · ·. "Come and get us if you have the balls."

The gangbangers open fire on the barricade, and the police respond in kind.

"Time to go," Dieter says.

"What about our friends?" David nods toward the gangbangers.

"They are expendable," Dieter says. "To the rooftops." With that, he lobs several smoke grenades into the alley. "Take the prisoner," he tells Peter. "I'll cover you."

Draping Luisa over his right shoulder, Peter clambers up a metal staircase to the roof, closely followed by David. Amid billowing clouds of black smoke, Dieter scales the fifty-foot brick wall with reptilian ease and vanishes into the night. Peering out from under the truck, Cochrane witnesses the German's escape, half-expecting the sono-fabitch to turn into a bat and fly away.

The gangbangers realize that they have been aban-doned about the same time they discover that the police have surrounded them. Snipers appear on the rooftops above, and a SWAT team has worked its way down H Street from the direction of Seventh Street to within fifty yards of the alley. The cop with the bullhorn orders the gangbangers to drop their weapons and come out with their hands up.

"Don't shoot!" Fuentes yells back. "I give up!" He tosses his AK-47 aside and walks into the street with his hands held high. Six others throw down their rifles and step forward. One lies face-down on the sidewalk.

"Is there anyone else?" the cop with the bullhorn asks.

"Right here." Cochrane crawls out from under the Z-71, gets on his feet, and raises his hands.

As the SWAT team searches and cuffs the gangbangers, Cochrane tells the cop who's frisking him that he's a detective. "My badge is in the breast pocket of my coat."

"Are you armed?" the cop asks.

"No."

"Where's your gun?"

"In the street. Somebody knocked it out of my hand."

"You're covered in blood," the cop says. "Are you hurt?"

"I'm a little banged up, but I'll—"

"Hey, man," one of the gangbangers interrupts. "What about me? I took a bullet in the arm."

The cop takes a look at the arm and shrugs. "The EMS is on its way," he tells the gangbanger. "In the meantime, shut your face." Turning to Cochrane, he says, "Here's your badge, Sergeant. Would you mind sticking around to answer some questions?"

"Sure."

A light drizzle begins to fall. Cochrane sees Jack Reynolds ducking under the yellow barrier tape.

"I got here as fast as I could, Bill." Reynolds places his hand on Cochrane's shoulder and whispers, "What the hell went wrong?"

"I don't even know where to begin."

"C'mon, let's get out of the rain." The two detectives walk over to Reynolds' car and climb inside. "Is it true about Steve?"

Cochrane nods his head. "Heath and Williams, too."

"Jesus Christ."

"That's not all. An entire FBI SWAT team is MIA."

"Come again?"

"One minute they're all there and—*poof*—they're all gone."

"Was it terrorists?"

"Maybe . . . I don't know." Cochrane closes his eyes and rubs his temples. "We were about to bust the gangbangers when these three guys show up with automatic weapons and an RPG. Two of 'em were dressed like secret agents, and they had German accents. The third guy looked like a teenage Antonio Banderas. He's gotta be the fastest thing on two legs I've ever seen."

"No shit."

"The German guys were twins—real superstuds. I shot one of 'em three times at point blank range. Then he lifted me off the ground. For a second, I thought I was a goner."

"You're lucky to be alive."

"If it hadn't been for Steve, I wouldn't be talking to you right now." Cochrane takes a deep breath and exhales. "It should've been me instead of him."

"It wasn't your fault, Bill. Shit happens."

There's a rapping on the driver's side window. Reynolds lowers the window all the way. It's Alonzo's boss, Captain Ellison. "Bill, are you okay?"

"I'm still breathing, John."

"Go home and try to get some sleep. That's an order."

"Okay, but there's something I've gotta do first."

"Why don't you let me send someone else? You've been through enough for one night."

"Steve was my partner," Cochrane insists. "I should be the one to tell Laura."

Cochrane notices a CSI team pass by and sees Cheryl among them. He jumps out of the car and catches up with her.

"Hey, I want to apologize for running out on you," he says.

"It wasn't your fault," she replies. "I'm just glad you're all right. Look, I gotta go. Call me tomorrow, okay?"

Cochrane turns to go and then stops. "You were right, Cheryl."

She gives him a quizzical look. "About what?"

"Everything."

As Cheryl walks away, Amanda Donovan appears with Mitch the cameraman. "Did you talk to her?" she asks with breathless expectancy.

"Who are you referring to, Ms. Donovan?"

"Luisa Santiago—who else?"

"I don't know what you're talking about."

"The hell you don't. She was standing right in front of you. We saw her, didn't we, Mitch?"

Mitch nods in agreement. "It was her, all right. I got it all on video," he says, patting his camera.

"Mind if I have a look?"

"Only if you've got a subpoena," Mitch replies.

"Look, I'm not gonna confiscate your camera. I just wanna see for myself."

"Then I suggest you watch the eleven o'clock news," Amanda says. "Let's go, Mitch. Time's a wastin'."

Cochrane returns to Reynolds's car. Captain Ellison is still talking to Reynolds, who is leaning against the driver's side door, burly arms folded across his chest.

"Was that reporter giving you a hard time?" Ellison asks.

"She's got video of the incident," Cochrane replies. "And she claims to know the woman's identity."

"Let me guess," Reynolds says. "It was Luisa Santiago."

"She's becoming a regular Elvis Presley," Ellison says. "Who knows where she'll turn up next?"

"Yeah," Cochrane says. "Who knows?"

Ellison takes out his cell phone. "It's the Chief . . . gotta answer this one." He raises the phone to his ear. "Go home, Bill. And I mean now."

"Mind giving me a lift?" Cochrane asks Reynolds.

"Sorry, Bill," Reynolds says. "I've been assigned to this case. Looks like I'm gonna be here for awhile. Why don't you get a cab?"

Realizing that he needs to clean up a bit before paying a call on Laura Alonzo, Cochrane rides a taxi back to his apartment. On the way, he reflects on his lie about not seeing Luisa Santiago. Or was it a lie? The red-eyed devil wielding that machete resembled Luisa about as closely as a tiger resembles a tabby cat. Tonight he discovered that the Luisa he knew was, for all intents and purposes, dead. Still, she did try to save him . . .

By the time the taxi arrives in front of his building, Cochrane is sound asleep. The driver has to shout to awaken him. "Wait here," he tells the driver and hands him some cash. Then he staggers up to his apartment to shed his torn and bloody clothing and throw on a clean shirt and slacks. Shoes and socks in hand, he runs barefoot into the cold and rainy November night, climbs into the back of the cab, and heads off to break the news about Steve to Laura and the kids.

Chapter Seventeen

DESAPARECIDOS

In his dream, Miguel is lying on the floor of the tomb beside Lady Morningstar. He plays dead while the soldiers slaughter every last woman and child of the royal retinue. The victims' screams and cries for mercy are heart-rending, but the silence that follows is downright deafening. Soon after the massacre, a stranger appears and walks among the dead, surveying the carnage. He briefly examines each body and nudges it with his foot before moving on to the next one. His ornate, jade-encrusted jewelry and quetzal-feather headdress denote a person of high rank. He carries himself like a soldier yet is unarmed. His face is hidden in shadow.

"You there!" The stranger addresses the commanding officer in Nawat. "What were my orders?"

"Noble Ahau," the officer replies, "you ordered us to bring Lady Morningstar down here and protect her until your arrival."

"Correct. But you disobeyed me."

"Ahau, I can explain—"

"Silence! Kneel before me."

The officer bows his head and drops to his knees.

"Lady Morningstar was to be sacrificed to Camazotz," the stranger says, "but I can't very well do that when she's already *dead*."

"Forgive me, Ahau!" the officer cries.

"I'll do better than that," the stranger says. "I'll give you a chance to redeem yourself."

"Thank you, Ahau!"

"You and your men shall play my team in the ball game honoring our conquest of this place. Of course, the losing players must forfeit their lives to honor the great Camazotz."

Still kneeling, the officer looks up at the stranger. "Then we are as good as dead, Ahau. Your team has never lost."

"At least it will be an honorable death. Or I could kill you now. Which do you prefer?"

"The ball game, Ahau."

"Done! Now rise and march your men to the palace and await my orders. I need some time alone."

The officer bows low and then leads his men out of the tomb.

After the soldiers have left, the stranger addresses Miguel: "You are dying. Can you give me one good reason why I should save you?"

"No man can save me," Miguel gasps.

"True enough. But I can."

"Then you must be a god."

"The stranger laughs. "You speak blasphemy! My name is Dark Sun, High Priest to Camazotz. If I deign to save you, how will you repay me?"

"Give me a blank wall and some brushes and paint and I will make you immortal."

He points to the murals. "Is this your handiwork?"

"It is."

"Then you might be of some use to me."

Dropping to his knees, Dark Sun lifts Miguel's head with one hand and his torso with the other. The fierce eyes of Miguel's savior burn bright red—they are the eyes of Tito Vazquez. He opens his mouth, exposing a pair of sharp fangs. "Don't be afraid," he says. "I'm going to make you stronger than you ever imagined."

As Dark Sun drinks his blood, Miguel feels his life ebb away. On reaching the portal to the Otherworld, he finds himself looking down at his savior and his body. A magnificent jade-colored butterfly emerges from Lady Morningstar's mouth and flutters beside him. Then it rises up an air shaft and soars far above the burning city and into the heavens.

Miguel awakens to find himself in his jet, which is parked on a runway at a private airstrip outside Charles Town, West Virginia. His cell phone is ringing. It's Tito.

"Have they arrived yet?" Tito says in Nawat, his version of code-talking.

"It's only midnight," Miguel replies in English. "They're not due for another hour."

"I thought we agreed to speak in our native tongue."

"Why?"

"Someone might be listening."

"To this nonsense?"

"All right," Tito says in English. "I'll check back in an hour."

No sooner does Miguel hang up than a black stretch limo pulls up beside the jet. The chauffeur gets out and opens the nearside passenger door. A pair of long, shapely legs encased in black stockings emerges from the darkness within. A willowy, raven-haired woman wearing a low-cut red miniskirt slides out of the limo and unfolds to a full six feet, spiked heels included. She is closely followed by Anna Schiller, who is back from an evening of baccarat, blackjack, and big losses. The gambling junket constituted a diversion in two senses of the word: momentary (albeit exorbitant) amusement for Anna and a feint intended to conceal the jet's true function as a getaway vehicle.

The two women sashay across the tarmac and then board the aircraft. Miguel is waiting for them in the doorway. The first thing he notices about the tall woman is her flawless pale complexion. The second thing is the large rock on her left hand.

"Miguel," Anna says, "I'd like you to meet Nadia. Isn't she lovely?"

Miguel glares at Anna. "Why in God's name did you bring her here?"

"And why are you being so rude to our guest?" Anna turns to Nadia and says, "Pay him no mind, *Liebchen*. Come inside and make yourself at home."

Nadia tries to enter, but Miguel blocks her path. "We're just about to take off. Anna should have told you."

"Don't be such an asshole!" Anna scolds. "The poor thing caught her fiancé cheating on her. She needed a shoulder to cry on, and mine happened to be available."

Miguel glances at his watch. "You've got ten minutes."

While the two women adjourn to the rear of the aircraft, Miguel tilts his seat back and closes his eyes. But his rest is soon disturbed by an insistent, top-of-the-Richter-scale bass beat. He opens his eyes and is treated to the sight of Nadia and Anna dancing to the Black Eyed Peas' "Party All the Time." Nadia performs some sinuous gyrations that remind Miguel of Luisa. Anna beckons him to join them. Then she rises on her tiptoes and kisses her new friend on the mouth.

Noting Miguel's interest, Anna shouts above the music, "You know what they say—two's company and three's a ménage à trois."

Miguel checks his watch and, picking up the remote, turns the sound system off. "Time's up!"

As the two women embrace, Anna sticks out her tongue at Miguel.

Without a word, Nadia brushes past Miguel and clanks down the metal stairs.

At that moment, a white Ford Econoline van screeches to a halt alongside the limo. The doors fly open, and three men dressed in coveralls jump out—two big, blonde guys and an average-sized Hispanic guy. One of the blonde guys pulls something bulky from the cargo area and hoists it onto his right shoulder. It's a woman's body. Nadia retreats into the jet and watches the action from a window seat.

Anna hurries over to her and says, "Stay right here and don't make a sound."

Miguel flies down the stairs, shouting, "Wait! You're carrying her like a sack of potatoes." He insists on helping the man carry the woman onto the jet. Once they get her onboard, Nadia hurries over and checks her pulse.

"Ohmigod! She's dead!"

"Not dead," Anna says. "Just sleeping."

They carry the woman down the aisle and lower her onto a sofa at the back of the jet. "Careful!" Miguel barks at the blonde guy. "Set her down gently."

Nadia notes that the two blonde guys are twins.

As he takes his seat, the first blonde guy points at Nadia. "What's *she* doing here?"

"She's with me!" Anna's eyes turn crimson to match her mood.

"I'm afraid you'll have to remain onboard," Miguel tells Nadia.

"Just where the hell are you taking me?" Nadia asks. "I have a right to know."

Turning his back on her, Miguel whispers something to Anna.

As Nadia awaits Miguel's answer to her question, she notices that the first blonde guy is covered in blood. "You're hurt!" She points to his midsection.

"It's just a scratch," he says.

"A few years back, I trained to be a nurse. I'd like to have a look at that scratch of yours."

The blonde guy looks at Miguel, and Miguel says, "Go ahead. This might be interesting."

Kicking off her heels, Nadia tells her patient to unzip his coveralls. Given his apparent blood loss, she's not surprised that he's pasty-faced and cold to the touch. Luckily, he's not exhibiting any other symptoms of shock—rapid heartbeat, shaking, confusion, loss of consciousness. All in all, he could be doing a lot worse.

Nadia asks Miguel, "Have you got a first aid kit?"

He tells Anna where to find it. Nadia opens the kit and takes out a package of surgical gloves, a pair of EMT shears, some alcohol pads, and a bottle of Betadine antiseptic wash. She wipes the shears with an alcohol pad and then scrubs her hands with Betadine back in the galley, briefly filling the cabin with the sharp odor of fingernail polish. Next, she puts on the surgical gloves the way she was taught in nursing school, taking care not to contaminate the sterile surface of either glove. Then she uses the shears to cut away the wounded man's blood-caked shirt. What she finds indicates that her patient is a fucking medical marvel. The guy may be built like a brick shithouse, but that does not explain why he can function with three gunshot wounds in the abdomen.

"So," Nadia begins, "when did this happen?"

"I don't remember."

"Tell her, Dieter," Miguel orders.

"About two hours ago."

Nadia whispers to Miguel, "Can we speak in private?"

"I want to hear what you have to say," Dieter says.

"Okay," Nadia begins, "here's the deal. Dieter's got three slugs lodged in his intestines, and he's lost a lot of blood. We have to get him to a hospital now, or he's a goner." Much to her surprise, Nadia's blunt diagnosis fails to impress anyone, least of all Dieter, who stares at her with steely-eyed nonchalance. She takes his pulse, hoping that the gravity of the situation will sink in. After a minute she looks up and says, "His condition is even worse than I thought. He barely has a pulse."

"I know you mean well," Miguel says, "but you have no idea what you're dealing with."

"Look," she retorts, "I don't care how much trouble you're in. This man needs a doctor."

"No more talk of doctors and hospitals. We have to leave, and that's that."

Nadia scans the others' faces: they're all drinking the same Kool-Aid. "Well, I can at least clean and dress his wounds. That might buy him some time."

Miguel shrugs. "I suppose it can't hurt."

Giving him a quizzical look, Nadia reaches into the first aid kit and pulls out some rolling gauze and compression bandages. "When I'm finished with Dieter, I'd like to see what I can do for the woman."

"There's no need. She's fine."

"Then you won't mind if I look in on her."

"Actually, I *do* mind. As I said before, you don't know what you're dealing with."

Even though this is the first field dressing that Nadia's done in five years, her fingers know just what to do. She even manages to coax a few words from her sullen patient. Noting the long scar on Dieter's left cheek, Nadia asks him how he got it.

"I cut myself shaving," is his deadpan reply.

The rest of the wound-binding session proceeds in silence. But when the last bandage is in place, Dieter says, "You have soft hands."

Given the source, she considers this a great compliment.

"Now it's my turn." The next patient in line is the Hispanic youth; he sports flowing dark locks and an irresistible smile. "I'm feeling very stiff. I was wondering if you could massage it out for me."

"Leave her alone, David." Anna takes Nadia by the arm. "Better find your seat, *Liebchen*. We're about to take off."

"Maybe she'd rather sit next to me," the youth says.

"Shut up, David," Anna says.

As she fastens her seatbelt, Nadia asks Anna where they're going.

"El Salvador."

As the jet takes off, Nadia gazes longingly out the window at the twinkling lights, wondering if she'll ever see her home and loved ones again. A virtual prisoner trapped among some desperate-looking characters, en route to a strange land without her passport and wishing that she'd paid attention in her high school Spanish class.

Having only the vaguest notion of El Salvador's geography, history, and culture, she supposes that it's:

A.) Somewhere south of Mexico;

B.) A place where foreigners regularly disappear and are never heard from again.

Nadia sinks into a tortured sleep. She dreams of running through a dense jungle. A huge black jaguar is chasing her, its fearsome red eyes glowing in the darkness. The creature leaps on her and suddenly becomes David. He starts to ravish her. In his ardor, he bites her on the throat and begins to drink her blood. She tries to break free, but he is too strong. She tries to scream but cannot make a sound. Then, from the depths of the jungle, a male voice cries out, "Wake up!" Blinking her eyes, Nadia looks over at Anna. She appears to be sleeping, but her headphones are pumping out "Welcome to the Jungle" at top volume. Nadia scans the rest of the cabin. Miguel is talking on his cell phone. Dieter is asleep. Dieter's twin brother and David are playing cards.

Wow, that was some nightmare . . .

Nadia gets up and heads to the bathroom. After splashing some cold water on her face, she examines her throat in the mirror. *No tooth marks. Thank God for small favors.*

When she opens the door, Miguel is waiting for her.

"I have a rather large favor to ask of you," he says.

"Ask away."

"Dieter has lost a great deal of blood—"

"And he needs a transfusion. I seem to recall having this discussion with you before."

"All right, I admit it. He needs blood, and he needs it fast."

"Then make an emergency landing at the nearest airport."

"There's no time for that. Besides, we have all the blood we need right here."

"You mean Dieter's twin brother. He should be a safe match."

"Not exactly. There is a problem with Peter's blood."

"What kind of problem?"

"The brothers have a rare blood type known as V positive."

"Never heard of it."

"As I said, it's extremely rare. A person with Type V can receive blood from any other group with the sole exception of another Type V."

What Miguel leaves unsaid is that over the centuries, vampires have developed an acute allergic reaction to other vampires' blood. Immediately after ingestion, the recipient's antibodies attack the donor's red blood cells. In response, the donor's antibodies begin to devour the surrounding vascular walls. This vicious cycle soon causes massive hemorrhaging. The victim succumbs within an hour of ingestion. There is no known remedy, and there are no known survivors. Vampires call it the Red Death.

"So," Nadia says, "I guess that leaves you, Anna, and the pretty boy, right?"

"Unfortunately," Miguel sighs, "we are all V positive, which leaves you, the pilot, and the co-pilot. Of course they can't be donors. They're flying the plane."

"But I'm a trained nurse. You need me to perform the transfusion."

"Dieter needs your blood."

"What if I told you I was HIV positive?"

For the first time, Miguel smiles. It's a nice smile. "All I ask is that you give Dieter a few pints of your precious blood. Just enough to keep him stable until we land."

Nadia takes a deep breath. "All right, let's get it over with."

Miguel has Nadia sit across the aisle from Dieter. He takes some syringes from the first aid kit and lays them out on a table in front of the patient. "I'm going to draw your blood, and Anna's going to inject it into Dieter."

"No fucking way!" Nadia says, rolling her eyes. "That'll take forever."

"Not the way I do it. Come here, Anna. I need you."

"Well, well," Anna smirks. "It seems our little darling is proving quite useful. I do believe an apology is in order."

"Ladies," Miguel says with an exaggerated bow, "I'm truly sorry for my rude and insensitive behavior. Now can we get on with the goddamn procedure?" In reaching for a syringe, his forearm brushes against Nadia's cheek.

That's weird. He's as cold as Dieter.

Miguel is true to his word. He and Anna work with astonishing speed and precision, their calm manner belying the blur their hands make as they pass the syringes back and forth. Nadia can't help smiling. *Just like playing a DVD in fast forward.*

"Look!" Nadia cries. "He's coming around."

"So he is." Miguel motions to Nadia. "Now, I want you to sit next to him."

"Why?"

"When he regains consciousness, he'll be a little disoriented. Seeing you there will reassure him."

"Whatever." Nadia rises from her seat, crosses the aisle, and squeezes in beside Dieter.

When he awakens, Nadia flashes him a great big smile to let him know that everything's all right. As she gazes into his pale blue eyes, she learns what it feels like to be on somebody's dinner menu.

"What the—"

Dieter grabs Nadia by the shoulders, bites her on the throat, and starts to drink.

"You fucking bastard!" she screams. Her terrified eyes start from their sockets. "You lied to me!"

"I'm sorry," Miguel says. "This is the only way he can satisfy his hunger. Relax. You'll be fine."

"How the fuck can I relax?"

But relax she does, for the narcotic transmitted from Dieter's saliva into Nadia's bloodstream soon takes effect. As Nadia slips into unconsciousness, she enters a fog-shrouded cemetery. Passing row upon row of headstones, she comes to an old, overgrown section of the graveyard. One marker is in a worse state of disrepair than the others.

Broken off near the base, the moss-covered marble slab lies hidden in the weeds. The faded inscription reads:

NADIA RACHEL LAROCHELLE
KILLED BY VAMPIRES
SHE FOOLISHLY THOUGHT
WERE JUST VERY PALE PEOPLE

Nadia awakens with a start. Dieter is staring at her with a smug expression on his face. "How do you feel?" he asks and then winks at his brother.

"Keep your hands and teeth to yourself," she warns, "or I'll hit you with my pepper spray." She gropes under her seat for her handbag. "Where the hell is it?"

"Are you looking for this?"

"Like I said," Nadia says, snatching away her handbag, "keep your hands off my stuff."

"Look," he says, "some souvenirs from last night." Opening his fist, he proudly displays fragments of the three 9-mm. slugs that had entered him just hours before.

"Who removed them?"

"They came out by themselves."

She peeks under the bandages and stares in disbelief. Overnight, the gunshot wounds appear to have done a month's worth of mending.

"That's what a little human blood can do," he gloats.

"Don't mention it," she replies, thinking it's his way of saying *thanks for saving my no-good miserable bloodsucking ass.*

The jet touches down at Comalapa Airport around 3:00 a.m. Central Time. The main door opens, and a young man in a navy blue delivery uniform hands Miguel a package. Tearing it open, Miguel walks down the aisle and presents Nadia with her new passport. "Welcome to El Salvador," he says.

"How'd you pull it off?"

"You can do anything if you have enough money and know the right people."

She tucks the passport into her handbag and looks Miguel straight in the eye. "Why didn't you just kill me?"

"Haven't you heard? We've become civilized."

A small fleet of pricey black vehicles awaits them on the tarmac. The twins load the unconscious woman into the back of a Cadillac hearse and roar off, closely followed by David on a Ducati motorcycle, leaving an Audi A8 and a Cadillac Escalade driven by a tough-looking hombre named Enrique de la Something.

"Enrique is a professional bodyguard," Miguel says, to which Enrique adds, "among other things."

"In addition to protecting you, he can show you around San Salvador," to which Anna adds, "especially the seamy side."

"Which side of San Salvador isn't seamy?" Enrique quips.

"When can I go home?" Nadia asks.

"Soon," Miguel says.

Anna hugs Nadia. "*Liebchen*, get some sleep. I'll call you."

Miguel and Anna wave goodbye as Enrique and Nadia drive off in the Escalade.

"You should've killed her on the plane," Anna says, "and dumped her body into the Pacific. What are you going to do with her now?"

"Enrique will look after her," Miguel replies.

"Tito won't like it."

"Well, Enrique doesn't like Tito, so that makes it even."

Miguel and Anna drive up to Tito's compound on the Volcán San Salvador. The place used to be a coffee plantation. The former owners belonged to one of El Salvador's oldest families. Tito says that he bought it because of the magnificent view. Miguel thinks that he is crazy for living on an active volcano. Tito keeps a chopper on the premises just in case.

The guard at the gate motions for Miguel to pass through. Armed guards patrol the perimeter fence and the grounds. The twins' Cadillac hearse and David's Ducati are parked in front of Tito's sprawling ranch house. Miguel opens the car door for Anna, and they walk into the great room together.

"Congratulations to you both!" Tito is stretched out on a large divan, surrounded by four young Salvadoreñas. There is a great fire blazing in the fireplace, for it is a chilly night on the volcano, and the women are scantily dressed. "This calls for a toast." One of the women places three wine glasses on a table next to Tito while a second presents her right arm to him. With a talon-like fingernail he pricks the vein in the crook of her arm and drains some blood into the glasses, which the women distribute to the vampires. Tito raises his glass. "To your continued success."

Anna and Tito drink, but Miguel sets his glass down. "Where are you keeping her?" he asks.

"Down in the wine cellar."

"May I see her?"

"Of course. Follow me."

The three vampires walk down a long corridor until they come to a heavy wooden door. Tito opens it, and they descend a creaking staircase into pitch darkness. The cool, dank air is heavy with a musty odor. Miguel hears the scraping of innumerable tiny claws as their unseen owners scurry for cover.

On reaching the cellar, Tito lights some candles. The flickering light reveals that the back wall consists of volcanic rock. The wine racks are covered by an intricate network of cobwebs. In a dark corner of the cellar stands a wooden bier. On the bier rests an open black coffin with a red satin lining. Inside the coffin lies the sleeping form of Luisa Santiago.

"She is so beautiful." Tito's fierce eyes are riveted on her face. "Had we met under more favorable circumstances, I might have fallen in love with her."

"What are you going to do with her?" Miguel asks.

Tito doesn't answer. He appears to be preoccupied.

Miguel turns to Anna and asks, "Is she in a coma?"

"She's in a state of suspended animation," Anna replies. "But you needn't worry about her. She's fine."

"How was it done?"

"She's been given hydrogen sulfide."

"I thought it was poisonous."

"It is in large doses. The British used it as poison gas during the First World War. But when given in small doses, it slows the vital functions without harming the patient."

Tito chooses this moment to announce, "I'm going to sacrifice her to Camazotz."

"Are you crazy? You don't even believe in Camazotz."

"At this point," Tito says, "I can't afford *not* to believe in him. I'm enough of a realist to know that I can't win the election. I'll have to steal it."

"For once, you're right, Vazquez." The voice emanates from a drainage pipe running under the cellar.

"Ah, *Profesor*," Tito shouts back. "I thought you were dead."

"Not yet. No thanks to you."

"Who is that?" Miguel asks.

"It's our old friend, Espinoza. *Profesor* . . . say hello to Miguel Maldonado."

"Now that you're both here, there's something I have to tell you face-to-face."

"By all means," Tito says. "We'll be right down."

Tito walks past the wine racks and draws a faded red curtain, revealing a circular staircase. Miguel follows him down the stairs until they come to a padlocked iron door. Looking over his shoulder, he sees that Anna is gone. He follows Tito through a subterranean passageway that narrows until it is little more than a slit. It opens onto a cave filled with women and children. At the far end of the cave, a group of them is sitting in front of a giant flat-screen TV watching *Avatar* through 3-D glasses. Four men armed with AK-47s stand guard. The scene reminds Miguel of the tomb at Ciudad Antigua.

"Why are you keeping them here?"

"Some election officials can't be trusted to do the right thing," Tito replies, "so I'm holding their loved ones as collateral."

"Do you really think you can get away with this?"

"I have so far."

One of the guards opens the main door for the two vampires. They enter another passageway.

"There's a network of caves down here you wouldn't believe." Tito is grinning with satanic glee. "You know how much I like caves."

They pass a number of doors on either side. "This is where I keep the troublemakers."

"You mean like Espinoza?"

"Exactly. The kind who don't know when to shut up."

"Why don't you just kill them?"

"They're more useful alive than dead . . . for now, anyway. Some of the politicos have even agreed to endorse me. And I keep Espinoza around for my amusement. Here we are." Tito opens the door to Espinoza's cell. The prisoner is lying on his cot, staring up at the ceiling.

"All right, Espinoza," Tito says. "What do you have to say for yourself?"

Espinoza squints up at the two vampires. Chained at the wrists and ankles, he slowly rises to his feet. "Only that

I intend to drive a stake through your heart and watch you die."

Tito backhands Espinoza across the face. "I ought to tear you apart." The vampire's eyes blaze a fiery red.

"You'd only be making a martyr out of a madman," Espinoza says, wiping blood from his mouth. "If you hadn't kidnapped me, I probably would've landed in the loony bin."

"Perhaps you'd like some company," Tito says. "I can arrange to have your family join you." Noting the fear in Espinoza's eyes, he says, "Just as I thought. You're only pretending to be crazy." He turns to leave. "Come on, Miguel."

"I want a moment alone with him."

"You're wasting your time," Tito says, slamming the door on his way out.

Miguel looks intently at Espinoza. "I knew your grandfather. He was a very shrewd man. He managed to keep his head at a time when many other men lost theirs. Do you know how he did it?"

Espinoza shrugs.

"He kept his mouth shut."

"You know what you can do with your advice." Espinoza flops down on his cot and turns to face the wall.

"I tried to warn you," Tito tells Miguel as the two vampires walk down the passageway. "I'm personally going to sacrifice that sonofabitch to Camazotz."

"We're even now. I brought her to you as requested."

"Not quite. I want *you* to sacrifice her."

"Why me?"

"She's your responsibility."

"I can't do it."

"I'm afraid you have no choice."

"She looks just like Lady Morningstar."

"That's because she *is* Lady Morningstar! She's come back to get her revenge." Tito slaps Miguel on the back. "Why so squeamish? You've already betrayed her once. It will be even easier the second time around."

Chapter Eighteen

IN MEMORIAM

A funny thing happens to Cochrane on the way to Alonzo's funeral. One minute, he's sitting in the back of a taxicab on Pennsylvania Avenue, stuck in traffic and getting royally pissed off about it. Then the exhaust on the delivery truck in front backfires—*BLAM!*—subjecting him to a heavy dose of diesel fumes, and *presto!* He's back in Fallujah, perched in the turret of Charlie 3-7's lead Bradley and waiting anxiously for attack orders. The first rays of the sun loom red and menacing over the battered city. He glances at his watch. It's 0700. Zero hour. Time to go.

Above the rumble of the Bradleys, Cochrane hears the shrill refrain of the *adhan*—the morning call to prayer—on a minaret loudspeaker. Before the *muezzin* can finish his chant, all hell breaks loose; the column is suddenly drawing heavy mortar, RPG, and machine gun fire. Cochrane immediately radios the battalion XO and tells him that they'd better get moving before somebody takes one up the wazoo.

"You're the man," the XO tells him. "Get in there and kill some bad guys." Cochrane gives the attack order, relieved that they're finally on the move.

As the Bradleys roll into the city, Cochrane checks his map and realizes that he ordered First Platoon to take the wrong approach route. He glances down at his map a second time to confirm his position and sees a blinding flash between his knees. As the turret fills with smoke, Cochrane realizes that the Bradley has been hit. Naz, his Iraqi interpreter, has a gaping hole in his chest, and Sergeant Kramer, his gunner, is missing his right arm. Cochrane crawls out of the turret and calls for a medic. Then his head starts to spin and he feels himself falling off the Bradley.

"Hey, Bill. Are you all right?"

Cochrane opens his eyes—it's Cheryl Lucas. She's got a worried look on her face.

"You're really freaking me out," she says.

"What happened?" he asks.

"You blacked out. Then you started yelling and thrashing around. I thought you were having a seizure."

The cab driver tells Cochrane to get out.

"I'm fine," Cochrane says. "Anyway, we're almost there."

"Get out *now*," the driver snarls as he pulls over to the curb, "or I call the cops."

"Look no further." Cochrane is decked out in his dress blues.

"I don't care." The driver jerks his thumb over his shoulder. "Get out."

"You idiot!" Cheryl pounds the Plexiglas partition with the palm of her hand. "How'd you like to spend the night in jail?"

"C'mon," Cochrane says. "Let's walk."

Luckily, they've washed up just a few blocks from the church. Before they enter, Cheryl insists on straightening Cochrane's tie, explaining that he'd tried to pull it off back in the cab. As they walk down the aisle, Cochrane scans the congregation. The mayor and the chief are there, and the MPD Blue is well represented. Cochrane is surprised that it's an open-casket funeral; on closer inspection, he discovers that Alonzo looks pretty good for a man whose throat was slashed from ear to ear.

The usher escorts Cheryl and Cochrane to the section of the front pew occupied by Laura Alonzo and her two small children, Julia and Stephen, Jr. Cochrane sits down beside Laura, and Cheryl squeezes in next to Julia. Stevie is seated between his mommy and his big sister.

The funeral is solemn and grand, befitting a policeman who fell in the line of duty. During "Amazing Grace," Cochrane starts to tear up.

Laura squeezes his hand and whispers, "Steve loved you like a brother, Bill." Then she pinches Cochrane's arm so hard it hurts. "But he'd tell you to stop beating yourself up and move on." Cochrane steals a sidelong glance at Laura. She's looking straight ahead, as if the exchange did not take place.

Laura Alonzo sheds no tears during the funeral or when her husband is laid to rest at the cemetery. During the reception, she barely utters two words. When Cheryl and Cochrane come over to say goodbye, she gives each of them a hug.

"Promise me you'll look out for one another," she says, her eyes filling with tears. For a moment, she is too choked up to go on. Somehow, she manages a smile. "I have a good feeling about you two. Don't disappoint me."

Once they're outside, Cheryl asks, "What was *that* all about?"

Cochrane shrugs. "Beats the hell out of me."

They walk in silence for what seems an eternity. Cochrane opens his mouth to speak just as Jack Reynolds catches up with them. "Hey, you two need a lift?"

"Sure," Cochrane says. Reynolds asks where they're headed, and Cochrane replies, "My place."

Reynolds's Crown Vic is parked a block away. Cochrane takes the front passenger seat, and Cheryl slides into the back seat. Reynolds looks into the rearview mirror and says, "There's plenty of room up front."

"That's okay," she replies. "I'm sure you guys have a lot to talk about."

"Now that you mention it," Reynolds says, "I've got a question for you, Cheryl." He starts the car and pulls out into traffic.

"O-kay," she says with a note of caution. "Ask away."

"Whaddya think happened to the two bodies that went missing?"

"I don't have the slightest idea."

"What bodies are you talking about?" Cochrane asks.

"Y'know," Reynolds says, "the two guys who showed up with Luisa Santiago the other night. We've got plenty of eyewitnesses who saw them get it—including you—but their remains vanished without a trace."

"That's strange," Cochrane says.

"Well, it gets even stranger. I sent some digital images of the two German thugs to Interpol. I figured if we're looking for Germans, Interpol would be a good place to start. So they ran a database search, and their computer found a perfect match, right down to the scars. Dieter and Peter Richter. There's just one problem. They're a couple of Gestapo agents for chrissake! Turns out they vanished over sixty years ago, back when Interpol was a branch of the Nazi secret police."

"So what do you make of it?" Cochrane asks.

"It's gotta be some bizarre coincidence. Or maybe they're related. Who the hell knows?"

"What about the gangbangers?"

"They're not talking. Not even after I told 'em that Vazquez had used 'em as bait to catch the Santiago woman."

"That's because they're all scared shitless."

"I don't blame 'em. My snitch says that an enforcer from El Salvador by the name of Arroyo told the locals they'd better get with the program or else heads would roll. Some poor bastard called his bluff and instantly became a head shorter. Now they all think this asshole is El Diablo himself."

The Crown Vic stops in front of Cochrane's building. It's raining hard, so Cochrane holds his umbrella over

Cheryl's head as they run to the door. On the elevator, she asks him, "Are you thinking what I'm thinking?"

"Well," he says with a leer. "I was thinking we oughtta get out of these wet clothes."

"Actually, I was thinking about the two Germans. They're *Nazi* vampires."

"Can it get any worse?" he says as the elevator door opens.

"What time did you say your friend was coming over?" she asks as they walk down the hallway.

"He should be here any minute." Cochrane unlocks the door to his apartment and tells Cheryl to get comfortable while he heads into the kitchen.

"You've got a nice place," she tells him from the living room. "But the walls are crying out for some pictures."

"I'm open to suggestions." He asks her if she'd like beer or wine.

"Some red wine would be nice," she says. Cochrane pours himself a glass as well. No sooner does he sit down on the sofa next to Cheryl than there is a knock on the door.

"That must be him," Cochrane says. He gets up and opens the door. "Professor Brower. Come right in."

"Call me Andy." He notices Cochrane's black armband. "I'm sorry about Lieutenant Alonzo. He was your partner, wasn't he?"

"Yeah, and my best friend." Cochrane asks Andy if he'd like something to drink.

"No, thanks," Andy replies. "I can't stay long. I'm heading straight to the airport from here."

"Wait a minute," Cochrane says. "I thought we were traveling together."

"There's been a change of plans," Andy says. "I'm meeting some officials down there tomorrow morning. We're going to need all the help we can get from the Salvadoran government."

"So what do *we* do?"

"You'll still fly down tomorrow. I'll meet you at the airport."

Cochrane introduces Andy to Cheryl. They shake hands and exchange pleasantries. Then Andy gets down to business. "Bill tells me you want to help. I have to say I'm against it."

"And why is that?"

"I don't think you're fully aware of the danger involved. We'll be facing at least half a dozen vampires and God knows how many of their goons."

"Don't try to scare me. I saw what they did to the detectives and the SWAT team."

"Have you ever done anything like this before?"

"Of course not, and neither have you, Professor."

"Don't say I didn't warn you," Cochrane tells Andy.

"Your point is well taken," Andy tells Cheryl. "We're all novices at this—except Bill, of course."

"Hey, I'm lucky to be here," Cochrane says.

"So am I," Andy says. "Maldonado paid me a visit not too long ago."

"Sometimes it's better to be lucky than good," Cochrane says. "All that matters now is finding 'em and killing 'em."

"I'll bet we're not the first ones to try," Cheryl says.

Her comment kills the conversation. Everyone stares at the flickering gas-log fireplace until Andy at last breaks the silence. "So, how does she look?"

"How does who look?"

"You know . . . Luisa."

"She's changed since you last saw her."

"Could you be more specific?"

"She's grown a pair of fangs."

"I was afraid of that."

Cochrane notes the sorrow in Andy's eyes . . . sorrow that erupts into full-blown hatred.

"It had to be Maldonado. That's one more reason to drive a stake through that vicious bastard's heart."

Chapter Nineteen

DEFECTION

On the way into San Salvador, Enrique tells Nadia that Miguel has instructed him to take her wherever she'd like to go. He recommends checking into a hotel, but she wants to go shopping first. Nadia's first stop is a pawnshop in downtown San Salvador. She has Enrique tell the man behind the counter that she wants to sell her engagement ring, which happens to be a two-carat Tiffany diamond. The man examines the ring and offers her a fraction of what it's worth. Enrique tells her that he knows someone who would pay her a much better price for it.

"I don't care," she says. "I just want to get rid of the damn thing."

Enrique shrugs and tells the man that the lady accepts his offer. Nadia gives the man her ring, and he hands her five crisp hundred-dollar bills.

"I guess we're both happy now," she says.

The man smiles and says something in Spanish. Enrique translates: "He says you're very beautiful."

Nadia smiles back and says, "*Muchas gracias, señor.*"

231

As they walk out the door, Nadia tells Enrique that she wants to go to the nearest shopping mall and buy some clothes. Enrique takes her to the Galería Escalón, a multi-level mall in downtown San Salvador.

Nadia begins shopping at Stradivarius. As she examines the dresses, an attractive young salesperson walks over and asks if she needs help. Catching the woman's scent in her nostrils, Nadia is filled with intense longing. In addition to the stirring in her loins, Nadia feels a strange tingling sensation in her mouth, around her eyeteeth.

The salesperson—ANITA, according to her nametag—speaks little English, and Nadia speaks even less Spanish, yet the sparks that fly when their eyes meet render speech superfluous. Carrying an armload of dresses, Anita follows Nadia back into the dressing room area. Nadia enters one of the dressing rooms, pulling Anita inside with her. As the two women lock arms and legs in a passionate embrace, the dresses—still on their hangers—fall down around their feet. Panting with desire, Anita presses up against Nadia and grinds her hips while Nadia showers her mouth and face with wet kisses. Working lower, she nibbles on the soft brown flesh of Anita's throat. Things get a bit hazy after that. Later, as the two women primp in front of the dressing room mirror, Nadia struggles to recall what had happened. An angry welt on Anita's throat indicates that things might have gotten out of hand.

After she fixes her hair and clothes, Anita returns to the sales floor. Nadia waits a few minutes before leaving the dressing room. When she reappears, Enrique says,

"You were back there a long time. I hope you found what you were looking for."

Nadia flashes him a Mona Lisa smile.

To show her gratitude, Nadia buys every item that Anita picked out for her. The five hundred dollars doesn't quite cover the bill, so Nadia pulls out a credit card that her ex-fiancé gave her. Much to her relief, the sale is approved. Anita writes something on the back of Nadia's receipt and hands it to her. It's Anita's name and phone number.

Enrique tells Nadia that he's going to take her packages out to the Escalade.

"Keep shopping," he tells her. "I'll be right back."

Nadia does exactly as she is told. An hour passes, and no sign of Enrique. She is concerned but not enough to start looking for him. She is at Nine West, trying on shoes, when David comes rushing in.

"There you are," he says, wearing a worried look on his pretty face.

"What are *you* doing here?" she asks.

"You're in grave danger." He holds out his hand. "Come with me."

"But Enrique told me to wait for him."

"He was called away on business and asked me to look after you."

David is mobbed by a group of young girls who mistake him for the star of a popular telenovela. Seeing her chance, Nadia makes a run for it, dashing out of the store and heading straight for the exit, only to find David waiting for her at the doors. He grabs her arm and leads her to the Escalade. She goes quietly, knowing that a cry for help would only endanger the person foolish enough to come to her rescue. For the first time in years, she prays: *O, God, please save me from this wild animal . . .*

David drives Nadia to a secluded spot north of the city. During the Civil War, it served as a dumping ground for *desaparecidos*. David drapes his arm around Nadia's shoulder and draws her close to him.

"I've been waiting for this moment since I first met you," he says.

"You just met me last night," she says.

"That seems like a long time ago."

"Are you going to hurt me?"

"Of course not."

Without further ado, David plunges his fangs into Nadia's throat. She goes under too quickly for her short but tempestuous life to flash before her eyes. As Nadia's blood mingles with David's, he starts to feel dizzy. This is a different feeling from the euphoria that usually possesses him as he drains his victims. But David is proud of his conquest and eager to boast about it. So he calls Dieter.

"You're joking, *nicht wahr*?" the German says.

"I'm perfectly serious," David replies. "She's right here."

"You goddamn fool!"

"Don't tell me you're jealous."

"Why should I be jealous? You just signed your own death warrant."

"What are you talking about?"

"I changed her on the plane, remember?"

"Why didn't you fucking tell me, you bastard?"

"Because Miguel told you. He said you didn't take it very well and warned me not to say anything to you about it."

"Maldonado is a fucking liar! He set me up!"

David screams and throws his phone out the car window. He looks into the rearview mirror and sees blood trickling from his right nostril like water from a leaky faucet. Then he glances at his hands: blood is seeping out from under his fingernails. Another peek at the mirror reveals that his eyes are shedding crimson crocodile tears. Seized with a violent coughing fit, he hacks up enough blood to soak the front of his shirt. Pretty soon, every orifice of his body is hemorrhaging. He is in the final throes of the Red Death. Drifting in and out of consciousness, David beholds the bearded visage of Enrique de los Santos peering down at him. Enrique produces a long-necked metal can and poises it above David's head, drenching him from head to toe with gasoline. Then he tosses a lighted cigar through the open window, and *whoosh*! The cleansing flames swiftly consume the dying vampire until only a pile of cinders remain.

As the jetliner makes its descent, the clouds part, revealing the shimmering blue Pacific below. The aircraft passes over miles of coastline followed by more miles of waterways, trees, and green fields before setting down in the middle of nowhere. Cheryl films the approach and the landing at Comalapa using her Nikon. She is talking to Cochrane again. During the flight from DC to Houston, she brought up Cochrane's episode in the taxicab, but he told her to drop it. She persisted, and they wound up having their first argument. During the flight from Houston to El Sal, they barely spoke to each other.

Cochrane doesn't want to dig up the past with Cheryl, but that's the only way that he can explain what happened in the cab. He doesn't want to tell her about what happened in Fallujah, or about how he used to lie awake at night in order to avoid the nightmares that haunted his sleep. The flashbacks were even worse—as he rediscovered in the cab—for they often struck without warning. Then there were the violent mood swings, which scared even him. Cochrane's girlfriend at the time told him to see a shrink or else she'd leave him. He did, but she left anyway. The shrink prescribed Zoloft, and it seemed to "smooth things out," as Cochrane put it. In time, the nightmares and flashbacks ceased to plague him, but the Chinatown disaster revived some of the old demons.

Comalapa looks pretty much like every other airport Cochrane has passed through, with Pollo Campero standing in for McDonald's. As he and Cheryl emerge from customs, Andy Brower is waiting for them. He's wearing a white shirt with rolled-up sleeves and a necktie loosened at the collar, looking out of place amid a sea of denim-clad Salvadoreños.

"I see you're traveling light," he says.

"Just a crucifix, some wooden stakes, and a change of underwear," Cochrane replies.

"I only wish he was joking," Cheryl says.

"So how was your meeting?" Cochrane asks.

"Not good," Andy says.

Andy's Land Rover is parked in front of the terminal. A distinguished-looking Salvadoran with silver-gray hair gets out of the vehicle. Andy introduces him to Cheryl and Cochrane as Juan Manuel Guerrero, a former Salvadoran minister of culture. "Welcome to El Salvador," he says. Then he takes Cheryl's hand. "It is indeed a great pleasure, Meece Lucas."

"Please call me Cheryl."

Cochrane isn't sure if it's the heat, but Cheryl appears to be blushing.

"Sergeant Cochrane, it is an honor to shake your hand. Andy has told me all about you."

"Don't believe a word he says."

Juan Manuel appears confused. "I don't understand."

"He was making a joke," Andy explains. "Well, we'd better get moving." They all pile into the Land Rover, Andy and Juan Manuel getting into the front seat and Cheryl and Cochrane taking the back seat.

Andy leaves the airport and heads north on the Autopista Comalapa, a four-lane highway to San Salvador. A wide, grassy median separates the northbound and southbound lanes. Overhanging trees, red guardrails, and large billboards dominate the scenery, broken every so often by a pedestrian overpass, a gas station, or a building. Andy slows down whenever he passes a bus stop or a pedestrian. Juan Manuel tells the group that he almost hit a man on horseback as he was crossing this very highway late one night.

"Juan Manuel and I met with the Minister of Justice this morning," Andy says. "We tried to warn him about Vazquez and Maldonado. But it was a waste of time."

"I've known the minister for many years," Juan Manuel says. "Although we've often disagreed, he has always respected my opinion. Today, he refused even to listen to me!"

"Maybe the rumors are true," Andy says.

"What rumors?" Cochrane asks.

"That Vazquez kidnapped his granddaughter."

"Since the government won't intervene," Juan Manuel says, "we must seek help elsewhere."

"Time for Plan B," Andy says.

"What's Plan B?" Cochrane asks.

"Two words," Juan Manuel says. "Sombra Negra."

"It means 'Black Shadow.'" Andy says. "They eliminate dangerous criminals the authorities either can't or won't bring to justice."

"You can't trust vigilantes," Cochrane says. "We're better off without them."

"We'd never get past Vazquez's bodyguards," Andy says. "There are too damn many of them."

"Andy's right," Juan Manuel says. "We need the *escuadrones de la muerte*."

"The what?"

"The death squads," Andy translates. "Juan Manuel has arranged a meeting with one of the leaders."

"I hate to interrupt," Cheryl says, "but I think we're being followed."

Cochrane points to a black Nissan pickup. "Is that the vehicle?"

Cheryl nods.

"I have a suggestion," Juan Manuel tells Andy. "We're approaching Olocuilta. Let's stop there. Our friends can try the rice pupusas, and maybe we can find out what the fellow in the truck wants."

"Good idea. I don't know about you two," Andy tells his backseat passengers, "but I'm starving."

"What's a papoosa?" Cochrane asks.

"It's a thick tortilla made from corn or rice," Andy replies, "and it's filled with ground pork, cheese, and refried beans. People in this region have been eating them for close to two thousand years. We know this because a batch of pupusas was found at Joya de Cerén, a Maya village that was buried under volcanic ash around 590 CE."

They take the exit to Olocuilta, the Nissan pickup following at a safe distance. Andy stops at a crowded open-air pupusería topped by a large green awning.

Cochrane scans the street. "Where's the truck?"

"Maybe we lost it," Andy says.

"I don't think so," Cheryl says. "It's been on our tail since we left the airport."

In Spanish, Andy and Juan Manuel order a dozen pupusas and a large bowl of curtido. Andy explains that curtido is a side dish similar to coleslaw. Juan Manuel also orders a round of Pilseners for everyone.

As they enjoy their meal, a well-dressed stranger wearing a black eye patch approaches their table. "My name is Ricardo Alvarez," he says. "Until a few days ago, I was Miguel Maldonado's attorney."

"We've met before," Juan Manuel says as he shakes Alvarez's hand.

"That was a long time ago. I assumed you'd forgotten."

"You are not easy to forget."

Cochrane affects his best tough-guy growl: "What the hell do you want?"

"I want to help."

"And why should we trust you?"

"I can see that this was a mistake. Sorry to have bothered you." With a slight nod, Alvarez turns to leave.

"Señor Alvarez," Juan Manuel says, "won't you join us for lunch? We can't possibly eat all these pupusas by ourselves."

That's because Cochrane finds that he detests pupusas and manages to eat just one.

Alvarez slides in between Andy and Cochrane. He takes a pupusa off the platter and bites into it. "Mmm," he says, smiling at Cochrane.

Cochrane glares back at Alvarez. "Try not to choke on it."

"My friends," Alvarez replies between mouthfuls, "I don't blame you for being suspicious. I would feel the same way if I were in your shoes. But like it or not, you need someone like me—someone who's rubbed elbows with the undead and can separate the truth about them from the bullshit and the superstition."

"We don't need you for that," Cochrane says. "I've already been up close and personal with 'em."

"Ricardo," Juan Manuel begins, "I must admit that I'm a bit skeptical as to your motives. You've been Maldonado's lawyer for ten years. Why turn on him now?"

"My friends, not only was I Miguel Maldonado's lawyer, but I was also his best friend—his *only* friend. I realize that he's done some terrible things, but I also happen to know that he's capable of great kindness and generosity. I had hoped that, sooner or later, he'd cut his ties to Tito Vazquez, and I did all I could to facilitate that. But something always prevented Miguel from making a clean break. Finally I had to say 'enough.' I now realize that he is just as dangerous as Vazquez, and that they both have to be stopped."

"I believe you." Juan Manuel rises from the table and says, "I hereby nominate Señor Alvarez to be our Van Helsing."

"I can't believe you're being taken in by this guy," Cochrane says. "He's Maldonado's lawyer, for chrissake!"

"I second the nomination," Cheryl says.

"All in favor say 'aye.'"

Everyone says "aye" except Cochrane.

"Motion carried. Welcome to our team, Señor Alvarez."

Once they're back on the road, Cheryl scolds Cochrane for being so rude to Alvarez.

"Give me one good reason why we should trust him," Cochrane says.

"Let me tell you a story," Juan Manuel says. "I first met Alvarez during the Civil War. We were enemies back then. I was an officer in the government army, and he was a guerrilla leader. One day, it so happened that our forces fought over ground that changed hands several times. At dusk, he and I arranged a truce to recover our dead and wounded. He was just a boy, but he kept his troops in check and held up his end of the bargain. The last thing he said to me was, 'If we should meet again, I hope it will be under better circumstances.' Then we saluted each other and went back to our lines."

"That's all very touching," Cochrane says. "But that was a long time ago."

"Just the same," Juan Manuel says, "I still trust him."

Cheryl and Cochrane arrive at their hotel with just enough time to check in and drop off their luggage before climbing back into the Land Rover. They're on their way to see Alfredo Lopez, the Sombra Negra leader that Juan Manuel arranged a meeting with. A former colonel in the Salvadoran army, Lopez's friends call him "El Coronel." His enemies call him "El Verdugo"—the Executioner.

"There are a few things you should know about the Colonel before you meet him," Juan Manuel says. "Miguel Maldonado killed his only daughter, and the man is obsessed with killing Maldonado. So I told him that I was bringing in a team of experts to help him destroy Maldonado and his nest of vampires."

"Why the hell did you tell him a thing like that?" Andy asks.

"The Colonel doesn't want an archaeologist, a politician, a woman, and an American detective who can't speak a word of Spanish. He wants professional vampire hunters."

"And he believed you?" Cochrane shakes his head.

"The Colonel is a desperate man. He's willing to believe anything."

"This oughtta be interesting," Cheryl says. "Just wait till he gets a look at us."

Andy takes them through downtown San Salvador en route to Soyapango. Juan Manuel points out the landmarks along the way: the Plaza Beethoven with its palm trees, fountain, and bust of a scowling Ludwig van B; the statue of Salvador del Mundo—in Cochrane's eyes a giant dashboard Jesus perched atop a massive blue globe; and the Cathedral of the Holy Savior, the site of Archbishop Oscar Romero's tomb, where forty-four mourners were killed on March 31, 1980 by gunmen who fired on the slain archbishop's funeral cortege.

It is almost 5:00 p.m., and the traffic is bumper-to-bumper. At one point, the passengers in Andy's Land Rover brace themselves for a head-on collision with a careening bus painted in gaudy colors, but the beast swerves back into its own lane just before impact.

They reach Soyapango at dusk. Off to their right, Mount San Jacinto towers above the city. Andy pulls into a McDonald's drive-through to pick up a Big Mac, a Coke, and an order of fries for Cochrane.

"Soyapango is a Mara Camazotza stronghold," Juan Manuel says. "I find it ironic that the Colonel has put his headquarters in their own backyard, so to speak."

They enter a neighborhood of modest houses. Andy pulls up in front of one long-neglected dwelling with an overgrown front yard, peeling white paint, and a torn screen door. Alvarez parks his Nissan truck behind the Land Rover. Juan Manuel walks over to the truck and says a few words to Alvarez.

"I told him to wait in the truck," Juan Manuel explains. "I don't think he and the Colonel would get along." Pointing to the house, Juan Manuel says, "Excellent camouflage, don't you think? Nobody would ever suspect that this was the Colonel's headquarters."

Juan Manuel leads the procession to the front door. Telling the others to stand back, he rings the doorbell. A man opens the door and says something in Spanish. Juan Manuel replies in Spanish while gesturing to the others. The man at the door turns and speaks to someone inside. A disembodied voice issues the command, "*Entrar.*" Holding the screen door, Juan Manuel waves the others inside.

Cochrane enters first, followed by Cheryl, Andy, and Juan Manuel. In the front room, six Salvadoran men are sitting at a rectangular table covered with maps and papers. When Cheryl enters, the men rise to their feet.

Though dressed in civilian clothes, their close-cropped hair, trim physiques, and erect bearing mark them as soldiers. Photos and sketches of men and women are pinned to the walls like wanted posters. Cochrane and Andy nod to each other as they recognize Maldonado's likeness among the many faces.

A tall man with salt-and-pepper hair steps forward. "I am Colonel Alfredo Lopez," he says. Lopez shakes hands with each of the vampire hunters. "Señor Cochrane," he says. "It is an honor. I also trained with the US Army, at Fort Bragg. But that was a long time ago."

"Tell me, Colonel," Alvarez seems to pop up out of nowhere, "how much training did it take to become an expert in butchering women and children?"

"*¿Quién es este pendejo?*" Lopez barks.

"*Me llamo es Ricardo Alvarez.*"

Lopez draws a handgun and points it at Alvarez's head.

"*Madre de Dios!*" cries Juan Manuel.

"*Salir de mi casa,*" Lopez barks. "*¡Ahora!*"

"*Oyeron al hombre.*" Juan Manuel seizes Alvarez by the arm and hustles him out the door with surprising speed. Cheryl and Andy follow close behind.

"I know that bastard! He's Maldonado's lawyer. Who invited him here?"

"He invited himself," Cochrane replies. "He says he can help us."

Lopez stuffs the handgun back into its holster. "And you believe him?"

"Why not?" Cochrane says. "What have we got to lose?"

"Just keep him out of my sight, or I'll shoot the sonofa-bitch." Lopez strokes his chin and looks Cochrane squarely in the eye. "The old man"—meaning Juan Manuel—"says you went *mano-a-mano* with a vampire. What was it like?"

Lopez's henchmen crowd around Cochrane, eager to hear his story. "There's not much to tell," Cochrane says. "The vampire came at me, and I shot him three times." Cochrane points his index finger and pretends to fire three rounds. "He was standing from me to you when the third bullet hit him, but he just kept coming. The bastard would've killed me if my partner hadn't stepped in. He wound up getting killed instead."

Lopez says something in Spanish to his men. They all file out the back door. "I told them to take a smoke break. Now I'd like to talk *soldado a soldado*. The old man says you and your friends are vampire hunters. The art of vampire killing appears simple enough to me—drive a wooden stake through the heart, cut off the head, burn the monster for good measure. It's a well known fact that bullets are no good against vampires, but all this seems to have escaped your notice. I must therefore conclude that you're either a fool or an imposter."

"Look," Cochrane says, "I never claimed to be a vam-pire hunter. I didn't even believe the damn things existed until last week."

"Then why are you here?"

"Same as you, Colonel. I want payback . . . and I'm ready for 'em this time."

"*Bueno,* we can use another strong arm . . . but a friendly word of advice. Send the lady home while you can. When the fighting starts, she will only get in the way."

"That's easier said than—"

A commotion in the backyard cuts short Cochrane's reply. There is much yelling and shouting, and several shots are fired. Lopez flips on the backyard floodlight and rushes out the door, closely followed by Cochrane. They find one of the men sprawled on the ground with an ugly throat wound. Lopez asks the other men what happened. They gesticulate wildly and chatter away in Spanish. Lopez tells Cochrane that the injured man was in the bushes taking a piss when a large, four-legged creature with red eyes came out of nowhere and knocked him to the ground. The man who fired on the animal said it looked like a jaguar. In the meantime, Juan Manuel, Andy, and Cheryl join the group, while Alvarez lurks in the shadows.

"*¡Ven acquí!*" Lopez yells to Alvarez. "Before that monster gets you too."

Alvarez approaches the group, kneels beside the man on the ground, and examines his eyes and mouth. Then he crosses himself. "He is no longer human. We must destroy him before he awakens. I'll need a mallet or hammer and a sharpened stake."

Lopez orders one of his men to get the necessary tools. Cochrane asks Alvarez if he can help. "I need two strong men to hold him down," Alvarez replies. Cochrane and one of Lopez's men kneel down on either side of the vampire. "Pin his arms and put all your weight into it."

"But he's just a little guy," Cochrane says with a smirk.

"Don't let that fool you. He will fight like a demon."

"You talk as if you've done this before," Lopez says.

"That's because I have." Alvarez places the stake on the sternum, directly above the heart. He exchanges glances with his two assistants. "Ready?" Each man nods in reply. Alvarez raises the hammer above his head and brings it down with all his might. As the point strikes home, the creature howls and thrashes about like a wounded animal, a jet of blood spraying from its punctured heart. Although Cochrane presses down as hard as he can on the vampire, he is lifted off the ground. Then the struggling ceases. The creature falls silent, and its contorted features settle into a calm expression.

"He's dead." Alvarez, his face and arms covered in gore, crosses himself once again.

"We should burn him," Lopez says.

"Why bother? Look." Alvarez points to the body, which is already decomposing. "There will be nothing left in an hour. The old ones shrivel up even faster."

"The Vampire War has begun," Lopez announces. "It will be either them or us."

Chapter Twenty

THE OFFERING

Cochrane's back in Fallujah again. He's lying flat on his back, half-buried in sand, wondering how the hell he got there. He tries to lift his head to look around but cannot muster the strength. The effort gives him an excruciating headache or makes him aware that he already has one. Someone or something is hovering over him, an angelic presence swathed in white light. "Just lie still, sir. The medevac chopper is on its way."

"What happened?" Cochrane asks the angel.

"You've received a concussion, sir. But you're going to be all right."

Blinking his eyes, Cochrane at last brings the angel into focus. "Wait . . . I know you. You're Maldonado! What the fuck are *you* doing here?"

"I had to speak to you, and I was pleased to discover that my subconscious and yours share the same frequency, as it were." Miguel sheds his medic's uniform, revealing a gray Armani suit underneath. He sits down in the sand beside Cochrane. "You must save Luisa Santiago."

"She's your problem. *You* save her."

"That's impossible. I'm being watched too closely."

"Where is she?"

"Vazquez has locked her away in his compound. He intends to sacrifice her."

"Seriously?"

"I'm afraid so."

"When?"

"Soon." Miguel rises to his feet and brushes the sand off his Armani suit. "You must attack Vazquez's compound tomorrow. If the attack succeeds, you might be able to save her." He surveys the war-torn landscape of Cochrane's dream. "I see that you are also haunted by your past." He trains his red eyes on Cochrane. "Remember, her survival is in your hands. Now, if you'll excuse me . . ." A huge dust devil suddenly whips in off the desert, engulfs Miguel, and carries him away. So ends Cochrane's dream.

Early the next morning, Cochrane calls Lopez and tells him about his "hunch" concerning Vazquez. Lopez is only too eager to swing into action. By noon, his troops are assembled at headquarters; he launches the assault on Vazquez's compound an hour later. The attackers use an armored truck to crash through the main gate. They meet far less resistance than expected. The gangbangers defending the compound are heavily outmanned and outgunned. Those who aren't shot down either surrender or flee into the hacienda.

Lopez and Cochrane follow the attackers into the compound. The two men approach a knot of prisoners.

Most of them are shirtless and covered with MC · · · and vampire bat tattoos. Removing his aviator sunglasses, Lopez addresses the gangbangers, "*¿Dónde está su jefé?*"

The prisoners' replies range from *no sé* to *how the fuck should I know?* That is, with one exception. A short, stocky man with *El Diablo* tattooed across his forehead says in Spanish, "He's in Hell . . . fucking your daughter!" The fellow grins up at Lopez, who puts his sunglasses back on while the other gangbangers double over with laughter. Lopez draws his pistol, presses the muzzle against the *El Diablo* tattoo, and squeezes the trigger. Blood and brains splatter the dead man's *compañeros*, and their laughter abruptly ceases.

"Now that I have your attention," Lopez says calmly, "can you tell me where Vazquez and Maldonado are?"

One of the prisoners says that he saw Vazquez leave in a chopper. Another says that Maldonado drove off around the same time.

Lopez says, "You didn't answer my question. Where did they go?"

To a man, the gangbangers say that they don't know.

Cochrane tells Lopez to ask them if they've seen Luisa Santiago. They answer in the negative.

"*Te creo.*" Lopez turns to the guards and says, "Take them away. You know what to do." The guards escort the prisoners to the rear.

A few minutes later, Cochrane hears a burst of gunfire from that direction. "Was that what I think it was?"

Lopez shrugs. "What would you have me do? If I turned them over to the police, they would be back on the street in a day or two. This way, they are no longer a problem."

Cochrane and Lopez approach the hacienda, taking cover behind the armored truck amid sporadic gunfire. Bullhorn in hand, Lopez orders the defenders to drop their weapons and come out with their hands up. One of the gangbangers tells Lopez to go fuck himself. Lopez drops the bullhorn, grabs his radio mic, and gives the order to fire the tear gas. Within seconds, half a dozen canisters crash through the windows. A few minutes later, a herd of scantily clad young Salvadoreñas rushes out the front entrance of the hacienda, crying, "Don't shoot!" They stampede past an assault team drawn up on either side of the doorway. The men wear gas masks and body armor and are armed with shotguns or M16s. Moments after the last woman has escaped, they burst through the front door with their guns blazing.

The fight inside the hacienda is soon over. As the casualties are evacuated, Lopez confers with several of his officers. He turns to Cochrane and says, "It seems the prisoners were right. Vazquez and Maldonado are gone. And they took Luisa Santiago with them." Just then, an aide salutes Lopez and addresses him in rapid-fire Spanish while pointing downward. Lopez tells Cochrane that Vazquez kept some hostages in an underground cave beneath the hacienda, and that his men are bringing them up. Cochrane takes out a photo of Andy's friend Espinoza.

As the hostages file past, he snatches the sunglasses off one man's face.

"Carlos Espinoza?" Cochrane asks.

"I'm afraid you're mistaken," the fellow replies, grabbing his sunglasses. He rushes past, avoiding Cochrane's gaze.

"Let's hope your friends have something to report," Lopez says.

The Colonel is referring to Andy, Cheryl, and Juan Manuel, who accompanied Alvarez to Miguel's mansion. Alvarez finds it amusing that his companions seem to fear Lopez more than they fear Maldonado. The vampire's lair commands a wooded hill on the western outskirts of San Salvador and overlooks a manmade stream, which doubles as a moat. They cross the stream by means of a remote-controlled drawbridge. Just to the right, the water plunges fifty feet into a pond. The house is perched above the waterfall. Cheryl says that the cantilevers jutting out over the water remind her of Frank Lloyd Wright's Falling-water. Alvarez replies, "Okay, but does Fallingwater have alligators?" He unlocks the front door using the key under the mat. After punching in the security code, he waves everyone inside, telling them to stay close together.

Andy peers into the dark, cavernous great room. "Do you think he's home?"

"If he was," Alvarez flips on the lights, "we'd already be dead."

Cheryl is drawn to the pictures on the walls. At first, she thinks that they must be some very good fakes of

Picasso, Cézanne, Matisse, Dali, Kandinsky, Kirchner, Klee, and a dozen other modern masters. But on closer inspection, it appears that she's standing in the middle of a mini-MoMA. "Who did Maldonado have to kill to get his hands on these?"

"Nobody," Alvarez replies. "Back in the 1930s, a Berlin art dealer paid him a lot of money to smuggle them out of Germany. The dealer was Jewish, and he was afraid the Nazis would confiscate them. As you can see, he never reclaimed his property."

"Why doesn't Maldonado sell them?" Juan Manuel asks. "He'd make a fortune."

"I once asked him that," Alvarez replies. "He said they don't belong to him, so they're not his to sell. Besides . . . he doesn't need the money."

"And yet he thinks nothing of buying and selling plundered Maya artifacts. What's the difference?"

"You'll have to ask *him* that. I was his attorney, not his conscience."

"Hey!" Andy calls out from an adjoining room. "You've got to see this!"

Cheryl, Alvarez, and Juan Manuel follow Andy's voice into a long room filled with large museum cases. Each case holds artifacts of a certain type: pottery, tools, weapons, jewelry, figurines. Each artifact is accompanied by a brief description and a provenience.

"Maldonado may be a thief," Andy says, "but he steals only the best stuff. This is the finest private collection of Mesoamerican artifacts I've ever seen."

"This is nothing," says Alvarez. "Most of his collection is in storage."

"Well, this case is empty," Juan Manuel says from a far corner of the room.

Andy walks over and looks inside. "According to the labels, it held a sacrificial bowl and some stingray spines and obsidian knives. Why would Maldonado remove them?"

"Maybe they were stolen," Cheryl suggests.

"Or maybe he sold them," Juan Manuel says.

Just then, Cheryl gets a call from Cochrane. He reports that Vazquez's compound has fallen, but that Vazquez and Maldonado are still at large, and they have Luisa Santiago. "What have you guys found?" he asks.

"Not much," she replies, "aside from a fantastic art and relic collection." Then she mentions the missing artifacts.

"Did you say 'sacrificial bowl?'"

"Yeah. Why?"

"No time to explain. Let me speak to Andy."

She hands Andy the phone.

"I know what Vazquez is up to," Cochrane says. "He's gonna sacrifice Luisa Santiago, if he hasn't already."

"Why would he do that?"

"How the fuck should I know? Look, we gotta track him down, and fast. You're the expert. Where would you go?"

"Well," Andy says, "if I was going to sacrifice someone, I'd do it at Ciudad Antigua. It's a great pre-Columbian site, and it's just down the road. They're still open. I'll give 'em a call."

Cochrane has to wait an eternity before Andy gets back on the phone.

"That's odd," he says. "All I got was a recorded message announcing a special benefit concert at the site."

"When is it?"

"Tonight."

"Benefit concert, my ass. We'd better get moving. We're outta time."

Margarita Salazar stands riveted to the porch of the visitor center. Long ago, she saw this happen before. A chopper swoops in low just above the treetops and touches down in a field, while a truck convoy rumbles up the dirt road leading to the site. On reaching the parking lot, several armed men jump out of the lead truck and gun down two security guards standing before the turnstile.

Margarita is roused by a tugging at her sleeve. It's Paquito, her eight-year-old son. The daytrip to Ciudad Antigua was his idea. Taking the boy by the hand, she tells him to run into the woods and hide there until she says that it's safe to come out. Then she gives him a hug and a kiss and sends him on his way.

Paquito does as he is told. He dashes across the open ground as fast as he can and hides behind a huge amate tree. He watches a tall, blonde man stride onto the porch, grab his mother, and hoist her onto his right shoulder as if she were a rag doll. Then he carries her off, deaf to her cries.

Paquito watches the spectacle unfold on the ancient site. Several men plant torches in the ground at the base of the pyramid and then place several large incense burners on the pyramid steps. The soothing citrus scent of copal soon fills the air. A caravan of cars, trucks, and buses crawls into the parking area. The crowd—a mix of locals and *turistas* from San Salvador—starts to gather before the main pyramid, where a ten-piece band is setting up its gear. Meanwhile, half a dozen gangbangers unload a coffin from the chopper and place it on the bed of a pickup truck, which hauls the box to the pyramid. A stocky, bald man appears to be in charge of the entire operation. He speaks louder than the others and makes extravagant gestures. A slender man with long, jet-black hair tied back in a ponytail leaves the convoy and approaches the bald man. His curiosity piqued, Paquito moves closer to hear their conversation.

"Miguel, my old friend." Tito spreads his arms wide and embraces his protégé. "You were right about David. Something had to be done. He was out of control. I blame myself . . . I was too indulgent."

"What's done is done," Miguel says. "He won't give you any more trouble."

"Thanks to you!" Tito claps Miguel on the back. "And to Enrique. Only I wish you had consulted me beforehand."

"There was no time. I had to act."

"Well, Enrique wasn't too busy to call—were you, Enrique?"

Enrique steps out of the shadows, a cigar clenched between his teeth. "*Hola*, Miguel."

"What are you doing here?" Miguel asks.

"He works for me now," Tito says.

"What brought this about?"

"He offered me your old job," Enrique takes a puff on his cigar, "and I accepted."

"You know what to do," Tito says.

Enrique plunges a foot-long stingray spine into Miguel's chest, and Miguel drops to his knees with a groan.

He looks up at Enrique and gasps, "You missed." But Enrique meant to incapacitate rather than to kill. Miguel draws the spine out, but the serrated edges tear up his insides. The pain causes him to pass out, and he drops the bloody instrument at Enrique's feet.

"Put him on the chacmool," Tito orders, "and be quick about it. We don't have much time." The chacmool stands before the pyramid. It is a large stone sculpture of a type common in the Postclassic Maya world, depicting a man reclining on his elbows and looking sideways. The legs are drawn up like jackknives, and the figure balances a large tray on his belly. Dieter carries Miguel to the chacmool and places him on it.

Tito, meanwhile, steps onto the small stage beside the chacmool and walks up to the mic. "My friends," he begins, "Good evening and welcome to Ciudad Antigua. Thank you for coming to tonight's concert. We have a surprise in store for you. Tonight a very special group of performers will re-enact captive sacrifices to the ancient god Camazotz, much as they were conducted at this site over a thousand years ago. A word of warning is in order. Due to their graphic nature, these re-enactments are not for the faint of heart. Thank you and enjoy the show."

During Tito's intro, Anna removes Miguel's clothes and paints him bright blue from head to toe. Tito returns to the chacmool and takes an obsidian knife from a leather pouch. He raises the blade high above his head, cueing the crowd to move in. Then he makes a deep vertical incision just below Miguel's sternum. Handing the knife to Enrique, Tito shoves his hand into Miguel's chest cavity and extracts his heart. The organ is still beating when Tito places it in a bowl that Anna has brought him. He raises the bowl above his head in triumph.

"I give you tonight's first sacrifice to Camazotz!"

The crowd roars its approval. Many of the onlookers are drunk and/or stoned. Most believe that this is a theatrical performance. Among those who suspect otherwise are American TV reporters Amanda Donovan and Mitch Andrews. They came to El Salvador to do a feature story on Maldonado and happened upon the vampire hunters as they were leaving his estate. Sensing that something was up, they followed Andy's Land Rover to Ciudad Antigua. Like many others in the crowd, Mitch is using his smartphone to film the sacrifice, a couple of gangbangers having "confiscated" his expensive pro-grade video camera back at the turnstile.

About fifty yards from the two reporters, Andy, Cheryl, Alvarez, and Juan Manuel are biding their time. The vampire hunters have just heard from Cochrane. Lopez and his men are stuck in a traffic jam on the Carretera Panamericana caused by a pileup near the Ciudad Antigua exit. Cochrane says that he and Lopez are riding ahead on a motorcycle taken from Vazquez's compound. "Lopez thinks he can get us there in about ten minutes," he says.

"Sure, if you can do ninety the whole way," Andy says.

"The bike's a Ducati," Cochrane says. "I don't think that will be a problem."

The crowd noise rouses Luisa. She rises from her coffin, wearing only a muslin dress. All eyes are on her. She sees Miguel's body on the chacmool. Under the spell of the synthetic psilocybin that Tito has injected into her bloodstream, Luisa believes that she possesses the power to revive him. She begins to dance around the chacmool. At first, her movements appear tentative and awkward, but as she limbers up, her dancing becomes more fluid and confident, inspiring the band to break into a bolero. The tempo accelerates as her gyrations become more frenzied. Slipping out of her dress amid a chorus of shouts and wolf whistles, she mounts the chacmool and straddles Miguel's corpse, smearing his blood on her face, throat, and breasts.

As Luisa cavorts on the chacmool, the vampire hunters are swept up by a wave of people pushing toward the front. Tito tells them to stop, but they keep pressing forward. He orders the gangbangers to drive them back and, forming a chain, they do just that. As the crowd retreats, Luisa realizes that she cannot bring Miguel back. A few tears trickle down her cheeks. She slides off the chacmool and begins a slow dance. As accompaniment, the band plays a stately pavane as old as Enrique.

"Somebody give her a dress!" Andy yells. To his amazement, near the back of the crowd, a little black dress is flung up in the air. It is passed forward, flung this way and that, until it lands at Luisa's feet. Andy calls to her, "Put it on, for God's sake!" She picks up the dress and slips it over her head. Then her eyes meet Andy's, and she beckons to him. He tries to break through the security cordon, but a gun-wielding gangbanger tells him to step back or die.

"What are you doing?" Cheryl has Andy by the arm.

"I'm trying to save her!"

Andy manages to break free, but Alvarez wrestles him to the ground. "She's past saving. You'll only get yourself killed."

Holding Margarita Salazar by the arms, a couple of gangbangers lead her up to the chacmool. Her wrists are Ty-Rapped behind her back. Machete in hand, Tito orders her to kneel before him, but she refuses. One of the gangbangers forces her down on her knees.

"This looks bad," Alvarez says.

"What are we gonna do?" Cheryl asks, wishing that Cochrane was there.

"I don't know," Juan Manuel says, "but we'd better think of something fast."

Bending down, Tito lifts Margarita's dark, shoulder-length hair off her neck and raises the machete above his head. As he does so, Paquito bursts out of the crowd and dives between the legs of an unsuspecting gangbanger. He jumps on Tito's back and grabs the arm wielding the machete. Tito tries to shake Paquito off, but the boy clings to his arm for dear life. A gangbanger wrenches Paquito loose and pins him to the ground.

Tito shifts his attention from the mother to the son. "You're a brave boy," he says, lifting Paquito off the ground and raising him up to eye level. "Just the sort of young man I'm looking for. How would you like to live with me? I'll let you stay up as late as you want and do whatever you like."

"I'll go with you," the boy says. "Just don't hurt my mother."

"No!" Margarita struggles against her restraints. "I beg you! Please don't take my little boy. Take *me* instead."

At that moment, a tremor shakes the ground, followed a few seconds later by a rumble suggestive of an approaching freight train. Then a second and even stronger tremor causes the spectators to tumble into each other. "Earthquake!" a man at the front shouts. The panic is complete—the crowd rushes *en masse* for the exit. Just a few enthralled spectators stay to watch the rest of the show. The band plays on, but only because the gangbangers are holding the musicians at gunpoint.

"We didn't sign on for this shit," the bandleader tells Enrique.

"Stop complaining," Enrique replies. "You're being paid well."

"Money's got nothing to do with it. This is about survival."

The three German vampires exchange nervous glances. Anna Schiller approaches Tito and says, "Maybe we should stop. The tremors—"

"Are a sign," Tito replies, "that he is coming."

"Who is coming?"

"Why, Camazotz. Who else?"

Anna resumes her place in the shadows between Dieter and Peter. "He's lost it," she says. "Let's get out of here."

Enrique slides in behind Anna and grabs her by the neck. "Not so fast."

"Release her," Dieter says.

"Finish the ritual," Enrique says, "and then you can go." He turns her loose.

"What's the point?" Anna says, rubbing the back of her neck.

"You may think this is all bullshit," Enrique says, "but Tito really believes in it."

Tito, meanwhile, senses that something is stirring in the dark recesses of the tomb. It has risen from the depths of Xibalba and is waiting for the right moment to reveal itself.

The time has come. Tito takes Luisa by the hand and leads her to the chacmool. He has her kneel down before the stone statue and bow her head as if in prayer. A swirling black cloud emerges from the tomb. It materializes into hundreds of flapping bat wings. "Behold!" Tito cries, raising the machete. "The great Camazotz has come to claim his sacrifice." Before he can bring down the blade, the vampire bats attack, tearing his flesh with their razor-sharp incisors and rending the air with their shrill cries. The old shaman realizes that *he* is the offering. Camazotz has betrayed him! Tito flails at the hairy little beasts with his machete and manages to cut a few of them down, but the rest just keep coming. He laughs at the absurdity of these midget vampires feeding on *him*, the greatest vampire of them all!

As Tito fends off the bats, Luisa grabs a long obsidian blade off the chacmool and plunges it into Tito's chest.

"This is for Aunt Rosa!"

As the black blade pierces his heart, a jet of bright arterial blood spurts from the wound and spatters Luisa's face. Clutching the blade with his left hand, he begins to draw it out. Luisa snatches Tito's machete from his right hand.

"And this is for Lady Morningstar!"

With one deft stroke, she slices Tito's head clean off, transforming his neck into a crimson fountain. Tito's headless corpse wobbles for a few seconds before pitching forward, the collision with the ground driving the blade deeper until the point protrudes from his back like the dorsal fin of a shark.

Amanda Donovan turns to Mitch Andrews and says, "For God's sake, tell me you got that."

"Hell yes!" He grins. "It's better than Zapruder."

The gangbangers gape at Tito's corpse as it decomposes with time-lapse speed. Anna turns to the twins and says, "I don't know about you two, but all this blood is turning me on." She rushes into the remnant of the crowd, grabs Mitch Andrews, and sinks her fangs into his tender white throat. As Mitch's body goes limp, the smartphone with Tito's death video slips out of his hand and falls into the grass.

Amanda Donovan screams, "Ohmigod, somebody please help!"

Juan Manuel is standing just to Anna's right. He wheels around and stabs her in the back with his crucifix. Though the shaft misses her heart, the sudden pain distracts her from Mitch's throat.

"That was very foolish," she says, licking Mitch's blood from her lips. She reaches over her shoulder, plucks the cross out of her back, and shoves it into Juan Manuel's right eye.

As she steps over Juan Manuel's corpse, Anna is knocked on her ass by a sledgehammer blow to the gut— Andy having fired his shotgun from point-blank range. On regaining consciousness, she tries to get up but can't because Alvarez has shoved a stingray spine through her heart and pinned her to the ground. The last image her dimming eyes capture is that of a sneering Cyclops with a handlebar mustache.

Dieter and Peter wade into the crowd, only to find Andy and Alvarez standing over Anna's corpse, each man armed with a sawed-off shotgun. Peter grabs Cheryl and uses her as a human shield while Dieter does the same with Amanda Donovan.

"Drop your weapons," Dieter shouts, "or the women die!"

"If you hurt either one," Alvarez points his shotgun at Dieter, "I'll blow your goddamn head off."

Just then, Lopez and Cochrane come roaring up on David's Ducati. Cochrane dismounts at the turnstile and jogs over to where the humans and vampires are facing off. He also brandishes a shotgun. "Turn 'em loose," he orders the twins.

"Drop your weapons first," Dieter yells back.

"Release the women," Cochrane says, "and we'll let you walk."

"Why should we trust you?" Peter asks.

"Because," Amanda points to Cochrane, "you've got his girlfriend!"

"You stupid bitch!" Lopez growls, having found an opening in the fence large enough to admit the Ducati. "I'll kill you myself."

He revs the motorcycle and rides straight for Dieter and Amanda. But the vampire eludes him with such élan that several spectators shout, "*Olé!*" Gritting his teeth, Lopez spins the bike around and makes another pass. Dieter dodges him again, using Amanda—who has fainted—as his cape. Lopez attempts a third pass. In his rage, he loses control of the Ducati and wipes out. He flips over the handlebars and lands on the grass at Dieter's feet, while the bike slides about twenty feet beyond the vampire.

"Too bad for him," Dieter says, kicking the unconscious Lopez. "He should've gotten a smaller bike."

"Leave him alone!" Alvarez yells.

Dieter kicks Lopez again. "Try and stop me."

Cheryl, meanwhile, struggles to break free of Peter's iron grip. When that fails, she bites him on the wrist—hard enough to draw blood. Grimacing, Peter takes her by the hair and yanks her head back, causing her to cry out. Then he bites into her throat.

"*Brüder! Achtung!*"

Dieter's warning comes just as Cochrane—having concealed himself behind the chacmool while Lopez tried to run down Dieter—plunges an obsidian blade deep into Peter's back. The vampire drops Cheryl and staggers backward, trying in vain to withdraw the knife. Alvarez then fires two shotgun slugs into Peter's midsection, knocking him on his back and enabling Cochrane to drive a stingray spine into his heart.

"Peter!" Enraged, Dieter tosses Amanda at Andy and steamrolls Alvarez as he charges Cochrane. Before he can reach his intended victim, Luisa leaps on him with a wild cry. As the two vampires wrestle, Alvarez gets on his feet and takes aim at them.

"Don't shoot!" Andy and Cochrane shout in unison.

Dieter flings Luisa aside and vanishes into the night before Alvarez can get off a shot.

Cochrane checks on Cheryl and is relieved to find her conscious and talking, while Andy hurries over to where Luisa fell, only to discover that she is gone. Alvarez, meanwhile, surveys the carnage. Four vampires—Miguel, Tito, Anna, and Peter—are dead. The two oldest—Tito and Miguel—have already moldered away, while Anna and Peter are still more or less intact. One vampire hunter, Juan Manuel, also lies dead. Alvarez kneels down beside him and plucks the crucifix from his eye. Then he crosses himself and says a prayer over his old friend.

Alvarez hobbles over to console Amanda Donovan. She is kneeling before Mitch Andrews' corpse and sobbing uncontrollably.

"I'm so sorry." Alvarez places his hand on Amanda's shoulder. "He obviously meant a great deal to you."

She turns and looks up at him with tear-filled eyes. "He's dead," she says between sobs, "and I can't find his fucking camera!"

Alvarez shrugs and moves on. He comes to Lopez, who is sitting on the ground and wincing. "I think I broke my collarbone," he says, gingerly touching his right shoulder.

"You're lucky," Alvarez replies. "The fall could've killed you."

"And you're limping."

"It's nothing—just a sprained ankle."

Lopez's men arrive on the scene as Tito's chopper passes overhead. Alvarez helps Lopez to his feet. "Better late than never," Alvarez says.

The two vampire hunters hobble over to the chacmool. The bullet-riddled bodies of four gangbangers are strewn around it. "I know them from the wanted posters," Lopez says. "They were Vazquez's lieutenants. Looks like they all wanted to be the new *jefé*."

Margarita and Paquito emerge from the shadows. She tells Alvarez and Lopez that a bearded man smoking a fat cigar took off in the helicopter.

"That would be Enrique de los Santos," Alvarez says. "Mara Camazotza's new leader."

"What's he like?" Lopez asks.

"He's a fucking vampire. Need I say more?"

Chapter Twenty-One

DEPARTURES

The vampire hunters are seated around a table in a crowded airport bar, killing time. Their bruises, bandages, and stitches draw a few stares, but they pretend not to notice. The conversation stops when a grainy image of Lopez appears on the overhead TV just a few feet away. The sound is off, but the Spanish subtitles scroll past along the bottom of the screen. Andy and Alvarez provide a running translation for Cheryl and Cochrane:

"Here's the latest on the Ciudad Antigua story. Police have arrested retired Army colonel and alleged death squad leader Alfredo Lopez and charged him with attempted murder. Witnesses say Lopez tried to run over American TV reporter Amanda Donovan with a motorcycle. Donovan apparently was rescued by a tall blonde man who later fled the scene."

"Can you believe that?" Cochrane shakes his head. "They've turned that Nazi bastard into the good guy."

Andy holds up his hand. "Wait, there's more."

"*Lopez led a daring raid on the compound of notorious gang leader Tito Vazquez. The raiders, reportedly members of the vigilante organization, Sombra Negra, rescued over a hundred hostages, most of them family members of prominent Salvadoran businessmen and public officials. Following the raid, Lopez and several accomplices broke up a ritual at Ciudad Antigua conducted by members of Mara Camazotza, the country's largest youth gang. Witnesses claim that the ritual involved human sacrifices to the ancient Maya god Camazotz. Police officials refuse to comment on the case, except to say that the three Americans held for questioning have been released.*"

"That would be us," Cochrane says.

"*The death toll at Ciudad Antigua now stands at fifteen. Two of the fatalities, however, remain unconfirmed. They are Vazquez and Miguel Maldonado, a wealthy Salvadoran businessman and reputed smuggler. Their remains have not been found.*"

"Yeah, but we know better," Andy says.

American police suspect Maldonado of kidnapping world-famous ballerina Luisa Santiago. A native of El Salvador, Santiago came to the United States during the Civil War. Her current whereabouts are unknown."

"What do you think will happen to Lopez?" Cochrane asks.

"He'll go to trial," Alvarez replies, "but no Salvadoran jury will convict him. The man is a hero in this country."

Cheryl and Cochrane exchange knowing glances.

"I have an announcement," Cheryl says. "Bill and I are engaged!"

"That's wonderful news!" Alvarez is all smiles. "Congratulations to you both."

"To Cheryl and Bill," Andy says, raising his glass. "May you have many, many happy years together."

The four of them clink their glasses together.

"Have you set a date?" Alvarez asks.

"Not yet," Cochrane replies. "I haven't even bought her a ring. This kinda happened on the spur of the moment."

Cheryl and Cochrane kiss.

"Of course you're both invited to the wedding," Cheryl says.

"I'll be there," Alvarez says.

"Me, too," says Andy.

When it's time for Cheryl and Cochrane to leave, they all get up and walk out to the concourse with Alvarez hobbling along on his cane. They try to make small talk, but it's no use. While Cheryl hugs Andy, Cochrane shakes hands with Alvarez, who then smothers him in a bear hug. As Cheryl and Cochrane walk hand in hand down the concourse, Alvarez wipes a tear from his good eye. Then he turns to Andy and says,

"I have to see a man about a dog."

Alvarez hobbles into the men's room while Andy returns to the bar. A woman is sitting at his table with her back to him. She is hopelessly overdressed, yet elegant enough to pull it off. He sits down across from her and says, "I'm so glad you're here."

"I want to apologize for disappearing on you the other night," she says.

"That's okay. It was a good thing you weren't around when the police showed up."

"Yeah, they always ask too many questions."

Her drink arrives. It's a Bloody Mary. Andy insists on paying for it. She picks it up, takes a few sips, and puts it down. Andy watches her intently.

"You look surprised."

"I thought you drank only . . . well, you know."

She smiles. "Don't believe half of what you see in the movies or read in books. There's a lot we can do that the legends say we can't."

"Like go out in broad daylight."

"Exactly—with certain precautions, of course." She flourishes her red scarf and Marilyn Monroe sunglasses. "It's all very stylish in a retro sort of way, don't you think?"

"It works for you. You've never looked more beautiful."

"You are so sweet to say it!" She leans across the table and kisses him on the cheek with ice-cold lips.

"A question's been nagging at me since the other night. How did you know the bats would attack Vazquez?"

"I didn't. I was just winging it, so to speak."

"So you just offered yourself up and hoped for the best?"

"Yeah, something like that. But I had a pretty good idea what they were."

"Vampire bats, of course."

"That's not what I mean. You've seen the skeletons in that tomb. You know that something terrible happened in there. Innocent women and children were massacred, and it was all because of a high priest named Dark Sun. You know him as Tito Vazquez. In desperation, the souls of the victims latched on to the bats and remained in the cave until they were avenged."

"Let's hope they've moved on to a better place."

Luisa takes another sip from her Bloody Mary.

"So how was Maldonado connected to Vazquez?"

"Miguel was one of Dark Sun's first disciples. He was the artist who painted the murals in the tomb. His work caught the High Priest's eye."

"That's impossible! Maldonado was a thief."

"Becoming a vampire has a way of skewing a person's character. Miguel went from being an artist to being an art thief. You might have noticed that my dancing has become freer since I changed."

"That's one way of putting it," Andy says. "So did you love him?"

"I suppose I did," she replies. "But he was such a bastard that I wanted to kill him half the time." Her eyes flash scarlet for a moment and then fade to black. "I miss him already." She takes Andy's hand in hers. It's as cold as her lips. "But enough of him. What are your plans?"

"Well, I'll be working at Ciudad Antigua through the summer. I'm also writing a journal article on the tomb murals. Then I'll be teaching a full course load next fall. And I'm putting together a big conference for next year. Oh, I almost forgot. I'm presenting a paper next month on—"

"I'm afraid I have some bad news," she interrupts. "It's about your friend Carlos Espinoza."

"Is he dead?"

"Yes and no. Tito was going to sacrifice your friend, but he changed his mind. 'Espinoza will make a pitiful vampire,' I heard him say. 'People will just laugh in his face.' It was all a big joke to Tito. He was cruel even for a vampire."

"I'll have to tell his wife. She's been through so much already."

Someone rushes into the bar and loudly informs the bartender that a dead body was found in the men's room.

"Jesus!" Andy is on his feet and heading toward the concourse. "Don't go anywhere," he says. "I'll be right back."

When Andy reaches the men's room, it's filled with curiosity seekers. He works his way to the handicap stall and peers inside. Alvarez is sprawled on the floor with a vacant look on his face and a gaping hole where his throat used to be. His eye patch is pushed up on his forehead, as if he was trying to get a better look at his assailant. His cane is still hanging from a hook on the door.

The police burst in and order everyone to reach for the sky. They subject Andy to a pat-down. A detective asks him some questions. When he returns to the bar, Luisa is gone and another couple is sitting at the table. Then it hits him: nothing will ever be the same again.

www.ingramcontent.com/pod-product-compliance
Lightning Source LLC
Chambersburg PA
CBHW050716180626
46814CB00002B/467